The Two Behind the Psychologist

By Courtland O.K. Smith

Table of Contents

Bill Just Passing Through

[Two weeks later]

My head is really beginning to hurt, I thought, touching a hand to my forehead. But it did not take long to realize that my head was not just *beginning* to hurt, rather it was beginning to hurt *more*. It had been hurting for days, years really, but the acute, sharp, focused, pins-through-skull kind of pain I was feeling at the moment was different, worse.

Should I be happy to finally be feeling something new? I wondered as I held my head in hands and sat uncomfortably on my metal chair in the small, rather dark, rather damp smelling visitation room, wrist shackled, elbows on the metal table bolted to the floor.

For years, twenty or even more, I had been stuck in a stagnant repetitive life, tumbling through an endless spin cycle, never to get clean, condemned to an existence where I was bounced around, knocked around, shaken into confusion, cleansed of all that used to be me, until I became nothing, no one. From the apartment to the bar to the office and back to the apartment, then repeat it all again the next day and the next. And for what? Professional success never came, a feeling of contentment never blossomed, and my marriage only deteriorated as the days cycled on and on and on.

Years of slowly becoming a ghost of the man I once was had driven me into an emotional fog from which I could find no escape. I was shrouded in a haze where I felt nothing but frustration then anger then frustration from the anger and back to anger, then repeating again and again. The foggy lens through which I viewed the world darkened its hue, sucked out the color, and left me with a grim palette of depression tinting my perception of the past, present, and future. Feeling something new, something different—even if it was just this acute pain in my skull—was at least a break from the monotony of frustrated anger and depressive emotion that had washed over me for years.

I'm dwelling. Head still in hands I shook it back and forth in disagreement with my previous thoughts. The past was done and I wanted to forget it, but this particular bit of the past was still uncomfortably fresh in my mind as Bill had convinced me to relive it in writing; he claimed it would aid his work with the lawyers for the trial.

"Where is he?" I said aloud, speaking quietly at first then repeating it much louder with my head up, hoping the guard would hear, hoping anyone would acknowledge. Bill was late; he had been making it a point to be tardy for our visits. The previous afternoon he had not even shown up, although I waited for almost an hour before the guard brought me back to my cell.

"Mind games?" I questioned aloud, but I pushed the thought from my head, which again rested in my hands, brought low by the weight of the relentless sharp pain.

Waiting for him in this visitation room, different from the previous day's, I decided I was owed an "I'm sorry" when he finally walked in. If those were not his first words, and heartfelt, I would withhold my cooperation until his sympathy could be more sincerely expressed.

But he's coming to help me. I needed to keep reminding myself that Bill was an ally. Even now he was working with the lawyers who were formulating a plan of action for the trial. I needed him and his help more than I needed anything else. I knew that not cooperating would be detrimental to my freedom. *But what is freedom?* I mused silently. Would I just go back to my cyclical, repetitive, never ending shuffle from apartment to bar to office and back to the apartment? Would I again absorb all of my patients' problems and allow it all to stew under the surface throughout the day and night, barely allowing myself a moment of rest, physical or mental? Was that really freedom? Or would it all be different after what happened? Would it be different without Julie?

I'm dwelling again, I thought, head back in hands. Two weeks in prison and I was already beginning to think unproductively; I would never exonerate myself without a clear head. *You aren't always the victim,* I reprimanded myself sternly. But the thought that I might bear the blame for all of it, for any of it, angered me. Or maybe it was just the frustration of waiting that angered me. Or maybe the aggravation from the constant pulsing pain in my head was the problem. In that moment, and for the first time in a long time, I did not try to discover the source of my emotion; I just felt it and allowed it to overwhelm me. Tense and restless in the metal chair bolted to the ground, I let myself become increasingly worked up. I had lost my wife, my patients, my life, my liberty, everything. *How can I go back to real life?* I thought. *Nothing will be the same, nothing is left.* The anger was a fire burning inside me that started small but rapidly expanded to an uncontrollable rage, flames building and building until the combustion grew too hot and powerful to contain and eruption was inevitable.

Then the door cracked open and my rage exploded. "Where have you been? Where were you yesterday? I waited an hour in one of these disgusting little rooms." I did not even wait to see Bill enter, just let my anger flow. "Idsaerraaaaahhh!" I shouted, trying to add something else, despite being overwhelmed with fury.

"Sorry about yesterday, Nick," Bill responded nonchalantly as he waltzed in and made his way toward the metal chair on the other side of the table. He undid the fastened button, the top one, on his two-button light brown suit jacket as he sat, no tie around the open collar of his light blue shirt. The suit fit him well, hiding the bulge of his stomach. My taut mid-section was, however, hidden shamefully beneath my increasingly loose dark blue prison clothes.

" 'Sorry'? That's it?" I questioned angrily. "Just 'sorry'? I'm in jail here, Bill." Pain and frustration deprived me of additional words so I repeated myself with varying emphasis. "I'm in *jail* here, Bill. I'm *in* jail here, Bill. I'm in jail here, *Bill.*"

There was a short silence during which Bill looked at me with concern on his face as he sat there in the chair. "Something came up yesterday," he finally said. "I called over here and told them I was not going to be able to make it. It probably took them a while to process the message and let you know. Sorry, Nick."

I scrunched up my face, forcing down the ferocity that still churned within. I wanted to hit him, beat him senseless with words or worse, but I continued to swallow the fury.

Bill leaned over the table and said, "Are you doing okay in here? You're acting a bit strange and you don't look well."

Not wishing to add Bill's murder to my pending charges, I remained tightly sealed, holding emotion and gut reaction in as I struggled for control. I kept my body motionless and instead thought about a suitable response that would accurately and adequately convey my disdain for the accommodations, loathing for the guards, sartorial distress, and overall extreme discontentment with the startlingly calamitous turn my life had suddenly taken two weeks earlier.

"I'll be fine," I responded, deciding to lie so the conversation could progress to something more productive.

Bill leaned back and nodded for a while. It was clear that he was thinking about something particular, but he would not say it aloud unless specifically asked to do so.

"Something on your mind?" I asked in a slightly strained tone as I fought down my demons.

"Nothing specific," he lied. "I'm just a bit concerned about your appearance. Are you losing weight?"

I was, but I did not respond. Instead, in an attempt to calm myself down, I tried to think about how it would be, how it *will* be, when I am again free. Things will be different for a number of reasons. Sadly I no longer have a wife, but perhaps some time alone will be cathartic. I will have to find another apartment, probably outside of Manhattan, perhaps away from New York altogether. Maybe I can take a teaching job; Professor of Psychology, it might suit me better than Psychologist. Certainly few, if any, of my patients will be waiting for me upon my release.

These thoughts of a simpler, less stressful life on the outside momentarily soothed my anger. I had previously perceived Bill's questions, as innocuous as they were, as attacks. However, after my short relaxation session, I was able to see the questions for what they were: inquiries into my well-being. It was rare that I could calm myself so quickly and effectively, but maybe my confinement was forcing me to develop this new and much needed skill, one that would have helped me immensely two weeks earlier. I would not be in jail at all had I been able to control my emotions that day.

"I might be losing weight," I responded evenly after my thought-filled pause. "The food they give us tastes like prison food."

Bill laughed as I allowed myself a smile, more for his sake than my own. And I hoped the joke would convey my acceptance of his subpar apology.

"How is the writing going?" he asked.

"You tell me," I responded quickly.

Bill squinted a bit and cocked his head. "What do you mean by that?"

I squinted back at him. "I've been sending everything to you after I finish writing each day. You've been reading it, haven't you?"

"Well," Bill began and cleared his throat. "Not exactly..." He trailed off sheepishly with a slightly apologetic smile on his face.

Remarkably, my rage remained fully curbed despite Bill's apparent determination to provoke me into attacking him in the disgusting, damp smelling visitation room. "If you haven't read what I've written yet, what are you doing here?" I asked calmly.

"I just came to talk, see how you're doing."

I blinked a few times before asking, "Do you have anything to report from the lawyers at least? Any new information for the trial? A new direction?"

He smiled and replied, "I'm just here to hear *you* talk. I want to know how things are going with you. How about we start with you telling me what you did yesterday."

I amazed even myself by keeping calm. "I am not and will never be one of your patients, Bill, so please stop treating me like one," I said softly.

"I understand how you feel, but why not just start by telling me what you did yesterday," Bill replied, still pushing his agenda.

"Yesterday, I waited an hour for you!" I said in a rather loud, almost threatening voice. "And I have been writing my report like you asked me to. Remember? You wanted to learn my perspective of the week preceding my 'situation.' "

Bill was silent for several seconds, as though making a note on his mental notepad, then asked, "And how *is* the writing going?"

I sighed at the question. I had had high hopes for this meeting, but it was clear that Bill had prepared in no way at all, just walked in from the street for a quick meaningless conversation as if we were meeting at the bar; Bill just passing through.

"It's been going fine," I said, rather defeated. At that point, I was merely waiting for a lull so I could inform him that I needed to get back to writing and that he should probably get back to work, maybe even read what I had sent him so far.

"I had a thought a moment ago…" He paused before continuing. "Courtland…" He allowed the name to linger in the air.

"What about him?" I asked warily. "Unfortunately he died three weeks ago; my first patient to do that to himself. Not much more to say about it. Not unless his parents are bringing me up on charges. Are they?"

"No, no, of course not," Bill responded quickly. "I just thought maybe you could try to focus more on his connection to everything when you continue writing about the week leading up to your *issue*." Bill's emphasis on "issue" was rather bothersome, but I magnanimously focused on his instructions instead of dwelling on it.

"What do you mean focus *more*?" I asked suspiciously. "A moment ago, you said you hadn't yet read what I had sent you."

"Well," he began slowly. "I kind of skimmed it."

Anger was again building inside me. "You kind of *skimmed* it?" I sneered. "So you lied earlier."

"It wasn't a lie. I said 'not exactly' when you asked me," he argued. "I think skimming falls under that category."

I could not disagree so I tried looking away and crossing my arms in protest, but the shackle around my wrist tightened and did not allow the full range of arm crossing so I gave up and placed my arms back onto the metal tabletop.

He continued. "I didn't want to tell you I had skimmed it because I thought that you would be more insulted by me skimming it than if I hadn't read it yet."

Again, his logic was sound so I could not and did not disagree, but still I wanted to argue. I wanted to scream and yell and shout at him. I knew, however, that none of that behavior would be productive in any way so I kept it in, sealing the lid tighter and tighter.

"How can I focus on him?" I asked. "He died a week before everything happened. He doesn't have any connection to anything. And anyway I'm just writing a straight account of that week. I'm not focusing on any particular person or event, just writing down everything I remember."

"I only ask you to pay closer attention to Courtland's connection to everything; to you, to your sessions, to your demeanor. Just something to keep in mind while you continue writing. He might hold the key."

I considered this for a second before telling Bill, "If you're suggesting that I was suffering from some kind of Post-Traumatic Stress Disorder, I do not think that defense will work in Court. Yes, I was stressed and upset by his death, but a jury will never believe that a psychologist didn't recognize he was going through something as debilitating as PTSD and instead allowed it to control his behavior. That scenario might be possible and even plausible to psychologists, but a jury would never believe it. Also, one week after the traumatic event is too soon for a PTSD diagnosis. When you read my report, you'll see that my wife suggested the same ignorant thing."

"So Julie pointed out your strange behavior also?" Bill asked.

"She always sought ways to tell me that I was the problem. That was just what she grasped hold of at the time."

"I see," Bill said slowly. "Well, I was not suggesting a PTSD diagnosis. I just think you should seriously think about Courtland's connection while you continue writing. And see how he may have also affected your relationship with Julie."

"Courtland and Julie never met," I replied quickly. "Courtland never met anyone that I knew. He was a patient and, like every other patient, he was never a part of my personal life, just my professional life."

"But he was a patient that you 'saw far too much of yourself in'?" Bill said, quoting my recent writing.

"Did you just skip to the parts where I mentioned my dead patient and ignore the rest?" I asked him, allowing a bit of the anger inside to seep into my tone.

"I am particularly interested in your perception of the relationship between the two of you."

I thought for a while before saying anything. Why was Bill so interested in my patient who killed himself a week before my arrest? What was he implying? What did this have to do with the trial; how could he use Courtland's suicide to get me out?

Bill interrupted my thought process. "Do you think it is strange that you identified so deeply with a patient that you diagnosed with Dysthymic Disorder? Do you think maybe you were depressed yourself?"

"I'm not on the couch, Bill," I said dryly. "And stop treating me like a patient. I am not and will never be one of your patients." I paused for a while, looking around the room and contemplating Bill's query, then continued. "I may have exhibited some of the hallmark signs of depression, but I was not depressed. That's all I want to say about that."

"Fine," he said, giving up on the topic far sooner than I had anticipated. "Just do me the favor of considering Courtland's potential connection to Julie and to you and what happened."

"Whatever you say, Bill," I responded, giving little credence to his instruction. At that point in the conversation, I wanted only to go back to my cell so I could continue to write.

Luckily, for once Bill and I had the same idea. "Well," he said definitively, "I should be getting back to the office."

"I should be doing the same," I joked, allowing forced joviality to maintain my sanity the best that it was able. "So you'll read what I wrote today or tomorrow?" I questioned as Bill banged on the door so the guard would allow him exit.

"I'll move it to the top of my list," he replied.

"How is it not already at the top?" I asked, a bit perturbed at my low priority. "I'm in jail, Bill," I added for clarification.

"To the top of the list," he said as he exited. "To the top of the list."

Wednesday Morning

My consciousness became aware of the damage before my eyes opened to examine it: my left arm was tingling painfully. Eyes still firmly closed, I decided I would be better off without a left arm. What did I use it for other than filling out the left sleeve of all my shirts and jackets?

I'm right-handed; that's the one that counts, I thought, preparing myself for whatever horror awaited when my eyes finally opened, focused.

Slowly, a tight squinting in reverse, my lids opened to a diffused yet intensely bright light. The day was overcast and the air was thick; humid like the previous night. As my eyes adjusted, I evaluated the invisible ailment with relief; nothing more than the result of hours being trapped beneath a hundred or so pounds of slumbering psychologist.

I rolled onto my back, releasing my left arm and revealing the unfortunate stiffness in my bones, more so than normal. I groaned at the humidity as I yawned out, sound bouncing around the small bedroom. Even the mere act of turning my head to face my phone on the nightstand yielded local yet excruciating and extreme discomfort. 8:54 a.m. I felt like I had been asleep for days, weeks, longer, but the fatigue still lingered in this never ending nightmare of pain.

I rolled back over, opening my mouth to groan again and discovering a scratchy throat against the humidity. I reached over and pulled the device close to my face to confirm. 8:55 a.m.

The elevated status of the thick wooden blinds in addition to my recently adjusted eyes allowed me a good look around the room. In the thousands of days I had slept in that room, very little time had been spent looking around.

Never satisfied, over and over Julie changed the color; at one time or another every hue of the rainbow had graced our walls. For years, pictures of the two of us together were proudly displayed, briefly relocating only to facilitate repaintings. Julie loved using her old camera, having the film developed. I saw it as wasted time, a useless hobby.

The pictures always returned to the walls when the paint dried, but in slightly different configurations, small updates and tweaks here and there. But over time the small updates and tweaks began to include paintings as photos of us rotated in and out. Before long, the paintings took over.

Looking around the room, the rouge walls were dominated by two large oil-paint abstract pieces.

Where are all of those pictures of our previous life? I asked myself.

I knew they had left slowly, gradually departing along with our love for one another, but to where?

"The basement," I said with a meaningless smirk and nod; they would be with the rest of our relics.

Julie once quoted Oscar Wilde to me after I had offended her; I had intended just a joke, but intentionally taken it too far. "Never love anybody who treats you like you're ordinary," she had told me before walking away. I knew I had been treating her wrong for too many years; I just wished I knew how to stop.

My eyes focused on the large abstract oil-paintings in an attempt to decipher them. I hated them; they had no place in a home.

These were gallery pieces to be gazed at by artists. And the deep rouge of the surrounding walls was overpowering, piercing into me and inducing a relentless throbbing in my head. I gave up any attempt to understand.

Back of my head to the pillow, an overwhelming feeling of emptiness was pulling me into the mattress. Emptiness then battled with fatigue to determine which would prevail in knocking me back to sleep.

But sadly, both warring forces were defeated by the birds chirping, the collective sound undulating from loud to louder then back to loud; all levels startlingly obtrusive. I sat up and leaned back against the headboard, the expanding feeling of emptiness filled my body, hunching me over. I interpreted the message; my body's way of silently crying out in hunger, or maybe just crying as it had been for days, weeks, longer.

The chirping began to fade through the absence of attention. My mind approached the fact that I was alone, utterly and truly alone. Julie's side of the bed contained nothing; some mangled and tossed sheets, several pillows, but not her. In the past, I would wake to a half made bed when she awoke first, but no longer. I sensed movement in the hallway approaching the silent stale stillness of the bedroom. The door open slowly and Julie's face appeared with a slight smile—apparently happy?

"You're up early," I said in a scratchy grumpy morning voice.

"I just couldn't sleep," she responded. "Tired from everything. How are you feeling?"

I did not think before answering, just carelessly allowed my mouth to move, allowed it to spew trite, but honest, idiocy. "Fatigued from fear of not living life…" A tone of sarcasm was underneath. I believed the words to be unintentional and the tone incidental, but it came across as mocking mimicry.

She paused, shook her head slightly, and then asked, "Do you want to go to breakfast? Maybe that place we used to go? I've been thinking about that lately."

"Thinking about what?"

"The past..." she said quietly.

I fought gravity and my achy bones to pull myself up and swing my legs around to the floor. "Sure," I said when finally I stood erect. "I'm starving."

"Shower and we'll head out," she said as she left me to the rouge walls, oil-paintings, unmade bed, and chirping birds.

Showering and dressing had become routine and uneventful, dull and monotonous, thus the absence of conscious awareness led to the absence of strong memory of the events that followed. In short, I daydreamed through my morning routine only to find myself face-to-face with a noticeably angrier Julie.

Stern, the corners of her lips were well below flat. "What took you so long?" she barked. "I've been waiting for you. I'm starving."

"Sorry, Julie," I said, uncomfortably aware that perhaps I had not been at my most efficient. But despite the extra time dedicated to the process of rising, I felt as though I was still ripping myself out of bed.

Determined to change the subject, I grabbed my checkbook from the counter. "Is there enough in the account to pay the office rent?" I asked.

"Why do *you* want to pay it?" she asked angrily, accusingly. Her face was red, as if she had just been crying. "I can do it online like I always do."

I thought for a moment before responding. "Because I want to feel like I have some control over *my* money."

"Well, you forfeited the right to control *your* money a long time ago."

I looked at her face, hurt covering it entirely. She did not deserve this. I needed to stop. I walked toward the door and opened it, stepping back for her to pass as a peace offering. She walked by me and into the hall. Without breaking her stride she continued down the winding staircase.

I struggled after her, trying to pull the door shut tight and push the key in while turning and jiggling.

"We need to get this lock fixed," I shouted down the stairwell, but no answer came back up, nothing except the slight faint echo of my own distressed voice.

Descending felt almost as draining as ascending. Shaking my head as I negotiated each downward step, I became somewhat angry at Julie for leaving me alone at the door.

As I entered the lobby, I saw her through the glass of the building's front door. She was looking up the street toward the park, the opposite direction of our formerly frequented breakfast café.

I approached the door, my reflection increasing in size. I wore a gray suit, lightly striped with slightly darker gray lines. My dark collared shirt was unbuttoned on top, no tie.

"Pin-striped," I said, unsure if it was aloud or in my head. Then "textured" was said, consciously aloud.

I had no recollection of donning the garments. Life had become one routine endlessly seguing into another to the extent that my mind increasingly dispensed with short-term memories. I merely acted and moved without conscious knowledge or thought, hoping I would end up where I needed to be, which seemed to happen more often than not.

As I opened the door, I was hit with a wall of humidity much denser than I had anticipated. The sky was thick with dark clouds, darker than they should have been given the amount of light that was sifting through. It felt ominous, like a prolonged anticipation of rain. The air was idle, no wind or movement at all; dead. Everything was in slow motion.

My clouded mind moved to a film history course I had audited in college. At some point, they were discussing the filming technique of reverse motion: filming actors while they walked or moved backward. That footage was then played in reverse, creating a scene out of place, impossible contradictory direction of action and characteristics, confusing to the eye and to the mind.

When used to convey extreme fatigue or a collapse in psyche as it frequently was in older foreign films, actors exaggerated their movements when filming then the playback was slowed, stretched out. This method led to an eerie, disquieting, and psychologically disrupting scene. My day felt as though it was a product of exaggerated reverse motion filming.

Julie's eyes were at no point directed toward me. As I approached, she maintained her forward stare and began to walk. I followed slightly behind.

Gliding along slowly, she strayed to the middle of the sidewalk. "Sidewalk meanderer," I used to call her years before when a playful jab was still perceived as a joke. Had I said it in that moment, she would hear my words as a personal attack. Maybe they would have been.

Her movement was slow, graceful but sad, with her head down. I sped my pace to draw adjacent.

"Why is your head down?" I asked, genuinely concerned, but with no concern in my voice.

"I like to see my shoes while I walk," she said in a shaky voice.

"Okay," I responded, quite satisfied with the answer, although her unshed tears cried out for help. "Are we going to the park?" I sped my pace again, pushing myself ahead, in front, in first place.

She responded with nothing and continued at her lethargic speed in the middle of the sidewalk, only to catch up seconds later at the corner where I was halted by the traffic light.

We said nothing; I, too uncomfortable with her inevitable puddle of emotion to ask her why she was so sad, and she, too proud or sad to express it herself. It was clear she felt that I should initiate the conversation; frequently she looked up at me with a disgusted expression, begging for acknowledgement.

When the light finally changed, taking far more time than necessary, we continued toward the park in silence; she again looking at her feet while I looked in every direction but hers.

The trees were full, countless shades of green clinging tightly to the browns and grays of the branches. The dead air from the front of the Brownstone was replaced by a warm, thick breeze.

A man pointed with both hands toward a large duck followed by six ducklings, her offspring, I assumed. I smiled then looked at

Julie without thinking. Still she looked no place but down, her face somewhat red and wet from tears. I looked away immediately.

I loathed our perambulatory position: walking, not only very slowly, but in the middle of the path. An older couple holding hands broke from one another, passed by us on either side, then reconnected ahead, only to turn and shoot angry looks back in our direction. Julie had turned me into the pedestrian I disdained most: a sidewalk meanderer. I was the obstacle to avoid.

The ground was soft beneath my shoes, cushioned by the uniformly green grass beneath. We approached one of the lakes in the park as I mentally recalled a youthful visit there with my aunt from Brooklyn; I had named it The Sea and the grass around it The Earth. No one then understood that I believed that I was The Creator.

Children were running around, playing, laughing. Their smiling faces were an innocent reminder of the conspicuous absence of joy in my life, further illustrated when Julie began to weep openly in the dimmed but intense sunlight.

"Look at all these people," I began. "It's sickening. They should be at their jobs, not running around like this." After I spoke, I felt like a coward, ignoring her tears and focusing elsewhere.

But Julie spoke to me, her first words for dozens of minutes, albeit broken and tearful ones. "They're just enjoying their nice day, Nick. They're happy. Everyone deserves to be happy."

My eyes remained forward, but I saw her wipe her eyes in my peripheral.

"No, they aren't happy," I responded as I searched my visual field for an example. Several seconds passed before I found something that did not ooze joy. "Look at her. At least she's not happy."

20

"Who?"

"That one, sitting there alone." I nodded to the left.

"Which?"

This time I used my right hand to point at a brown-haired teenage girl with a pad and pen sitting comfortably on a small grassy hill.

"What," Julie asked, "you think she's working and therefore unhappy?"

"No, she's not working at all and she is definitely not happy," I responded confidently.

"She's drawing or writing and enjoying the nice day. She looks happy," Julie insisted.

"She's revising her will," I said bluntly.

Julie looked up at me, in the face, in the eyes. Her face was pink and swollen from the tears but she was still lovely. She paused, then let out a guilty laugh and with that, her unknown reason for crying was forgotten, or at least swallowed. We continued to walk quietly.

As one does when one walks for more than five minutes in New York City, we passed a homeless man asking for change. I ignored his desire to be acknowledged as a human by looking away and continuing on. Julie, however, apologized to him for having no change.

I was happy to pass unscathed, but dissatisfied with Julie's compassion. I turned to see what harm the homeless man would inflict in our wake.

A young man, likely a college student given his overly collegiate look, bent down and handed the homeless man what appeared to be a plastic container with what I assumed to be food inside. Then, to my astonishment, the college student proceeded to sit down and talk with the homeless man, shaking the homeless man's right hand then patting the homeless man's right shoulder. Despite my conviction that I wanted no knowledge of where either of those homeless body parts had been, I could not help but sickeningly imagine.

I continued on with Julie, walking forward, but the majority of my attention was still behind us. Suddenly, I felt sad for that lonely soul, having to bring a homeless man a meal so he would have someone with whom to talk. It was the only way the young man could procure a captive audience. I averted my gaze and faced forward again, shaking my head.

"Poor guy," I said aloud. Julie may have assumed I was referring to the homeless man, but she knew me better than to assume that.

A woman passed by, jogging with a baby stroller and a dog. Her tight black, blue, and green spandex stretched as she moved by quickly. I feared for the well-being of the child forced along on the trip. The earphones with wires bouncing against her side ensured that the baby's cries went unnoticed.

As she disappeared from view around a corner, she came precariously close to hitting a man crouched near the ground. The man was tracing shadows of everything that had one. Bikes, trees, poles, branches, garbage on the ground, the benches. His medium was chalk, all colors.

Julie stopped to ask him some questions, her artistic side taking over. I ignored their conversation and focused on his work more closely. It was shockingly creative. The colors, the compositions, the depth he was able to create by marrying a picture with the backdrop of the real world. All by doing something as simple as tracing shadows.

I was, however, frustrated by the fact that it would wash away at the first rain. Maybe even blow away from a good consistent gust or wear away from being walked on. I was further frustrated to see no signature, no mark to indicate the artist. Why would he do something so beautiful and time intensive, creative and painstaking for no recognition, no reward? Only for it to be destroyed moments after completion? It was too temporary to warrant the effort, and for nothing? I did not understand and it bothered me.

"Come on, Nick," Julie called from several steps away.

I pulled myself up and backed away, giving the thumbs-up to the anonymous artist as he created for the mere sake of it.

As we continued, we noticed a handful of protesters handing out fliers and attempting to engage passersby. One shouted, "Stop the violence," to an unreceptive walker. To what violence he was referring, I had no idea.

"Let's go this way," I said to Julie, directing her away from the enthusiastic youth. I knew walking through their blockade would prove to be hazardous, and I might have punched one of them to the ground had they harassed us. The irony would likely hurt them more than the blow itself.

As we walked on, Julie's attention drifted off the path to the right, which inevitably pulled her feet in that direction. The change in course was unintentional, evidenced by her almost colliding with a swiftly approaching jogger.

"Julie," I shouted to alert her to the impending impact.

The jogger avoided Julie's inattentive wandering at the last second, Julie still oblivious.

"What?" she asked to the shaking of my head.

She did the same thing while driving, frequently seeing something on the side of the road then drifting in that direction without realizing. When she checked the adjacent lane before changing lanes, she would drift into it before she determined the path to be clear. And she had the audacity to question my desire to not ride with her.

She pointed toward a tree. "Look," she said. "It's a Cape May Warbler."

"What?" I asked as I followed her off the path.

"A Cape May Warbler! It's a bird, Nick."

I looked up where her arm was still pointing and saw a little object twitching around with a twig in its mouth. "How do you know what kind of bird that is?" I asked.

"I've always been interested in birds. You knew that."

I spent several seconds evaluating the veracity of her statement. "I did not know that," I informed her. "Oh, wait!" I said as I grabbed her arms and shook her still. I tiptoed up to a group of birds milling around only a few feet from where we stood. "What kind of bird is that?" I whispered, pointing toward one hopping around and looking rather deranged.

"That's a pigeon," she said loudly, startling some of them.

"Wooowwww," I responded mockingly. "Do you prefer 'ornithologically inclined' or 'bird lady'?"

Julie looked at me, face half angry and half laughing, and walked toward a bench upon which she then sat. I followed her lead, a foot and a half separating our movements. There we stayed in silence, taking in the surroundings and forgetting about the other.

A young family came by; a father, mother, and a daughter of no more than four years in age. The father handed a lollipop to the daughter. Wide eyed and with a bright smile, she took the candy from her father and, before placing it into her mouth said happily, "I love you, Daddy" in a little voice.

"Aw, that's so cute!" Julie exclaimed. "That little girl is the cutest little thing. Nick, isn't she cute?"

"No," I said sharply, a bit angry at what had transpired. "Those people trained their daughter to respond like that. She doesn't know what love is, she has no idea. If she did, she probably wouldn't love her parents; the people who enforce all of those rules and regulations that govern her life."

"Fine. You win. She's not cute then."

Julie and I went back to focusing on the environment while not acknowledging the other in any way. I began to notice the alarming number of people walking around and lying in the grass who, by all indications, appeared to be alcoholics. Some enjoyed their beverages from the ubiquitous brown paper bag while others brazenly waved around their alcohol, drinking direct from the wine bottle, no cups in sight. I was certain that few of them would accurately recall that hazy warm summer day.

At that point, my mind became very conscious of my body's absence of nourishment. The physical vibrations which began in my stomach and moved through to my head enticed me to grumpily ask, "Can we go and eat, please? I thought we were going to go to breakfast, not waste my time in the park."

Without words, she stood and began to walk.

"Fine," I said before standing and following after her. "Where are we going?" I called out in a subtle attempt to show her that we were headed in the wrong direction given our previous decision to dine at our formerly frequented café.

"We're going to get food," she said with her head facing forward, away from me.

———

Insecurity

I was still walking behind Julie when we finally made it out of the park. We were at its bottom corner, far from where we had entered and farther still from the café. I looked around at the busy intersection, at the cars, at the people. My eyes were drawn to a muscular young man carrying numerous high-end clothing-store shopping bags with an older woman by his side. I assumed at first that he was her son.

I allowed my eyes to move around the crowds of people and cars and buildings then settle again on the helpful progeny carrying his mother's bags. They had not changed position or physical relation, but my perception of the situation began to evolve. It became clear that he was robbing her, blatantly demanding money from her purse as he pointed aggressively and shouted.

I scoffed aloud at the workings of the criminal mind playing out in front of hundreds of people on the busy city street. I wanted to shout, "Just take the purse, you idiot." But after some thought, I made the assumption that the robber just did not like that brand of handbag. Seconds later he ran past Julie and me, fear on his face and bags on his arms. I smiled at him, a thanks for the lesson in sociology.

"Where are you taking me, Julie?" I asked.

"Can we just go into here for a second?" she said, leading me toward one of the buildings.

"Do they have food in there?"

"I just want to look around," she replied.

"What is this place?"

"Curiosity killed the cat," she said.

"Luckily I'm not a cat," I parried.

"I don't think that adage was meant to warn cats," she responded as we entered.

The doors were guarded by two extremely large muscular men in tight black shirts with tags that read SECURITY.

"Those tags should probably read, INSECURITY," I whispered to Julie. She laughed.

The interior, a large square space, was well lit with glass displays arranged in several rectangular sections. Salespeople stood on the inside of the different displays which, I realized, were filled with jewelry.

"Is this a jewelry store?" I said loudly.

Julie turned to me with a disturbed look on her face. "Shhh!"

Everyone in the store was whispering and moving around very deliberately and quietly. It was a significant decibel level change from just a few steps behind us, although that fact became blatantly obvious to me only after Julie shushed me into guilt.

She began to look around as I scanned the room for somewhere to sit. My eyes settled on several tired looking men sitting on a bench on one of the far off walls so I gravitated toward them, leaving Julie to browse on her own.

With a dramatic rolling of the eyes and a resigned shrugging of the shoulders, I acknowledged the idiocy that was our wives to the seated men as I silently joined them. Not one of us talked because all knew that not one of us had the desire. There was a mutual, unspoken camaraderie.

We sat for what felt like hours, elongated by my growing hunger. My eyes lost Julie in the smattering of jewelry browsers for at least two dozen minutes before she finally reappeared, rounding a corner and making her way slowly in my direction.

She was smiling as she said to me, "Say good-bye to your little friends, dear."

Feeling like a child being picked up from daycare by my mother, I left the sandbox and followed after her before turning back to send an upward nod to those less fortunate.

We moved quickly through the displays then up some steps then around corners where I found myself face-to-face with a gleaming, extravagantly suited salesman standing proudly behind a thick sparkling bracelet delicately arranged on one square foot of black velvet on a display table.

"What's this?" I asked.

The salesman began to explain, "This, Sir, is one of our most exquisite pieces. A timeless combination. Four and a half carats of precisely cut diamonds delicately set in a platinum…"

"Okay," I said, interrupting him. Then I turned to Julie. "Why is this man talking at me?"

"Can I get it, Nick?" she asked, shocking me silent with such an absurd inquiry.

As I stared at her with visible disgust, creating an uncomfortable situation for all, the well-dressed salesman stood placidly as though it was his sworn duty to stand his ground, some kind of sales tactic.

I looked at him with his Cheshire cat grin and politely said, "No, thank you, Sir."

"Please, Nick," Julie said in an attempt to change my already made up mind.

"Please, Nick," said the salesman, beginning to get on my nerves with his rude and inappropriate sales tactics.

Feeling as if I was being quickly backed into a jagged corner, I retaliated with what I knew would control Julie's desire; I attempted to embarrass her.

"You know we can't afford something like that, Julie Alicia Douglas Thesiger." I spoke loudly so that all who were around could hear.

I assumed my words would bring an uncomfortable expression to her face. I hoped she would adopt a timid posture, head lowered into her shoulders and arms pulled in as she tried to make herself small. My intention was for her confidence to fade away thus allowing me to easily lead her out the door like the neutered puppy I needed her to be, but that I should never have treated her as. She then did something that I did not in any way expect.

She laughed. She laughed loudly and, with a jovial sinister smile, she said, "Of course we can!" Apparently I, not she, would be the neutered party.

Julie turned to the consistently grinning face of the salesman and instructed, "Please wrap this one up, Jacob." She then turned back to me. "Nick, please give Jacob a credit card."

She looked straight at me, intensely, confidently, peering deep and with no intention to blink. Questions filled my mind. *How can we afford this? How can I pay for this? Why is she doing this to me? What should I do?*

"Ahh," I stammered. "I don't have my credit cards on me, dear."

"What do you have then?" she demanded.

"I think I have my checkbook," I said, immediately questioning why I admitted to it.

"Fine then, write this man a check," Julie demanded.

Again, questions filled my mind. *How much is this bracelet going to cost? Will we have enough in the account? How could we have enough in the account? Why is Julie doing this to me? What is going on? How had I lost?*

As Jacob turned to quietly pack up the bracelet, I stepped in close to Julie and said, "This check is going to bounce."

"Don't worry about it," she said, unfazed by my words.

For some reason, even though I knew that there could not possibly be enough money in the account for the bracelet and our monthly expenses, I obeyed and I did not worry.

Jacob placed a small box with an artful bow in front of us on the glass display table, square foot of black velvet removed. I took out my checkbook and bent down to fill it in using the pen Jacob had already conveniently placed in front of me on the glass display table. I made the check out to the name on the box.

"What is the total?" I asked.

"Fifteen thousand, one hundred, seventy-two dollars, and fifty cents, Sir," he said happily.

I turned my gaze from the check to his face. Because he was grinning the same grin, I was unsure if he was attempting to make a joke at an inappropriate time or if he was indeed telling me the outlandish price of the bracelet.

"Are you kidding?" I asked.

"No, Sir, I am not kidding. As they say, you can't put a price on happiness."

Still looking at him, I said, "I couldn't agree with you more, Jacob, yet... here we are." I then wrote in the astronomical amount on the check.

I looked at Julie before adding my signature. She nodded me on so I continued. I then wrote *Screw you* in the memo line before tearing the check from the checkbook and putting it on the clear glass display.

"Thank you, Nick, Julie," Jacob said as Julie picked up the box with the tiny bow and put it into her purse.

"Go to hell, you grinning bastard," I muttered under my breath as I walked back the way Julie had dragged me.

Down the stairs then squeezing between the extremely large men, I found myself filled with questions, anxiety, and anger. Julie was taking her time exiting the store so I pulled my phone from my pocket to check the time. 11:03 a.m.

Knowing there was not enough time and knowing well there was very little chance of a civilized breakfast between the two of us in the near future, I decided to go straight to the restaurant to meet Bill.

"I'm going to the office," I said as she emerged onto the sidewalk, bombarded with the decibels of the surrounding sound.

"What?" she asked.

Even though I was sure that she heard me, I repeated myself. "I'm going to the office."

"What?" she asked again.

I followed her example and pretended not to hear as I walked away, up Fifth Avenue. She said nothing thereafter, just let me walk away from her.

My mind bounced and then mixed words into interrogatives. *What will happen when the check bounces? Will I have to return the bracelet? Will this further damage my credit? What was she thinking? Why did she do that to me? How did she do that to me?*

A man on the street was playing a trumpet, tones just sharp enough, just out of tune enough to irritate my senses. It brought to my mind a light blue kiddy pool in Brooklyn filled with lukewarm water from my youth. I had been pulled from it and hauled up the stairs carelessly, then deposited in the hallway, left there for an eternity. I looked up to see the mirrored ceiling creating the reflection of infinity of me; a disconcerting and perplexing sight for a young only child. The effect made it appear that I was not really alone, that my support system of endless identical relatable understanding individuals who could positively shape my being was there for me. But I knew I was alone. I am alone.

The street signs pulled me back into reality, into the present after I had walked far enough from the tone-deaf musician. They informed me that I was a long way from my intended destination, but I did not need a sign to know how far off course I was. I thought about a cab, but I decided to calm myself with the long walk.

The sidewalk along Fifth Avenue was suspiciously clear, tensing me, raising my anxiety. *Where are all the people?* To calm myself, I allowed my thoughts to wander as I moved seamlessly uptown, slowly emerging from the decibels under which my mind had been buried.

Wednesday's Drinks

I looked at my phone before pushing on the door to enter the restaurant. I smiled as the digital display changed from 11:59 a.m. to 12:00 p.m.

The restaurant rarely appeared as dim, dreary, and dark as it did that day. The headache I immediately developed from my painfully adjusting eyes indicated that the overcast sky outside allowed through far more of the sun's rays than I had squinted for. There in the entrance I stood, holding my head and hoping the pain would soon subside.

Six people went about their business acknowledging me in no way. Two men eating together smiling and laughing; three others, two women and a man, ate separately at scattered tables, interacting with their various electronic devices.

I began to walk to my stool when somehow, someway, I lost my way. My feet may have stuttered on the step down into the restaurant, precipitating a slow but cascading effect on my stride. My eyes may have not fully adjusted to the indoors, decreasing the accuracy of my depth perception. The long walk up Fifth Avenue may have adjusted my stride, resetting the way I moved my legs so my movements were out of sync for the task. But clearly something was off.

Tumbling down, my legs froze and caused my head to lose altitude rapidly before hitting the floor, luckily cushioned slightly by my left hand which I was able to swing around just before impact.

I scrambled on the floor for five, six, seven seconds before the man who was sitting alone came running awkwardly over on his tiptoes.

"Gosh, are you okay? I was sitting across the restaurant and I saw you fall. Did it hurt?" He spoke quickly, with a small smirk on his face, and an exaggerated inflection. I suspected he was mocking me, but, since he helped me up, I took his gesture of goodwill to be genuine.

"Thanks, I'm fine," I said as he righted me with his right hand in mine, pulling me vertical. I looked at my hands which were covered in dirt and dust and small rocks. One never realizes how dirty floors actually are until one is literally face-to-face with them.

"Will you be okay?" the Good Samaritan asked.

"Yeah, sure. Thanks," I said, brushing myself off.

"You better check yourself out. Your nose is bleeding," he informed me, pointing at my face.

I slid my dirty left finger across the bottom of my nose then pulled it away to reveal mucusy red blood dripping over the digit. "Oh, look at that," I said.

"Yeah, why do we fall, right?"

"Sorry?" I responded, confused.

"You know, why do we fall down? To get back up." He smiled at me. I smiled back and thanked him for his help with a nod and a small wave.

As I passed by my stool on the way to the bathroom, I thought I heard faintly behind me, "Did you have a nice trip?"

I did not turn, but continued to the bathroom.

"See you next fall," I thought I heard as I opened the door to the bathroom, left hand flipping up the light-switch on the white tiled wall. Scattered laughter that may have been in my head followed and was cut off as the bathroom door swung to a close.

The water was cold against my skin. My face, hands, arms, knees, shins all throbbed with pain. The white porcelain sink swirled blood through the water round and round and round until it disappeared down the drain. I stuffed toilet paper in each nostril to help stop the bleeding, but after several seconds, the two wadded up pieces were heavy with red and in need of replacement. This treatment was repeated five times as I stared into the mirror wishing to better recognize what was staring out.

When I finally sat on my stool, last round of toilet paper crammed in my nose, Bill was there waiting.

"Didn't think you would be coming from that direction," he said while facing the brick wall behind the bar. He then turned to me, face tightening from shock at my appearance. "What happened to you? Who did this to you?"

"T'was a lonely soul," I responded in the nasal voice one adopts when air is restricted to the nose. "Throughout life, this individual had been walked all over, manhandled. Took it out on me, an innocent passerby. Didn't even see it coming. Hit me like a brick wall, but a wall that was too lazy, too cowardly, to stand up…"

"What are you talking about? Did one of your patients do this to you? Did you get mugged?"

"I don't want to talk about it," I said, looking away and shaking my head.

Bill pursed his lips and withdrew from the fight for information. He was worked up about my condition, but gave me the courtesy of privacy.

The bartender, a three day veteran of the job, came over. "I saw you fall on the floor earlier. Looked pretty bad. You okay?" she asked.

Bill smiled at me, content and condescending. "You tripped?" he asked declaratively.

"Two beers, please," I said politely.

"Thanks, Carly," Bill added.

She immediately slid two mugs of beer toward us, poured moments earlier as she had inquired about my condition; she already knew the drill. I turned facing forward and drank. Bill, seeing that I was in no mood to be made fun of, did the same. Without words we sat there for five minutes. Bill's face suggested that he was mentally reliving my words which all suggested the culprit to be the floor. At least I had the satisfaction of having given the answer in as clever a way as possible.

"So," I said after the bout of silence, "how are you doing?" I posed the question less as a sincere inquiry into his well-being than as a passing nod to another noon hour in the restaurant, drinking, sitting, staring.

Before Bill had a chance to answer, the door swung open wildly and hit the empty maître d' podium that stood behind it, making a crashing sound when whatever was perched atop came tumbling down to the floor, the dirty floor. The man, the same very large man from Tuesday and Monday, looked at it, then waddled his way to his customary table.

Bill and I looked at one another and shook our heads. The man lowered himself slowly onto his chair which I was sure would not be capable of taking yet another day of such abuse. I feared for the menu which the man snatched quickly from the waitress's hand as she politely offered it.

Bill and I watched him as he searched for acceptable sustenance while continuously shifting around uncomfortably. He never stopped moving, as if he would die if his body was not in constant motion. He shouted something unrecognizable as words to the waitress before struggling to take a lingerie catalogue out of the right front pocket of his oversized brown shorts, exposed when he lifted the bottom of his yellow and green Hawaiian short-sleeved shirt.

"Shopping for his wife, I'm sure," I said sarcastically.

Bill let out a laugh as we both turned back toward the wall, silent again for a long while. Drinking, sitting, staring.

This time Bill broke the silence between us. "Stuck. I just feel stuck," he said.

"Stuck where?" I asked. I was surprised to detect a tone of disgust in my voice that I hoped Bill had not perceived. Another person who was about to complain about life, a repetitive story I heard every day from every person around me. I wanted nothing more than to sit and relax, saying and hearing nothing.

Bill then allowed his frustration to come out in words. "Stuck in my job. It's going nowhere. I'm going nowhere. I'm getting to the point in life where I'm asking myself, 'What's next?' You know? And I'm looking at it all and I'm not liking what I'm seeing, not liking where I'm going.

"I thought by now I would be a tenured professor somewhere, lecturing to a room full of bright students who truly respect me. One would raise his hand; he has a question. I call on him. He stands up and asks some impressively insightful question about the day's lesson. I would stand there at the front of the room for a moment as he seats himself, you know, bringing my hand to my chin; thinking. Then I would answer. It would be something,

38

something amazing. He would start nodding his head, the one who asked the question. Suddenly he 'gets it now.' Cue the inspirational music. Cut to the blond, also nodding. Then to an Asian fellow smiling at the epiphany. Pan out to the rest of them while I continue to speak, reaching everyone, each feeling like they and I are the only two people in the room, like I'm talking directly to them, changing their lives forever."

Bill paused for a moment, allowing space for my reaction to his oddly vivid fantasy, but I remained quiet so he began again and kept going for a while. Something about his job and how he had become disenchanted and felt as though he was going nowhere. I began to tune him out when I felt that his words were repeating themselves. The last one I heard was "shark."

My attention slipped toward my reasons for showing up every day to meet Bill. *What purpose does he serve? Where do I fall in his life? Why does he keep coming back each day?* I began to think about what we still had in common after all of these years.

In our profession, we frequently had to act as the model to patients, give them someone to look up to. This meant determining what kind of model best suited different patients, figuring out what kind of person they should be looking up to, then becoming that person. It was oftentimes the only way to connect with them. But, it became confusing. Who am I today? It was easy to get lost in our assumed identities.

We both came back each day to that restaurant because we needed a place and a person with whom we could be ourselves so that that most essential part of us was not lost; so we would not forget who we were.

It was always difficult to surrender to the need for the reversing of our professional identities, for the psychologist to become the patient; but we performed this necessity each day, if not for ourselves, then for the other.

"Quid pro quo," I whispered to myself, verbally responding to my thoughts.

As Bill went on, my mind drifted toward Julie, the bracelet, how we would pay for it, if we had the money. Julie had been handling our finances for years. Maybe she had been quietly saving, but for what? A bracelet? Why this? Why now?

When I returned my attention, Bill had just completed his rant. *"Nada mas..."* he said vigorously shaking both fists.

"What?" I asked, puzzled at how his rant had somehow changed languages during the short time of my attentional blink.

"Oh, sorry. I've been thinking in Spanish a lot. We have a new patient at The Institute; he speaks only Spanish to his hallucinations. I have to translate for some of the other doctors."

I knew Bill slipped into Spanish merely to allow an opening to mention that he knew one more language than I did; a souvenir from his summer after junior year spent in Italy and Spain, a trip I was monetarily incapable of undertaking. I smiled and blurted out one of the few words I knew in Spanish. *"Fuego."*

Bill paused for me to respond to what I could only imagine was a well thought through rant filled with complex metaphors and bits and pieces of several more languages. But I said nothing. I just sat there, staring at the wall.

"Nick?" Bill began. "You weren't listening to me, were you?"

"No. Sorry, I've been in my head a lot lately."

"Jeez, is my life that boring?" he asked.

"Unlike my credit card, I have a low rate of interest," I said with a smile.

Bill paused for a moment before laughing in a monotone, mocking laugh. "Ha ha ha… I guess I walked right into that one, didn't I?"

"Couldn't help myself, sorry."

"So now that you've ignored me and insulted me," Bill began, "you have to tell me what your problem is. You're not yourself. You haven't been for days, weeks. Always shrugging off the question when I ask it."

My instinct was to immediately deny Bill's accusations, but instead I considered for a moment why my urge to deny was so overwhelmingly strong. He was right, after all. At that moment, years of slowly sliding downhill from a failed ascent to the unrealized peak of a genuinely happy man had led to the resentful burnt-out angry bitter man I had become and toward… I could not even imagine where I could possibly be headed when I further descended on this path. How had my life become this? And why? I had done everything right and my life was still a mess, a desperate depressing mess. I responded to Bill with what neither of us were expecting: my honest opinion.

———

Job

"You know the book of Job? From the Bible?" I asked. "Long 'O,' " I added for clarity.

"Yeah, of course. Extremely pious guy. Prosperous. Seven sons. Three daughters. He was such a good guy that he spent most of his time giving offerings to God because he thought there might be the slightest chance that his sons may have sinned. Then out of nowhere God tells Satan to destroy Job's possessions and kill his family. Just completely out of nowhere."

Bill was getting a bit worked up by his summary of the ancient scripture so I allowed him to continue even though I knew the story well. As he spoke, I checked my nose after removing the red drenched toilet paper. No dripping. I leaned over the bar and tossed the wadded up paper into the garbage in the corner.

"And what does Job do?" Bill continued. "He takes it and continues to praise God. And what does God do? He tells Satan to torture Job as much as Job can take without dying. And all of his friends were telling Job to stop praising God, to stop praising the guy who did all this to him, but Job wouldn't have it. He just kept on praising God. And his last words in the story: 'curse the day I was born.' And that's it!"

"Thank you for that detailed summary, Professor," I said.

Bill, suddenly aware of how emotional he had become when telling the story, sheepishly smiled an embarrassed smile. "Sorry. That part of the Bible really bothered me. You do everything right and all you get is abused and for no reason whatsoever. And you're left with no explanation whatsoever. An explanation would have been nice even if it was something like, 'Oh, I was just bored and wanted to pick on somebody.' But, nothing. The reader gets nothing."

"Well, there is a moral in there somewhere," I said. "I think it's supposed to suggest that people should worship God no matter what is happening. You know, for better or for worse? And no matter what happens, there is some greater reason for all of it, you just might not be able to see it. That scripture is cited whenever there is a natural disaster or something that kills a significant amount of innocent people."

"Whatever," Bill said quickly. "I've heard the scholars' explanations. None are good enough for me. How did we get on this in the first place?"

"Actually, I was going to equate my life to Job's," I said, expecting Bill to explode in a burst of laughter, mocking my self-centered, self-pitying, and possibly blasphemous interpretation of life.

But, to my surprise, Bill said calmly, "I can see that," before drinking from his mug. Then he added, "But Job wouldn't accept his fate; you seem to have accepted yours…"

I sat back for a while, drinking, thinking, staring while Bill did the same.

"I just had a fight with the wife. Been fighting with her a lot lately," I said, astonished that I spoke those words. Only later did I realize that Bill had slipped quietly into the role of the therapist, agreeing with my ridiculous statement because he knew that I did not want him to. This caught me off guard and lowered my defenses; I felt subconsciously comfortable enough to blurt out what was actually bothering me.

"You've mentioned it in passing, but I never knew it was this bad," he said. "I guess when it comes to havoc, nobody reeks like you?" Bill laughed aloud at his pun, terrible in quality and timing. "That was my retort to your credit card interest joke. I feel it was appropriate, equally unfunny…" he added, pronouncing each word with precision.

Suddenly, a high-pitched sound ricocheted around our mid-day relaxation space. As if Santa was begging for money in front of a department store in December, violently jingling bells rang the ears of everyone in the immediate vicinity simultaneously forcing us all to reflexively cover our ears. I thought it may have been the smoke or carbon monoxide alarm alerting us to immediate danger, but quickly realized that it was the sound of the large man's cellular phone. It took several more rings than it should have for him to finally pick up.

"Hello," he shouted, almost as loud as the ringer itself.

"Could he have chosen a more earsplitting ringtone or a more obnoxious setting for it?" I asked sarcastically and loudly to Bill, but directed at every member of our immediate vicinity.

The man's voice mercifully faded into the background as he continued his conversation.

"So what's going on with your wife?" Bill asked, as any good therapist would, keeping us on task despite interruptions or tangents.

"The lady doth protest too much, methinks," I said, quoting Shakespeare, consciously taking the words out of context, applying a modern definition to "protest," and thus completely misusing the quote just as the vast majority of people usually do when Shakespeare is invoked.

Bill played along. "Doth she?" he inquired.

I took a long drink from my mug, keeping it on my lips for several seconds longer than necessary, allowing the absence of my voice to linger and my thoughts to gather.

"What was it that you were talking about? You said you were dissatisfied?" I tried to change subjects. I had always found it shockingly easy to divert Bill's thought process.

"It's about respect. I don't get any respect at The Institute, never did," he said, seeming to completely forget about my problem. "Ever since I started there, I haven't been anybody important. No one gave me a second look. I was forced to do all the menial stuff, paperwork, statistics, running numbers, data input, never leading a study."

Disgusted, Bill finished the remaining beer in his mug, almost half. Feeling suddenly challenged, I downed whatever portion was still lingering in my own mug, which turned out to be much more than I had anticipated, some flooding down my cheeks and onto my shirt.

"Carly!" I shouted, respectful volume. "Another round!" She came around swiftly filling then sliding over two mugs without question or comment.

Bill continued. "It's been like this since college. Even then no one respected me except you really."

"Me?" I questioned.

"Yeah, you. I'll never forget during our freshman year, there were a group of us trying to come up with nicknames. Remember that? It was the second or third month. Cool Guy, Big Mike, J-Dog, Special K, Red Hatter, Viper..."

"Ahh, that's right!" I exclaimed. "How are those guys doing?"

"No clue," Bill responded. "Haven't spoken to any of them since we made up all those nicknames we never used."

"Oh," I responded.

"Anyway, when it came to the two of us for nicknames, someone said that I was the Goose to your Maverick."

"Oh yes! I remember that," I said, recalling something I had long filed away.

"Do you remember what you said afterward?" he asked.

Bill answered his own question before I had a chance to think. "You said 'No! Bill isn't Goose. If I'm Maverick, Bill is

Iceman.' That's what you said to me, to everybody. You said I wasn't your subordinate wingman; I was your equal."

The fact that Bill had been so emotionally affected by this alcohol induced conversation all those years before did not stop me from laughing at his misunderstanding.

"Bill, we had just watched that movie, *Top Gun*. Iceman and Maverick were competing throughout the entire thing. Iceman thought he was better than Maverick, but it turned out that Maverick was vastly superior. They weren't equals!"

The smile on Bill's face began to fade.

I continued to berate. "The eight of us had literally just finished watching that movie when we had that conversation. How could you not know what I meant?"

Bill looked forward as he contemplated his mis-thought, probably questioning our entire friendship; the look on his face suggested that its basis had been this assumed statement of equality.

"I guess I wasn't paying enough attention. I never did like those old action movies." He spoke quietly, obviously hurt. He gulped down half of his replenished mug.

"Sorry, buddy," I said, apologizing with little sincerity. "I thought you knew. It was just a joke anyway. A joke made years ago."

"Whatever," he said, dismissing my words.

"It doesn't mean anything," I offered. "And come to think of it, I do remember wondering why you were so happy to be designated as an inferior competitor."

"Whatever," he said again cutting into my last word. "Let's just forget about it."

I chuckled as I watched Bill's disgust over the old misunderstanding grow. Humming a couple bars from the *Top Gun* soundtrack did not help the matter, but I did it anyway.

"What about this?" I offered. "I think I remember someone saying you were the Huckleberry Finn to my Tom Sawyer at some point."

"More like Holden Caulfield," Bill muttered, mouth on his mug.

Again, we sat staring silently at the brick wall behind the bar. Drinking, thinking.

"College was fun though," Bill said into his mug. "Remember our Psych 1 professor?"

"Ohhh yes! How could I forget Dr. Greene?" I responded.

"Yes," Bill said. "How could you? The rest of us were a little bit jealous of your little tryst with her."

"Indeed, I did, didn't I? That was what got me interested in psychology! I was just taking the course to fulfill an academic requirement."

Bill laughed. "Lucky man. You know she had two children."

"She did?" I had not known.

"Yes, she did. They weren't much younger than we were. Twins, a girl and a boy. I think they were two years behind us. You know the girl. I forgot her name. And her husband was in the department also. Professor Nelson."

"Really? He was her husband? I had no idea. No wonder he was so hard on me in class!" I laughed. "The things you learn twenty-some years later…"

Then I thought for a second as we both drank from our mugs. "I remember the first day of that class. She told me I looked familiar to her. 'Do we know each other?' she said to me. I told her I didn't think so then she said, 'Maybe we knew each other in a previous life; maybe I was your mother?' Then she told me she was a Freudian. I hadn't realized until she lectured on Freud that she was coming on to me."

"Fantastic!" Bill said of her aggressive behavior. "College was good to you."

"It certainly was. What comes before Part B?" I asked.

"Part A!" we both sang in unison as we hit our mugs together, splattering beer onto the smooth wooden bar.

Laughter in between gulps as we finished off what remained was met with me shouting, "Another round!" I assumed Carly would respond appropriately. She did.

"Remember Sophomore Spring when we dedicated three days each week to becoming bowling experts?" Bill reminisced.

"Eh, what were we thinking?" I exclaimed.

"Someone told us it would be a good networking tool for business. 'The new golf' or 'racquetball' or 'tennis' or something," he said.

Shaking my head, I said, "What a waste of time that was, but endlessly entertaining."

"We were able to perfect that curving trick-shot thing," he said proudly.

"Wonder if we could still pull that one out if we had to…"

"Maybe if money were involved, but I have a feeling I lost that ability years ago," Bill lamented.

Then I remembered. "How about that terrible little diner all the students would go to at 4 a.m. after drinking too much, then forcing one person to sober up just enough to drive there?"

"They had great pancakes."

"They did, didn't they?" I agreed. "But it was like ten miles away. I feel like there must have been a closer place to get pancakes."

"Not at 4 a.m. in New Hampshire. Oh, and our midnight tennis matches?" Bill asked.

I laughed. "Who knew they had glow-in-the-dark tennis balls and tape to mark off the court and to line the rackets? Genius inventions."

Smiling, nodding, we drank and drank, bobbing our heads at the good times past. Then we simultaneously recalled the same classic part of our College Experience, something no student could forget because all partook. We looked at each other, smiling and nodding.

"Two Dollar Margaritas!" Again we hit mugs and laughed.

"Remember when we had The Lazy Competition?" I asked.

"How could I forget," Bill responded reluctantly.

"Hilarious!" I insisted.

"Oh, yes," he said sarcastically. "Hilarious… No one reads the textbook for that class we were all in together. Which class was that?"

"Psych 26," I responded quickly. "Physiological Psychology."

"That's right, that's right. We went to class so few times it was hard to remember what the title or number was."

"Well, that was part of the contest. Who could put in the least amount of work and still get a good grade," I reminded him.

"Yup, and we all failed except for you," Bill said, again reluctantly.

"Indeed! Read the book right before the exam, a couple hours of work; that's all ya need!" I told him.

"That's all *you* need. And you got an A. Much deserved," he added again sarcastically.

I laughed aloud at the recollection of my triumph.

"That was before you told us you had an eidetic memory," he recalled with reluctance.

"I knew if I told you beforehand, you wouldn't get involved with the contest."

Bill shook his head. "You are a cruel man. A cruel, cruel man."

"Indeed," I said smartly.

We took a short break to drink, thinking of more fine times from the past.

"How about The Chicken Beard Contest junior winter?" Bill asked.

"Wow, that's right. We all looked foolish for those three months," I reminisced.

"I don't recall you winning that one," Bill said in an attempt to knock me from my high horse. "I believe you were the big chicken."

"Bahcauw!" I called out, mimicking a chicken. "I didn't win that one, but I won all the female attention that you all scared away from yourselves with your ridiculously ugly facial hair."

Bill's response was delayed several seconds as his face displayed the emotion brought on by the long overdue realization.

"You planned that out, didn't you? Suckering us into a competition to make us increasingly unattractive so you wouldn't have any competition for the girls?"

I put my hands up, palms toward him. "Guilty as charged."

"Wow," Bill exclaimed, impressed in spite of himself. "Criminal mastermind. Evil genius."

"What can I say?"

We went back to work on our beers, slower than before.

"You were pretty popular with the ladies back then," Bill said, interrupting me from nursing the contents of my mug.

"Yes, indeed; 97 percent of them were real winners," I recalled.

"Wow! Listen to you! Ninety-seven is a prime number. That means you would have to have dated one hundred girls to get to that exact percentage."

"*At least* one hundred," I corrected with a smile.

"Womanizer," he grumbled into his mug, still smiling.

"I agree, but that was how we measured ourselves back then. We were in college."

After a sip, Bill said, "I suppose you're right, but I still don't think youthfulness is an excuse for that kind of immaturity."

"By definition, I think it is," I said before recalling. "You remember how it caused such a fuss among some of our female friends?"

"What?" Bill questioned. "Dating so many girls, you mean?"

"No, dating the girls I dated," I corrected. "The quantity wasn't what they found issue with. It was the quality. All the other girls were disgusted. You don't remember this?"

"No, not at all," Bill admitted.

"Yeah, they always thought of me as an intelligent, well rounded, sensible individual."

"And modest," Bill added.

I laughed his sarcastic assertion off. "They found fault with the fact that I would only date the stereotypically good looking girls who happened to be not the smartest. They were generally legacies at the school whose financially successful fathers had married models. They got into the school solely because of their familial connection to it. The ones who spent more time on their appearance than they did on their academics or really anything else."

"Well, where is the problem with that?" Bill asked.

"I guess our friends, the girls, thought I was better than that."

"Better than what?" Bill asked, still not fully grasping where the conflict lay.

"They felt that my thought process was being controlled by society's influence over my desires for the stereotypically ideal looking woman. They thought someone as intelligent as I should be dating intelligent sensible women, not chasing the good looking ones who happened to be less than brilliant. They thought I would desire more intellectual stimulation than that."

"Hmm. I never realized anyone had an issue with the people you dated," Bill remarked.

"It was a big problem for me back then. I lost some great female friends over it. They really made me think about the whole thing. Were my choices so very controlled by societal pressures? I thought I liked those girls for who they were, but maybe their looks were as far as it went; there really wasn't very much substance to a lot of them.

"But, honestly, how much is anybody *not* controlled by societal pressures or their culture? And, if I were, that would still be me: my likes, dislikes, desires, my personality, right? Does it really matter that the origin of some of my preferences *may* have been sourced in what society told me I was supposed to be attracted to? In high school, in college, you date the kind of people you are supposed to like, not the ones you actually like. But, for me, it happened to be the same group. At least that's what I convinced myself. To this day, I'm still unsure of the truth."

Bill nodded in agreement as I spoke.

"I questioned myself a lot about those choices. I became really self-conscious. I feel like I was no more influenced by society or our culture than anyone else, but I still felt bad dating who I did. Like I was letting everyone down or something."

"I never knew any of this," Bill admitted.

"I suppose I didn't really talk about it. I wasn't used to feeling insecure. Why would I tell anyone I was? You know?"

"I hear ya," Bill echoed from inside his mug. "It's like thermometer or thermostat."

I looked over inquisitively and saw he was already done with another mug. I quickly caught up just in time for Carly to slide two more toward us.

"What do you mean?" I questioned after a sip.

"Are you controlled by your environment or do you control it? Thermometer or thermostat..."

I nodded, drank, stared at the brick wall as he did the same for several minutes.

"We used to go through girls like we went through tissues," I said of our lives past.

"So now you found a handkerchief?" Bill asked in an attempt to bring our conversation back on track.

"I suppose I did. And nice continuation of the simile and conjoining use of a metaphor, I might add," I said in an attempt to shift the focus to Bill's wit.

He could not resist adding to his already impressive intellectual score card for the hour. "I believe it was Mark Twain who said, 'What is human life? The first third a good time; the rest remembering about it.'"

"Indeed!" I responded, impressed with my own ability to shift the focus of the conversation away from what I had little desire to discuss. "Happiness makes up in height what it lacks in length," I added.

"Robert Frost, I believe?" Bill proudly labeled.

"Bravo, my good man." And it was left at that. We swiftly drank most of what had just filled our mugs.

An uncontrollable smile overwhelmed my face when my mind recalled and then pushed to my mouth, "How about, during the warm months, when we would throw the baseball back and forth in front of the dorm?"

"Yup, and doing it inside the dorm during the cold months?"

"Yeah, that was dangerous," I said slowly.

"Remember the girl?" Bill asked, knowing well that the girl of whom he spoke was difficult to forget.

My voice moved toward defensive. "She should have looked both ways before barging out of her room into the hall like that!" I responded, absolving myself of any wrongdoing.

"Poor girl had a black eye for weeks. I never knew black eyes stuck around for so long," Bill said. "I suppose some lasting damage is inevitable when you step in front of a ball moving at such a swift pace."

"You're the one who called for a fastball! One finger, straight down," I shouted, blaming him for the collision.

"Oh, don't try to put this on me!" Bill responded, pushing aside responsibility. "Retrospect: we probably should not have been practicing pitching in the hall like that."

"So let's call it a learning experience," I said definitively pushing the blame off the pitcher's mound.

"Agreed," Bill responded. Then he began work on the beer in his mug, swallowing most of what remained.

I made an attempt to catch him. But before I could, Bill said, "Remember that girl you dated right before Julie? She was a real beauty. I only met her twice, I think. You were together through graduation then for a couple months in the city that summer. I had started my graduate program before you started yours and we didn't really see each other too often so I didn't really get to know her. What was her name again?"

"Oh, yes," I responded remembering immediately to whom Bill referred. "The one you guys called 'the smelly girl,' right?"

Bill laughed aloud. "We did call her that, didn't we. I suppose *she* wasn't really smelly per se. It was the perfume she always wore."

"Sometimes you have to stand back to admire a work of art," I insisted with a smile. "Rebecca was her name."

"Oh, that's right, that's right," Bill recalled. "Rebecca Nelson."

"Oh," I said. "I don't think I ever knew her last name."

"How could you not know her last name? That was Dr. Greene's and Dr. Nelson's daughter," Bill informed me.

"No, she was not, was she?" I exclaimed.

"Of course she was. I thought you knew. How could you not know? Her parents never came up in conversation?"

"I guess not," I said, thinking. "But her father's hatred for me is becoming more and more understandable. Did he have any sisters that I dated? Maybe his mother?"

Bill laughed. "She would probably have been at least eighty back then, but I wouldn't put it past you."

"Thanks, buddy," I said, smiling into my mug.

"Hey, I've got a joke for you!"

"Go ahead," I encouraged, still thinking about the odd parental coincidence.

"I like my women like I like my pasta," Bill said, setting up his joke.

"And how's that?" I asked, rather skeptical of his ability to pull off a good ending with a beginning like that.

"Al dente!" he said with a laugh.

I thought for a moment before responding. "With teeth. Clever." Then I asked, "Do you remember how the two of us broke up? Rebecca and I?"

"No. How? What happened?" Bill asked.

"You don't remember? This was a defining moment. It was rather poetic, beautiful, simple, mutual…" I said, trailing off.

"What happened?" Bill asked, craving the story.

I looked up and away as I spoke in a narrator's voice. "Tragically we simultaneously lived at two different and opposing ends of the city. We had two completely different schedules, two completely different groups of friends. From two different worlds really, we were. Living two completely different lives, parallel action. We had nothing in common, nothing but our love for one another.

"We wanted nothing more than to be together, to be in each other's arms, but it was too difficult to bear, just impossible. We knew it, but it was a tacit kind of knowledge; never spoken, but fully understood.

"One day, when we pushed aside our obligations for the moment, we met in Central Park, the midway point between us; we walked, smiled, admired the beauty that surrounded us. We knew what was happening, what needed to be said so neither of us spoke. Silently we walked, walked for hours, hand in hand, no direction, no destination, just experiencing the love.

"We reached the subway station without conscious desire, were forced onto different platforms. As we stood across the tracks, we waited for our different trains which would take us to our different and soon to be separate lives. Across the tracks we stared at one another, trains simultaneously arriving with a screech. It was an almost impossible situation to re-create; her train and mine soon to be headed in the same direction for only a short time before arcing off on their opposite paths. It had to be that specific station, those trains' schedules, those track configurations, and those two subway cars; they all needed to match up for our silent farewell to be so poetically perfect.

"We walked in, never breaking eye contact, watching the other through the windows. The doors closed behind us. The trains moved together, our eyes locked as they accelerated. Slowly, as they moved north and the tracks began to curve off in opposite directions, I could see her begin to cry as our proximity decreased. Scattered structural beams blurred the image. The light became sporadic. Then suddenly, as quickly as she had entered my life, she was gone. A concrete wall separated the two sets of tracks, the two trains, the two of us. Darkness and nothing more."

"Nice, Nick," Bill commented.

"I call it 'Distance: Not Measured by Geography Alone.' "

Bill laughed and drank. "You've always been quite the raconteur."

"Why couldn't things end like that?" I asked without thinking.

"You think things are ending?" Bill questioned.

Caught off guard, I buried myself in the mug until it was empty.

––––––

More Drinks

"Another round?" I asked Bill, pointing to my empty mug with my left hand.

"Another round," he agreed.

"Another round!" I shouted to the waitress who had already started pouring from the tap.

"Thank you, Carly," I said graciously.

Bill, never one to give up the opportunity to use alcohol as an excuse to harass women, tried some of his best lines. "Carly, you must be a speeding ticket because you have 'fine' written all over you."

She ignored him completely, barely looking up after filling one mug and starting on the next. I laughed.

Bill tried again as she finished up. "If I could rearrange the alphabet, I would put 'U' and 'I' together."

Again, completely ignoring him, Carly walked away silently.

"You, Bill, are like school in July," I suggested.

"What do you mean 'school in July'?"

"No class," I answered.

"That's why they call it fishing, not catching," Bill said as he raised his mug to his lips. "But I haven't been reeling them in like I used to. You're lucky, Nick. At least you still have your looks. What do I have?"

"A point," I responded quickly.

Silently sitting, staring, and drinking followed.

After a duration of silence, broken by the occasional sultry slurp amplified by Bill's mug, I blurted out what was on my mind; something I would not have done had I not been filling my empty stomach with beer. "I remember how we first met."

Bill looked at me, confusion on his face. "You and me?" he asked suspiciously.

"No, no!" I shouted before realizing that I was shouting and said quieter, "Me and Julie."

"Fair enough," Bill responded with a bit of a wobble in his stool swivel. "Let's hear it."

I began the story. "It was when I realized she was perfect for me. Same time. We had a mutual friend who was having trouble with his girlfriend. You remember Carlton, right?"

"Right, right, Carlton," Bill said, even though he had never met Carlton.

"When they broke up, Carlton and his girlfriend, that is, he cried and whined about it for days, weeks even. It was hard to listen to him go on and on, but he needed a friend so I was there."

"You're a good man," Bill said, beginning to slur his words.

I paused for a moment after noticing Bill's slur and quietly signaled to the bartender to stop pouring us drinks with a flat hand waving fingertips across my neck. Then I continued. "He was truly sad and wanted nothing but to have her back in his life. I could feel his pain so clearly. I met him at a coffee shop downtown one night to talk about his loss; it was a Tuesday.

"While we were there, she walked in. I saw her and immediately was attracted to her beauty. She started walking toward me and she had this walk, you know? This confident powerful stride, each foot placed concertedly to the ground. Each step I fell deeper and deeper in love. Then she touched his shoulder. 'Hi, Carlton! I haven't seen you in forever. How're things going?' Then she said the two words that changed my life, 'Who's this?' "

Bill started laughing at how those were the two words that changed my life. "That's great! I don't ever think I've heard this one. Go on, go on!" he said loudly, craving more.

Ignoring Bill's low tolerance for alcohol, I continued. " 'Beth dumped me,' was all Carlton said. He didn't even introduce us. Selfish... Then Julie said something which solidified my newly found feelings for her. You know what she said?" I asked rhetorically. " 'So move on and get over it!' That's what she told him."

"What happened next?" Bill asked, engrossed in the story.

"Well," I began, "Carlton was too delicate to take the much needed straightforward tough-love advice. He reacted with anger, getting up and storming out, slamming the door to the coffee shop behind him."

"Carlton was always one to overreact," Bill said. "Then what happened? She didn't run after him, did she?"

"No, of course not. She turned to me and asked in the most adorable way possible, 'Too soon?' "

Again Bill burst into laughter.

I pushed his mug away from him with the back of my left hand, then continued. "I told her that it needed to be said. Then I told her my name, asked for hers, asked her to sit down."

"What did she do?" Bill asked, hanging on my every word.

"What do you think? She sat down. We talked for a while. Back then she was more Marilyn than Madame. Rebelling against her posh upbringing. I offered her something new, something different, something exciting, something she wanted apparently." I stopped talking for a moment and became unexpectedly sad, thinking about how things between my wife and I used to be, how everything was past tense.

Bill pulled his mug back and finished all the beer inside, yet surprisingly did not request another. There he sat, not looking at me but at the wall behind the bar. I assumed he had drifted into a drunken stupor, lost in his own alcohol induced thoughts. His absence of attention allowed me to speak my thoughts unfiltered, without the fear of being harshly judged.

"All she wants to do now is embrace her family and whatever they want her to do, follow the path they want her on. But she's held back by the residue of her past rebellious life—yours truly. Judging from the way they talk about me, the way they despise my very existence in their precious little Julie's life, I fear that they're pushing her to wash herself of me."

Bill mentally checked back in just long enough to inquire, "What did she say next?"

Unfazed by his inability to hold focus, I continued. "She asked me about myself. And I asked her about herself. We talked for some time. Basically just had a conversation."

"That doesn't sound like the way you would snag them back in those days," Bill commented.

"Well," I said, ready to indulge him, "as we were leaving, I asked her if she wanted a ride back to her place. Then she said, 'You have a car? Why would you have a car in the city?' She couldn't believe that I kept a car."

"What'd ya tell 'er?" Bill slurred.

"I told her, 'Some days, when I'm feeling low, I just get in my car and drive. No destination. No navigation system. In no particular direction. Just turn off my phone and drive. Let the road take me where it may.' "

"Aaaaahhh! She musta loved that!"

"You know she did!" I agreed. "It wasn't hard to figure out what she wanted to hear, what she needed to hear."

"What happened next?"

"I asked her if she knew how to drive," I said to Bill.

"What'd she say?" Bill's attention was fully on me.

"Well, she said pretty suggestively, 'I bet I can drive your car.' "

"Aaahhhh!" he exclaimed again. "What'd you say?"

Now, somewhat enjoying the rather flattering progression of our back and forth, I turned toward Bill and spoke in a more dramatic excited voice. "I said to her, 'You know how to drive a stick shift?' Then she paused and frowned before smiling and suggesting, 'Only if you teach me…' "

"Awesome!" Bill responded, loving every second of the story. "You said yes, right?"

"Of course! I told her, 'It's much like dancing.' Then she said, 'I guess that's why I drive an automatic then…' "

I paused for Bill's response, but he froze for a moment before saying, "I don't get it."

"She was implying she couldn't dance," I informed him. "Then I questioned her, I said, 'You? You look like you got more moves than a monkey on twenty-three feet of grapevine.'"

Bill burst into a bout of uncontrollable laughter from the sheer ridiculousness of my strange combination of words.

"Yes," I said. "She had the same reaction. Then I told her, 'So, I'll pick you up at seven then...' And the rest is history."

At that, I finished what was left and released my mug onto the dark wooden bar from two inches higher in elevation than would have been appropriate. Hearing my unintentionally rude finish, Carly began to approach from across the restaurant, but I waved her off with the same cut-off motion I had used before, flat hand waving fingertips across my neck. She stopped, nodded, and returned to her previous post.

Bill was nodding his head, showing his respect for the story. "Well done," he praised over and over. "Well done."

"I remember those days so clearly," I told him. "When we were getting to know one another. I was so amazed by her, by everything about her. I remember asking what kinds of movies she liked; and I've never heard a better answer."

"What did she say?" Bill asked.

"I don't remember," I admitted. "But, it wasn't her exact answer that made it so great. It was that, when I asked her whose movies she liked, she responded with the names of directors, not celebrities. It was just so beautifully refreshing, so cultured, intelligent, magnificent..." I trailed off.

Bill, not fully understanding my point, nodded and repeated, "Well done," a handful more times.

"You know," I began, "I could always tell when a girl was interested in me because strong emotions make your pupils dilate." I pointed at me left eye with my right index finger.

"That's right!" Bill shouted. "Affective Neuroscience, junior year."

"Indeed," I agreed. "I saw it in Julie every time I looked at her. Now, nothing. We rarely look at each other these days anyway. And, when our eyes do meet for a fleeting moment, hers are likely to be filled with tears."

Bill had tuned back out, face focused on the bricks and pulled tight, as if he was desperately trying to will himself sober because he realized he would have to return to work soon.

"None of this is relevant now," I said. "I don't even know why we're talking about it."

"Nick," Bill began, "you know what Shakespeare said…"

"I'm unsure as to which of his many relevant lines you refer. Enlighten me."

" 'What is past is prologue,' " he responded with a theatrical twist.

"Meaning?" I asked, giving Bill a drunken chance to decipher and relate.

"Meaning whatever has happened in the past has led us to the present day events. Sort of setting the stage."

"I don't remember Shakespeare saying that," I said, having given myself some time to think.

"It was in *The Tempest*. Act 2, scene 1, I believe," Bill responded confidently.

"Really? How'd *you* remember that?" I asked, surprised.

Bill gloriously and triumphantly said, "You're slipping, Nick."

At that moment the door of the restaurant opened slowly with a low creak, turning us on our stools to see a long legged, lush lipped, lovely looking lone lady glide in as if on a cloud. We stared as one stares when one somehow finds oneself to be in the presence of an individual so unbelievably attractive that one is endlessly lost in the act of admiring the beauty of that person.

After looking around the room, she settled her gaze in our direction, peering practically through us with no change in her somewhat stern expression. I knew it was me she was interested in, but Bill also knew he was the lucky one.

She then did something neither Bill nor I nor anyone could have predicted or even believed possible. She walked directly to the large man's table, big beautiful smile beaming, attempted to get her arms around his corpulent body—a body incapable of standing to properly greet her—then kissed his sweaty left cheek before blessing the seat across from him with the pleasure of the presence of her posterior.

The two of us looked at one another bewildered at what had just occurred. Our initial astonishment at her beauty was wiped away and replaced with confusion at the incomprehensible pairing of this man and this stunning woman. But the fact that we had previously seen him with other extremely attractive women made the situation a rather fathomable one.

"He must be paying her," I said aloud.

"Must be," Bill agreed as he shook his head.

We swung back around to sit in silence, staring at the bricks and pondering the affordability of the large man's suddenly much more desirable lifestyle.

"I knew what I was getting us both into from the start," I finally blurted out.

"What do you mean, Nick?" Having noticed that his drunken internal state was affecting his behavior, Bill spoke slowly, clearly, deliberately, making a concerted effort to appear less inebriated.

"Our entire relationship was based on a fatal mistake; we relied on each other for everything. We were essentially all that the other had. Her family, most of her friends, they all kind of disowned her. Well, not really 'disowned' per se, but they cut her out of parties and events when she should have been included. She had to turn to me for everything. And what did I do? I forced her to mend things with her family so I could climb the social ladder with their help. That was really what I wanted from her, to raise my social status. But they began to influence her and slowly pulled her back into their world while pushing me out." Outwardly stoic, I felt a strong emotion twisting and turning in my stomach and mind, something I rarely experienced.

"Well," Bill began, still speaking with deliberate intent. "I'm sure that wasn't all there was. I'm sure you loved each other." Then he turned to me and asked, "You did love her, right?"

"Of course I did and I still do!" I insisted loudly.

Bill then steadied himself with both hands on the wooden bar, and asked, "Why?"

I turned away, toward the brick wall behind the bar to gather my thoughts before I spoke. I knew I loved my wife, but why? How does one answer that question? I spoke calmly in a low even tone.

"Julie was the love of my life, my companion, she was even my teacher. She *is* those things. When I met her, I knew nothing of the workings of New York society. I was never wealthy, privileged." I looked around the room, but focused on nothing. The discomfort that my honesty brewed impeded my ability to sit still.

I spoke with frustration in my voice as I quoted Emerson, " 'All things through thee take nobler form...' That's what she was to me. I saw the world differently, better. I learned more from her than I did from all my years in school. Not by sitting down and being lectured to, but by watching what she did, who she talked to, how she talked to them, her expression, her characteristics, the way she held herself, the way she dressed, the way she spoke and captivated a room. Without her, I would be nothing but a lower class poor kid who was smart enough to get some degrees, nothing more, just another semi-success story, but the kind of success the ignorant poor perceive as success, not real success."

"Well, that's not fair," Bill interjected. "Just because you came from a poor neighborhood and a poor household doesn't give you the right to call all poor people ignorant."

Startled at Bill's clearly made point, I thought before speaking. "Maybe it doesn't, but I can assure you that they would look at me and consider me a success because I got out, went to college, graduate school, received prestigious degrees, and never returned. But they have no idea what else there is, no clue how much further I have to go to truly 'make it,' plus the fact that I could never and will never make it because I came from where I did."

"So you don't consider yourself a success?" Bill asked.

"No!" I shouted angrily. "I'm not a success. I'm nobody. My apartment is minuscule and I can barely pay its rent and my office rent. I don't have a vacation house to escape to. All I have is my office; I go there to get away from my frustrating life, ignoring the fact that my office is my life."

I rolled my eyes out of anger, anger at his question and anger at my response. Then I asked, "Do you know how that feels?"

Bill did not respond, just looked at the wall, so I continued. "My car is probably going to be repossessed. My client base is dwindling quicker than ever and it wasn't sufficient to begin with. And all I do with them is bounce meaningless thoughts back and forth because they can't find anyone else to do that with. And, out of everyone that I know, my patients are the ones who respect me the most."

As I spoke, I became more and more angry at Bill for asking, at Julie for evolving beyond me, at my patients for complaining, at the years of school I wasted, at myself for everything.

Bill then completely ignored my rant and again startled me with another emotionally stimulating question. "Were you ever really in love with her?"

"Pardon me?" I asked, knowing well what he had just asked, but giving him a chance to phrase it in a manner less confrontational. Then, before he had a chance to respond, I added, "I loved her so much her voice would narrate my dreams if I still had any."

Out of all the things Bill could have said, he said the one thing I did not anticipate, the one thing for which I had no ready response. "It doesn't sound like you were ever *in love* with her," he said. "It just sounds like you were fixated on the way she made you feel about yourself and what you believed she was capable of offering you in the way of social status and success."

I looked at him, shocked at his words, shocked at his poise and calculating tone. Had he been playing drunk to lull me into a comfortable state, one in which I would speak freely? Or was it the inebriation that allowed him to be blunt?

"Wow, Bill…" I finally responded. "That assessment really makes me sound like a self-absorbed ass."

We filled the resulting awkward silence with the healer of time.

As we sat there I began to think about what I believed I would gain from confiding in Bill my feelings of dissatisfaction. I was incapable of believing what I found myself saying to patients over and over: "Sometimes it just feels good to tell someone, get it out of you."

It was good advice, but only when the person being told is not a friend, but an unbiased observer paid to accept the conversation and objectively attempt to guide future actions. I was attempting to squeeze the failure of life out of my head and my emotions dripped onto the dark wooden bar in front of Bill.

It was a mistake that exposed the fragile state behind my confident façade. I had always held the upper hand with Bill, but, after this conversation, in that moment of silence following it, I felt as though Bill was the one wielding the power in our friendship. I sensed the coming shift in positions; I would be forced into submission while he moved to the top rank. I knew, after that, nothing would be the same between us.

———

Not a Novice Eater

When silence falls upon all the participants in a given conversation (argument), the ambient sounds too quiet to previously be perceived are suddenly, in that silence, magnified. Without looking at each other, Bill and I turned our heads slightly to peer behind us. The large man sitting at the table was ferociously sucking on and gobbling up the chicken legs he had ordered. The beauty across from him did nothing, but watched intently, longingly. What she saw in him, I could not understand, but the more I thought about it, the more likely it seemed that she was indeed being paid. I began to fear for her life as he quickly became closer and closer to finishing what was on his plate.

"This guy is really beginning to get to me," Bill said, clearly jealous of his companion.

"Want me to do something about it?" I asked hollowly.

"Like you would do something," Bill responded jokingly, with a slight smile. The tension from our conversation had been massaged away by our mutual disdain for the large man's inexplicably good fortune.

"You're right," I admitted. "I wouldn't do anything. Why don't you?"

"Maybe I will," he responded.

"You couldn't scare a child," I joked.

"What?" he asked. "Who would want to?"

We both smiled at the thought of intentionally trying to scare a child to prove a point. Then the large man's dining experience became infinitely more infuriating when Bill and I, heads still turned to watch him, witnessed him intentionally toss the chicken bone, cleaned of meat, to the floor.

"Oh, I would murder that guy if I had the chance," I fantasized aloud.

"Don't say that out loud!" Bill warned. "Say 'redrum' instead."

"That's impressively cryptic, Bill," I commended. "But I'm pretty sure if someone hears me say, 'I want to redrum that guy,' they're not going to assume I want to buy him a drink." I thought for a moment then asked, "Does red rum even exist?"

"Good question."

Silence again fell over us. We watched two people leave the restaurant, one come in and order food, and another go through a cup of coffee and ask for a refill. The large man ordered his next course, an additional entrée: steak.

"What are you thinking about?" Bill asked, breaking the silence between us.

I thought for a second before responding with a complex and vague non sequitur. "The endless abyss of never ending dissatisfaction with life is continuously refilling the void left by whatever it was that I was missing inside."

Bill, seemingly too embarrassed to ask me to repeat, nodded. We then returned to silently sitting, breathing, staring at bricks, occasionally turning to scoff at the indulgent jealousy-inducing man behind us.

After a handful of minutes of nothing, the absence of our conversation was interrupted by the sound of a screaming woman.

"My husband is choking! My husband is choking!"

Bill and I look at one another before swiveling our stools to see who could possibly be choking.

"Who else?" I said to Bill.

"Should we help?" he asked.

I responded with wise words. "Aristotle would tell us that '...we learn to be just by doing just acts.' "

"Well, that's *just* stupid," Bill punned before we spun around on our stools to face the brick wall behind the bar once again.

I laughed then asked, "Can you believe that's his wife?"

Bill responded, "I chose to ignore that part for my own preservation. And I doubt that guy is even choking."

We turned back around to examine the man wiggling in his chair, swinging his arms around the best he could, while his wife jumped around frantically from table to table looking for help.

"Why not?" I asked as the man flopped to the dirty floor from his thankful chair.

"Novice eaters choke, babies or extremely skinny people, people who haven't eaten much in life. This guy is a pro. No way he would make a mistake. He's obviously had a great deal of practice."

I laughed aloud in agreement. "So what do you think is wrong with him, Doctor?"

"I don't know; heart attack maybe?" he whimsically diagnosed.

"Could be," I agreed. "But, look, he's grabbing his throat, not his chest. And he seems to be having trouble making sound and breathing. It's got to be choking."

"Oh, look at that," Bill said. "You're right. Must be choking then."

After watching for several more seconds and seeing a man and a woman, other restaurant patrons, ostensibly come to his aid, but instead merely ask him absurd questions such as, "Are you choking?" and "Should we call the hospital?" Bill asked, "Should we do something?"

"Naaaa," I responded.

Then Carly, leaning over the large man, pointed to us and shouted, "Doctor! Come help!"

Bill and I attempted to shush her, both quickly pulling a sole index finger to the lips, but the false hope had already been passed around the restaurant.

"Oh thank God!" the beautiful woman exclaimed. "Please help my husband."

I then could not help but ask Bill again, "Seriously, can you believe she's his wife?"

"Should we tell her we saw him with that blond girl yesterday?" Bill asked me.

"Please!" she shouted from her husband's spot on the floor. "Please help us."

"Oh, we're not doctors," I said finally.

"I thought you told me you were a doctor," Carly shouted angrily.

"Well," I began, somewhat embarrassed. "We're psychologists."

Carly then asked, "Why didn't you specify?" She was clearly perturbed by our lack of medical degrees.

I shrugged my shoulders as my expression indicated that I did not know.

Bill leaned toward me and said, "You are what you eat."

"What do you mean?" I asked him.

"You are what you eat," he repeated. "And this guy must have eaten a ridiculously fat person!"

I laughed at Bill's inappropriate joke even though it was not very funny or well thought out. "What comes after asphyxi-seven?" I asked Bill.

"Uh… asphyxi-eight?" he said aloud, then realized the joke and laughed heartily.

I joined in on the laughter. "Asphyxiate; that's hilarious," I gloated. "You know this happened to me before?" I began. "A woman went into labor in a restaurant and they tried to get me to help because they thought I was a medical doctor."

Bill then asked, "What happened?"

"Let's just say the mother didn't end up naming the child Nicholas," I responded.

Then the man whimpered loudly as he punched his tight right fist into the middle of his chest. "My chest! My chest!" his voice straining. "Help me, please!"

"I don't think he's choking anymore," I proudly diagnosed to all. "I'm pretty sure he's talking which means he couldn't be choking. That's not how choking works. Pretty sure choking obstructs that pathway. He should be fine."

"Heart attack! Heart attack!" he pushed out forcefully.

Defeated, I looked at Bill and muttered, "Looks like you were right."

"Nice!" Bill celebrated verbally.

"Oh, please help my husband! Please help my husband!" the beautiful woman shouted in our direction.

I looked at Bill who put his hands up, palms toward me, to exclude himself from what he knew I was tacitly suggesting we attempt: to help her husband. I got up from my stool out of sheer desire for the man's absurdly beautiful wife to stop shouting. Up close, he was even larger than I thought he was.

"What should I do?" I asked.

"I don't know, you're the doctor," the beautiful wife said.

I looked at her and gasped at her beauty. "Really?" I asked aloud. "*You* are married to *him*?"

"Yes!" she shouted angrily. "Can't you do something? You said you were a doctor!"

"I told you, I am a *psychologist*." I said the word "psychologist" as condescendingly slowly as possible. Her high level of beauty and choice of spouse suggested a low level of intelligence so I continued to explain. "I have a PhD, not an MD. It's an academic degree, mostly research. My training was in analyzing people's thoughts and behaviors and scientific methods of helping them change their behaviors. I have no more knowledge of the human body or medicine than you do. Well, maybe a bit more than *you*."

She froze up, either because she was trying to process all the large words I had just bombarded her with or because she was shocked that psychologists can call themselves doctors without being what most people consider "real doctors."

"Do something!" she yelped finally.

"Fine," I conceded. "Well, there's no way I'm going to perform CPR on this guy. Uh... I remember reading somewhere that chest compressions were a more effective method anyway."

"But he's not choking," Carly yelled in my left ear.

"Gosh!" I exclaimed. "You don't have to yell. Nobody has to yell. There are very few people here and we can all hear each other if we speak with inside voices. Please!"

Everyone looked at me as if I was suggesting we fill the restaurant with beer and go swimming. The large man's condition appeared to be getting worse as he was no longer huffing and puffing but was instead wheezing and sputtering.

"Do something!" someone still sitting across the restaurant shouted.

"You're not even standing up," I retorted.

I then began to work on him, pushing against his chest and hoping it would somehow do something to improve his situation.

"Why isn't it working? Why isn't he breathing?" His wife was shouting hysterically.

As I continued to work on the large man, I could hear one of the restaurant patrons chewing gum, creating bubbles, and popping them. It infuriated me.

"Does anybody have an aspirin?" I asked.

Carly shouted back, "Can we deal with your headache at some other time?"

"It's not for me. It's for him!" I responded angrily and almost as loud. "And inside voices please," I added.

"How do you know he has a headache?" asked his extremely beautiful but unhelpful wife.

After a quick eye roll, I responded, "I don't. It's supposed to thin the blood, helping it pass through the arteries and heart. It gives him a better chance statistically."

"How would you know? You're not a doctor!" Carly hissed in every direction.

"I am a doctor!" I shouted proudly. "I'm just not a *medical* doctor."

"Exactly!" Carly shouted back.

"Fine," I said, becoming more and more frustrated with what I was dealing with.

I began to work faster and with more force, pushing with a great deal of strength. My nose began to bleed again. The blood stained the large man's yellow Hawaiian shirt, saturating it with red drops layering over the barbecue sauce from his chicken. I wiped my nose with the cuff of my sleeve and continued.

"Bill!" I shouted before questioning in my head why I shouted so loudly. "Come over here. Give me a hand."

Bill jumped from his stool. I could see in his face he was, as he was about to say, "Ready to rock!"

I stopped and looked up to shake my head at him. His eyes said, *It's my time to shine! I'm in the game!*

Bill descended upon the now unconscious man and fumbled around the man's oversized stomach, pushing in and out, slapping his face back and forth. It was quite obvious that Bill had no idea what he was doing.

"Has anyone called an ambulance? Have they given us any instructions?" I asked Carly.

"Uh, no…" she admitted after looking around at everyone hoping for a "yes."

"Okay," I said. "Someone is going to get on that at some point, right? Just a suggestion."

Carly got up and ran to the phone.

"Maybe he's a diuretic?" Bill offered as he continued to work on the man's stomach with excessive force.

"What?" I asked. "You mean a diabetic; like he needs a cookie? Passed out from low blood sugar?"

"Yes, that's what I meant," Bill said a bit embarrassed.

"No!" his wife shouted. "He's not a diabetic."

"That diuretic thing made me think of something," Bill began. "Maybe he needs to go to the bathroom. Maybe he's too full?"

"What? No. That makes no sense," I said. "He had a heart attack."

"No, no, he might have stuffed himself to the point where some of it needs to come out. I've seen it happen on TV, that medical drama on Wednesday nights. They base episodes on real stuff, real medical conditions. It happens sometimes to obese people."

"You're kidding me?" I questioned.

The man's wife pushed me away shouting, "You don't know what you're doing. You're going to kill him." She may have added, "And you're crazy!" toward Bill.

"You told us to try to help," I retaliated.

"Just get off him," she said as she began to cry at the sight of her motionless husband.

Bill stood and began to make his way back to his stool while I, still crouching, quietly checked the man's pulse before standing and observing the despair that had fallen over the room.

"Can anyone help my husband?" the beautiful woman shouted through her tears.

The silent responses from the restaurant patrons left a haunting hole in my mind; everyone was looking down, looking away, or just staring. We all knew that no one could help her husband anymore, trained or untrained. The hysterical sobs of his wife lightly echoed in each of our ears as she held him tightly.

"Can anyone help my husband? Please?"

Nobody could have helped the man, but, even if they thought they could, they were unlikely to step up for fear of the real possibility of a lawsuit, no matter what the outcome of the attempt to aid.

"Can anyone help him? Please, can anyone help my husband? He's going to die!"

Herbert Mellon Levine died after momentarily choking which led to a massive heart attack. He was thirty-six years, four months, and five days old. Paramedics arrived forty-six minutes after his passing and pronounced him deceased without even attempting to revive him. It was forty-six minutes spent in a numbing, deafening silence broken only by the cries of his widow.

"Can anyone help my husband?"

We left the restaurant one by one, saying nothing to one another, looking everywhere but into anyone's eyes. I do not know if we were afraid of what we would see—fear, shock, a fleeting memory of what had just occurred—but there was not one person in the restaurant who wanted to find out.

Bill and I said nothing to one another. I stood close to the man, watched him lying there. Bill sat at the bar, observing from a dozen feet away. The paramedics needed help hoisting the man onto the stretcher. Being careful not to meet eyes, the manager and I assisted, fumbling as we worked together out of sync.

The man's wife travelled with him in the back of the ambulance with no hope of ever seeing her husband breathe again. I swung closed the back doors to the vehicle, one before the other, and saw her lovely face through the window. Her expression was much as it had been when I first saw her glide into the restaurant, stern and emotionless. Shock had set in; hysteria had drained away a half hour earlier.

Bill had already left, so I went back into the restaurant to settle the bill, but the manager waved me off as I approached, shaking my hand, then hugging me tightly for a moment longer than was comfortable.

My walk to the office was slow, humid, sticky, as the sky became thick and dark with clouds. The clogged streets offered no comfort, just the wafting heat and mismatched smells from all the bodies.

The crowds were where I focused my emotion as frustration and anger set in. I scorned the obnoxious and oblivious shoppers, bags occupying three times as much horizontal space as they should, swinging off arms and hands. Tourists who travelled all the way to New York City to eat at a chain restaurant. Those with enough intelligence to sample the New York City restaurants, but opted to sit outside, pushing those on the sidewalk into the street with their tiny outdoor tables. Thieves pushing counterfeit merchandise. Beggars pleading for my hard earned money. Police with that cocky air about them frowning menacingly at any who ventured a look. Bike messengers jumping up and down from the sidewalks and streets, weaving between everything as just another obstacle. Children, too short to be seen until already underfoot, impossible to negotiate.

None knew of my troubles. I knew nothing of theirs. It was only fair that we were muted to each other, incapable of hearing or seeing anything in the other's life past a fleeting glance at the façade of the present.

The doorman opened the door, spotting me on approach from several yards away. I moved slowly, throwing off his timing. He held the door open for far longer than he anticipated, allowing cold air to rush out while warm filled its place.

Why do doormen and pilots dress exactly the same? I thought as I passed without an exchange of words, without even a glance in his direction, as if the door was automated. The door was as good as automated. It should have been automated.

Guilt, an unexpected and out of place emotion, followed me up the empty elevator. I questioned whether my confusion about how to emotionally react was being experienced as guilt for ignoring the doorman. He deserved more respect than he received from passersby, from delivery men, and especially from the owners in the building.

Trying to justify my feelings of guilt and definitively assign them to my rude behavior to the doorman, my mind transported me to when I had first acquired the lease for the office. It had been early enough in our marriage that Julie still took part in my life.

Each Christmas, she made sure to send me with cards for the doormen. Shocked and grateful, they thanked me, confiding that they never received genuine gratitude from the owners in the building. They began to treat me like one of the guys: fist bumps or hand slaps when I walked by, off-color and crude remarks about residents' wives and daughters for my ears only, a disgusted look or roll of the eyes toward me when another resident would ignore a friendly hello.

It took little time to realize that my camaraderie with these men only dragged me deeper beneath the other residents in the minds of society. Scared of that prospect, I began ignoring them when residents were around, treating the doormen like the residents did, like they were nothing, like the door was automated. The doormen realized the level to which I had moved them in my hierarchy and began treating me with a façade of respect just as they treated the rest of the residents. These were genuinely good people who I pushed away for a sliver of a silver spoon, a step up the social ladder.

As I exited the elevator, I decided that the guilt was well identified and its origin was well labeled; thus I dismissed it.

Wednesday at the Office

The sound of the office door locking behind my back was satisfying, bringing some semblance of serenity, a moment of satisfaction, but I could not shake the image of the man lying on the dirty floor of the restaurant. I thought about the soft mushy surface of his chest as I had pushed it again and again, hard, over and over and over and over.

My mind slipped toward Courtland, my unfortunate suicidal patient who was with me one week earlier, smiling, fine, alive. The office was dark, light choked dead by the clouds that had grown thick.

I saw him on the couch before I flipped the light-switch on the wall next to the door. He turned to me, looked right into my eyes, no words. The switch illuminated his absence, but his presence was still palpable, following me around every inch of that office, every inch of that city, every inch of my life. He would never leave.

Before collapsing into the large leather chair behind the mahogany desk, I filled the carafe with filtered water and set it on the coffee table between the couch and seats. I then spent some time shaking off the residue of death, fresh and stale alike.

I rolled my sleeves up, rolling the bloodstains out of sight. The screens flickered from darkness before I signed in and examined my minuscule workload. The corner of the screen read 1:39 p.m.

———

Winston

The first message was from a relatively new patient, Winston, a response to Tuesday's message in which I had, at his request, rather carelessly informed him of my preliminary assumptions for diagnosis, always a mistake.

I opened it without pausing to further examine my own emotions and how they might bleed into the day's sessions.

—

Good Wednesday, Dr. Thesiger,

Thank You For Your Honest And Open Answer. I Read Over It Several Times. I Then Spent Seventy-One Minutes Reading About Those Disorders And Have Come To The Conclusion That I Have Ocd.

I Have Spent A Number Of Hours Attempting To Create A Suitable Response To Your E-Mail, And Have Decided That I Would Prefer To Have A Video Session. May We Do This On Monday At 4 P.m.? These Are The Only Numbers That Match Up Properly For Me To Be Comfortable So Hopefully You Will Be Free.

Briefly, I Would Like To Explain What I Believe The Origin Of My Disorder To Be…

When My Father Was Alive, During My Childhood, He Was Never Really There. Always Busy For Some Reason Or Another. Always Away On Business, My Mother Would Tell Me. It Was Not Until Much Later, After He Passed, That She Told Me They Had Been Separated For Most Of My Childhood.

During Those Days, He Would Call Me Every Day At Exactly The Same Time; Right After I Would Arrive Home From

School. I Used To Look At The Clock And Count Down To 4 P.m. Each Day Of Every Week, The Phone Would Ring And I Would Pick It Up And There He Would Be. We Would Talk For Thirty Minutes Until 4:30 P.m.

I Miss That More Than Anything Else In The World. Having An Event That Occurred At The Same Time Every Day Was What Kept Me Calm. Now I Have Found Something Else Which Keeps Me Calm; Capitalizing Each Word That I Type.

Please Let Me Know If We May Speak Via Video Session At 4 P.m. On Monday. And Please Let Me Know If We Can Make It A Weekly Session Time.

Thank You, Doctor.

-Winston

—

The middle finger and thumb of my right hand distorted my vision as they rubbed against my eyelids. It did nothing to help the headache I had developed while reading Winston's message.

My response was short and urgent.

—

Winston,

I am quite concerned about the jump you made from yesterday to today. I feel as though you are being influenced a great deal by my description of the disorders you mentioned in your previous e-mail.

My intention was not for you to try to relate to those disorders and try to fit yourself into the descriptions, but it appears that is what you have done.

Monday at 4 p.m. is a fine time to contact me for a video session, but I encourage you to contact me sooner, by phone, e-mail, or you could try me for an impromptu video session. Try me anytime. Do not try to see if the numbers line up or if they are "comfortable."

Best of luck to you, Sir Winston.

-Dr. Thesiger

—

After proofreading and checking the spelling on my response message, I paused before sending to consider if maybe Winston did have obsessive-compulsive disorder. It would be hard to accurately diagnose or be sure of the absence of the disorder through e-mails or video conversations alone. Even analyzing the results of his personality tests, which I was yet to do, would not yield an adequate amount of information for an official diagnosis. I had no doubt that he was playing into the disorder, but maybe I was wrong.

I stopped my potentially harmful thought process, which appeared to be moving toward questioning my entire way of practicing psychology, with a quick tap on the "send" button.

As quickly as the message left the screen, Winston and his eccentricities were out of my conscious mind only to be replaced by my next patient's perceived issues.

———

Arthur

A video attached to the next e-mail from Arthur rested below Winston's recently replied-to message. I took a deep breath before bothering myself with Arthur's exaggerated dramatization of real life.

As a college senior with too much free time, he frequently communicated with me via overly dramatic vignette. I ignored the fact that I was being disturbed from several different angles and that viewing Arthur's video would only add another and allowed the impending disturbance to take over the screen.

—

The setting, almost always different from video to video, was a lush outdoor area. Clear and sharp with detail, the video was shot with a higher quality camera than previous videos. The far background was dark, shaded by the leaves of the surrounding tall old trees.

"Must be in the woods for some reason," I said aloud. Then I leaned in closer to the screen, "But why is it so well lit?" I asked myself of the middle section.

Arthur began off camera; I assumed this was done to enhance the dramatic effect of his entrance and not because he had to press the record button given that he held the remote for the camera in his left hand.

When he finally sauntered into the frame, he was wearing a long cloak with a hood and holding a long stick in his right hand, using it to lean on as he walked, slowly, assisted.

His brown hooded cloak changed from dark, almost blending into the background, to well-lit as he neared the middle of the frame. It became obvious that he had found a nice quiet dark spot in the woods then brought his camera and additional lighting equipment so he would be well illuminated during taping. The amount of energy Arthur put into these productions was alarmingly high. He really was trying entirely too hard. For some reason, he probably thought that, because I live in New York City, I must know somebody on Broadway with whom I might share one of his videos.

I shook my head as he walked in circles before reaching the middle of the screen, marked on the ground with an X formed from bright yellow tape, probably not intended to reach the final cut.

After circumnavigating the yellow X, Arthur jumped onto it and threw off his cloak, hood getting stuck briefly on his head before being flung off by his left hand, still clutching the remote. The removal of the cloak revealed what I hoped were his street clothes (as opposed to the cloak being his street clothes), brown shorts with large pockets above the sides of his knees and a dark blue T-shirt with the word STAR on it in pink lettering.

"I suppose that's better than the cloak," I said aloud.

"Disgrace!" he shouted. "A damn dirty disgrace!"

The camera zoomed in as he ran toward it, effectively simulating the camera rapidly approaching. I nodded my head at the surprisingly good cinematography so far.

"Impenetrable really…" he said, his tone turning to that of an intellectual as he looked away from the camera, pondering.

He continued after a moment's thought. "The psyche of the uninformed, the mere civilians, the pedantic plethora of pathetic poopieheads." He looked directly into the camera at "poopieheads." I laughed aloud.

"You, Sir Doctor, my good man, my guide through this thing we call life, you are most likely wondering why it is that I am so strapped for patience, so filled with distress, with rage…"

"Actually, I am," I said, realizing that Arthur seemed to do an impressive job of asking rhetorical questions during his videos and pausing just long enough for my responses.

As he spoke he zoomed the camera out slowly to reveal that he was sitting on a large throne. I questioned where he had gotten a large throne, how he had moved it into the woods, and how he had managed to maneuver it into the frame with himself on it and without the knowledge of the viewer.

"What's past is this," Arthur began. "Got into an argument with a friend earlier in the day."

Immediately I checked the time stamp of his e-mail, 9:47 a.m. "Pretty early for an argument..." I said aloud.

He continued after a dramatic pause. "Ha..." he laughed condescendingly. "So above her, I am. Knowing more than she does, I do."

Again, I laughed aloud, this time at his misuse of the English language.

"The breadth of her intolerance and ignorance was inevitable. The argument of which I speak, it is over the insatiable... Cooking that is."

"Cooking?" I asked the prerecorded video.

"Yes, cooking," Arthur responded as if he knew I was going to question it.

"I have, Dr. Thesiger, decided that I would pull back a bit on my involvement in the arts, performing, and take some classes in the arts, culinary. The decision came after watching your last response. The words of the great Thomas La Mance. Life is what happens while you are making other plans. I realized that all I was doing was making plans. Show business was what I was planning. It was what I wanted in life, all I wanted, the only place I saw myself, the only thing I planned for."

Arthur then looked into the camera with a ponderous expression. "Yes," Arthur finally said, starting up after a dozen seconds lost to thought or the illusion of thought. "I had made the decision long ago that I would have some backups, something to fall back on, but I never took any of them into consideration until now."

Arthur then zoomed the camera out a little more and swung both legs over the right arm of the throne, turning his body 90 degrees to his right in the process. As he spoke, far behind him, a young man wearing a backpack walked into frame, looked at the production taking place, shook his head, then continued to walk on.

"Now, the argument," Arthur began. "Ohhhh, I was so frustrated. She doesn't know much of anything, an ignoramus. She and I got into a bit of a conversation about why I was pursuing cooking as opposed to acting. I told her I feel like acting is selfish and actors are selfish people. Cooking, on the other hand, is generous. I'm giving people nourishment. Everyone needs nourishment. People gotta eat! Am I right?"

Arthur left his throne with a hop and began walking back and forth in the frame. "And at that, she became furious. Yelling at me, shouting that I was stupid. Saying acting wasn't selfish. 'What kind of moron are you?' she asked me angrily. 'How is cooking any better or worse than acting? How can you compare the two?'

"Of course I retaliated by slapping her in the face, slapping the silly from her, and then running away. I showed her! Who did she think she was, telling me I was a moron? But, I have since calmed and I never intend on seeing her again."

Arthur then hopped back onto the throne, arms resting on the armrests and both feet on the ground. The camera began to zoom in slowly.

"Gosh, the people I have to deal with... But, deal with I do. This, Doctor, was what my morning consisted of. Talk about starting your day off on the wrong foot!"

His elbows left the throne armrests and moved to his thighs as he leaned forward, hands together with fingers intertwined around the remote. The camera adjusted the shot to re-center his figure and zoomed in slightly.

"I thank you for your help through the hard times, Doctor. And I will speak more about my new classes in the culinary arts soon. Maybe I can cook a dish to be sent in your direction? Stay tuned."

His figure, filling the frame, jumped quickly to stand on the throne. The camera zoomed out and adjusted to keep him fully on screen. "Arthur out!" he shouted before pointing the remote at the camera. The video ended abruptly.

—

I sat back in my large leather chair and swung around to look out through the window onto Central Park. It was dark, gloomy. Then I swung back around to the screen. Possible responses were absent in my mind. I was blank inside, unable to make even a doodle on my mental notepad.

I began to put myself in Arthur's place. I declined to ask myself the obvious questions of why I had just shot a well-produced video in the woods with a throne. Questions about why and how I got into an argument about acting and cooking began to come. Then the slap hit me.

"What was I thinking?" I said aloud.

Without additional thought or any planning, I hit the record button, responding to him via his choice of medium.

—

I cleared my throat on screen then began. "You slapped her? You slapped another person and a female at that? What were you thinking, Arthur? What were you thinking? You don't resort to physical violence. Don't swing unless swung upon, or *slap* in your case. And never hit a girl. Just walk away unless your life is in danger and, in that case, you run away."

I adjusted in my large leather chair and moved the camera to keep myself well centered.

"Do you know why you resorted to the most primal and juvenile of reactions after your belief was questioned? Because you hit a wall in your thought process, in your backward logic, which you did not want to break through.

"You didn't even question yourself? You didn't ask yourself why you had no response other than slapping then running? Think about it, Arthur. No, no! Seriously think about it because this is important. This is what you have to do when you feel the urge to slap someone when there is no actual reason to do so."

I stopped for several seconds, giving him some time to think. "Can't come up with anything? That's because of that wall I was talking about, the one you don't want to break through. You slapped your female friend because you chose not to even consider the possibility that you might be wrong, that she had a good point and your argument was meritless. You had nothing, no good response, so you slapped her. Real mature, Arthur.

"Do you know why you were able to come up with not one piece of support for your argument? Now I'm going to have to ask you to really think about it this time because this is really important, it's at the root of your problem; your inability to appropriately question your motives. The answer is this: no support exists for your argument.

"Now, Arthur, think about this for some time. Why would you say something, argue it even, if it made no sense?"

I paused, allowing Arthur to think again, really think about the question.

"Come up with anything?" I asked obnoxiously. "I didn't think so. Here is the answer: you are a failure. You failed in acting, never getting past being an extra in one TV commercial and getting only company parts in school plays, never the star despite what your shirt might say. You knew, maybe consciously, maybe subconsciously, that you would never really make it as an actor, so you were soured by it, allowing anger to increase in pressure and intensity until it came out as disdain for the entire acting industry. So you convinced yourself that acting is negative, is selfish, but think about that. Is acting selfish? How the heck is acting selfish? How is performing for other people selfish?

"Did you know that there is not a culture on this planet that doesn't have some form of recreation and entertainment and music? Not one. Human beings, with our level of intelligence and complex brain structure, need it and you're calling it selfish in comparison to preparing food? How can you compare the two?

"You can't. That's the answer, in case you were wondering. You're only doing it because you failed as an actor and now you've latched on to cooking relatively arbitrarily and you can't just admit that you failed. Well admit it, accept it, and live with it, Arthur. You are a failure. A true, real life failure. Not until you admit it will you ever be able to get on with your life, make appropriate decisions, and learn to think about why you feel a particular way about something. Maybe you'll even stop hitting girls."

—

I touched the button to stop recording, furious and shaking. Without giving myself time to think, I hit the "send" button. I did not want to consider the pros and cons of what I was doing. He angered me so deeply that I felt it completely necessary to retaliate by putting him in his place without consideration of consequences.

"Maybe this kid does have what it takes to make it in New York City," I muttered to the desk.

———

After the message was sent, I justified it by mentally labeling that session as "reality therapy"; a successful and effective method used with substance abuse patients and addicts of all kinds. Bombarding the patient with harsh realities and brutal honesty were at its core.

The sound and feeling of my stomach grumbling in addition to the low-blood-sugar-induced angry message alerted me to the fact that I was completely empty and had gone without food for the entire day.

I brought up the screen with restaurants that delivered, but nothing looked appetizing. Nothing even caught my eye. Pizza was the default upon which I very rarely fell, but indecisiveness forced my hand. Three slices would arrive within thirty minutes.

My head hit the small tan pillow on the couch. It provided little cushioning, pulling and twisting my neck uncomfortably. Quickly I realized that napping was not a viable option while waiting for sustenance. I thought about how Arthur could save my life with his cooking, but darn well could not do so with his terrible overacting.

My back hit the patient couch, by the window, the ergonomically contoured classic psychologist's couch in the constant lying back configuration like a chaise lounge. No patient had ever used it. I knew none would. It was for show, custom-made to incite the illusion of the office of a professional psychologist. The room needed to fit the part and I had spent accordingly. The hundreds of thousands paid to fulfill my request for an upscale office were never recovered, never would be. Still I paid the loan payments when I could, barely covering the interest, borrowing more money just to stay afloat.

The large leather chair behind the desk supported me upright, completing my bout of musical chairs as I attempted to find a level of comfort I knew was gone forever. I turned to the park and lost myself. The clouds parked overhead were bulbous, angry, ready to split and spill, but they held tight. The trees moved in dueling waves sourced from every direction, crashing into one another, maybe winning over the competitor or maybe losing, but all were ready to fight the next battle.

I turned back toward the real world, revived the screen, then selected the message below Arthur's. The video I had sent minutes earlier encouraged me to consider my own emotions while analyzing, but it felt difficult and uncomfortable to do so. I ignored my feelings and went on.

———

Dave

"Dave" read the subject.

—

Dr. Thesiger,

It's been some time. I've been studying for finals. Our first summer session is ending. I'm nervous. Don't know what to do. I've been studying, but I'm still unsure. Any words of advice?

Thanks.

-Dave A.

—

I always described Dave as a "good kid" in my mind. Had never done anything wrong to anybody, never performed a bad act. His only problems were hardly problems at all, but could be more accurately labeled as characteristics that his parents found alarming. I had been hired to keep a watchful eye on him and guide him in the right direction when he needed. His parents, terrified of his timid self-conscious behavior, believed themselves to be too busy to take his calls from college so it was up to me to deliver when he needed some encouraging words.

My response was one which I had used many times with other students, but would tailor to fit the specific situations.

—

Hello Dave,

There is something that I would like to remind you of as you go into finals. You would not be at your school if you could not succeed there. In high school, you were a strong student, successful academically, and a standout member of your community. If that was not so, you would not have been considered for admission, much less admitted.

Yes, there have been some bumps in the road, but suffering a setback in a course, having difficulty with a chosen major before changing to another, or being told (explicitly or implicitly) that you cannot make it by an external negative force in your life does not define you. You define yourself.

Do not forget about all the work you did to get there and who you are. All the things that made you someone your school wanted to have and all the people who have supported you and continue to support you; that should be in your mind as you enter this stressful time.

I would say good luck, but luck is the last thing you need. Skill and purpose are what you have and what you shall use to succeed. Be well, Dave, be well.

-Dr. Thesiger

—

Spell-checking was quick and painless, executed with a three second scan of the screen. The message was added to the sent message folder, on its way to assure Dave that he would not only do well on his finals, but do well in life.

————

Gabriel

The message below Dave's in my rarely empty inbox had a subject of "Gabriel." A master's student in psychology, he was interested in doctoral programs, but unsure of which specialty or focus within the discipline to concentrate on. His professors suggested that he consult with a therapist so he could better understand his psyche, his behavioral patterns, and his strengths and weaknesses to help him decide what to concentrate on within a doctoral program and to allow him to experience psychology from the point of view of the patient, watching a therapist in action.

Gabriel decided I would make a good guide for him because his schedule only allowed him time for an e-mail here and there and in-office sessions once a month or so.

His e-mails generally consisted of long, drawn out theoretical questions about psychology as a philosophical endeavor. My role was to act as a professor reading an assignment. Some days it was nice and almost refreshing to respond to academic questions about the profession, but it was not some days.

—

Dear Dr. Thesiger,

For years, I have had the utmost respect for psychologists. . As an idealistic naïve boy, I felt that the purpose of psychology was solely to help people with their problems by offering advice through therapy. Growing up and undergrad classes taught me that there are many facets of psychology other than therapy. All I did for the four years of undergrad was learn about neuropsychological research and memorize the empirical facts of psychology, behavior, and the mind.

Now that I am in graduate school, I am finally learning about psychotherapy and I am surprised to discover that there are so many different forms and methods. This is, of course, a good thing because no two patients are the same and no two problems are the same. Different approaches are more appropriate for different situations.

Despite the numerous forms of therapy, I assumed that there would be one aspect that was present in all: advice. I was under the naïve impression that patients receive advice during therapy sessions. Don't people go to therapy to get help *and* to receive helpful advice? I was surprised to learn that patients do not receive advice during psychoanalytic therapy (for example).

Psychoanalytic therapy, the classic Freudian kind, requires patients to lie on a couch and talk about whatever comes to mind while the psychologist merely asks questions; this method appears to be more interested in finding the origin of people's current problems and making assumptions about why people are the way they are based on what is learned in sessions about their unconscious mind. These assumptions are merely assumptions and nothing more.

In psychoanalytic therapy, rather than getting advice, patients receive some kind of higher knowledge about their past and how it is assumed to relate to their present. And, as crazy as this sounds, that "knowledge" appears to help people with their problems even though the problems themselves were not discussed. Given that psychoanalytic therapy does appear to help people with their problems, it is almost as if psychoanalytic therapy is the placebo in an experiment to prove that other forms of therapy work.

It may be harsh to refer to psychoanalytic therapy as a placebo. The fact is that this form of therapy does help people (placebo effect). But, does merely talking to people with problems also help them (control group)? The experimental group in this hypothetical study would likely receive Cognitive Behavioral Therapy which is much more focused on the problem and methods to improve it and behavior. How much more or less would any one of them work or would they help patients the same amount? And where do other forms of therapy fall on the spectrum?

It is impossible to compare and try to validate a specific method of therapy (and invalidate the others) for so many reasons including the countless variables that would be impossible to control for, especially the loose and inconsistent way in which therapy is practiced (from what I hear). We will probably never be able to scientifically test which one is the *real* therapy, which works best. Maybe all are. Or rather, maybe none are. But, none of this changes the fact that therapy and therapists help people even though some of them are using methods that may be no more helpful than just a friendly conversation.

-Gabriel

—

I bugged out my eyes and rolled them dramatically around the room. I did it twice more because it felt good to mock the boy on the beginning of his path to become me. He believed that he had an original thought, but all who go through the training question the methods. I did not intend to allow my assigned protégé to fall into the trap of all that came before him.

—

What's up, Gabe?

How are the events of your life treating you? How about your perception of them? And the perceptions of others about those events and their own as they relate to you and as they do not?

Your message shows some good insight, but unfortunately, it's insight that few in your place do not share. Everyone wonders if any of these things actually work or if one is better than the other. The quick and dirty answer is that running some research experiment comparing them would be useless. Even if you came up with a winner, a therapy that worked better than the rest, that wouldn't translate to the real world for several reasons. Different forms of therapy work for different people and their different problems at different times with different therapists.

Think about the fact that your patients are different from one another. Their pasts, their presents, and problems are all unique. Additionally, they will all react differently to the same thing. Another important factor is the therapists themselves. Every therapist is different and patients react differently to different therapists. The rapport between a patient and therapist is a key factor in the question of success in session.

It feels good to think that you've come up with questions that you believe nobody has asked and I am glad you are bringing these presumed to be earth-shattering questions to me, but don't get too excited. Very very very few people will ever come up with a novel thought in their entire lives.

Consider this, when I first started having ideas and voicing them, a very smart woman told me that there are billions and billions of people on earth today and they are all descendants of billions and billions of people. All of these people had a lifetime of thoughts, dreams and desires, education and experience. They had spent a lot more time than I had thinking about the world, the way it works, and pretty much everything imaginable while coming up with good and bad ideas alike.

This woman told me that there is no way that I could possibly think of some kind of special new novel idea. Statistically, it just couldn't happen. Whatever I think of is not new, but has been thought of by potentially millions, even billions, before me.

She told me that everything I think and do is a copy so I should just go with the flow and let life take me where it does. I should follow the beaten path and not try to stand out with my ideas because there's no way that I have a novel enough mind to surpass tens of thousands of years of thought from billions of people. Who am I to think I am that intelligent and unique?

That woman was my second grade teacher. She said this all to me after I raised my hand and asked her a question which completely derailed her inconsistent lecture on Native American farming practices. Her intention was to shut me up and make sure that I never made her look stupid again, in front of a room full of second graders or anyone else.

Interestingly enough, I took her little tirade as a challenge. Let's see if I can beat the odds and come up with something new and special. Let's see if I can create something that changes the way people think, live, love... Ever since then I have spent my life intentionally trying to think outside the box.

Gabe, I commend you for thinking this way without being yelled at by an obnoxious self-conscious second grade teacher. You need to continue thinking in that manner and you will come up with something great; you *will* change the world.

Use your frustration with what currently exists in the field of psychology as motivation to improve it. Consider this: the best toolmakers are frustrated artists. They want to paint a masterpiece, but the right brush does not exist. They have to create it themselves.

Create that brush then create that masterpiece. And, if you're wondering how my pursuit of novelty has turned out, so far I'm still striving to get there. But, I can tell that you're already years ahead of where I was at your age. Hopefully I can be the first to hear something truly new in this modern world in one of these emails from you.

-Dr. Thesiger

—

The message was sent without reading over it to check for spelling or grammatical mistakes because I felt suddenly submerged under a strong wave of fatigue. The absence of food was first on the list of culprits, but I dismissed that quickly. My thoughts went to the common practice of fasting for religion or blood tests or to fit into a too small pair of jeans, maybe look good in that bikini at the beach. My energy-deprived mind projected pictures of jeans and bikinis all over my consciousness.

Before passing out from hunger, I made the conscious decision to allow myself to slip away, assuming the pizza delivery person would wake me. I guessed that I would have time to eat before my three o'clock arrived.

The blurred image of the outside world faded away into a dizzying abstract painting, bringing my mind to the "art" newly installed on the apartment living room wall; reds, browns, blues, greens, grays, purples, pinks, yellows.

Zipping through the fuzzy state one goes through while being jerked out of sleep, my first and illogical assumption was that the light tapping I heard was someone trying to get in through the window. The tapping was high-pitched and sounded like glass was involved in some way.

My head began to throb immediately upon returning to the wide awake world. Standing was a chore, but a necessary one. The clouds had become thicker and darker, but my passing glimpse at the outdoors led me to believe that no rain had fallen.

"Made the mistake of napping with the sun," I mumbled quietly to myself.

———

Ernest

Looking out of the peephole I spied, not the pizza man, but Ernest. I shuffled quickly over to the computer to check the time before returning to the door. 3:02 p.m. I knew there was no chance that my sleep had been so deep that I slept through the knocking from the pizza delivery or the resulting call from the doorman. It likely had not yet arrived.

The high-pitched tapping tore through my mind, third round louder and sharper than the first two. I opened the door to see Ernest standing with a smile.

"Dr. Thesiger!" he shouted rotating and swiveling his head side to side for seemingly no reason.

"Ernest." My voice was groggy and uninviting. "Please come in."

He sprinted into the office and hurled himself into one of the chairs opposite the couch, slamming it into the wall, and, unbeknownst to him, leaving a noticeable scuff mark.

Ernest, a frequently entertaining man in his mid-fifties, was one of my two patients who required regular supervision and therapy to ensure his safety. His condition put him at risk constantly, regardless of how he actually felt.

He was easily described in my initial report as "a bit of a firecracker." One could never predict his mood or his behaviors on any given day. There were days when he came in spewing profanity, paranoid about all that was around him. There were others when he was polite and pleasant, happy and energetic, forgoing sleep to dispense that energy in any myriad of ways, many of which were unfortunately dangerous and life threatening. And there were still other days when he arrived at my office in the deepest depths of depression, barely eating, barely moving, leaving his bed only to defecate. But, surprisingly and amazingly, he always made it for our session, Wednesday at 3 p.m.

I invariably felt that his appearances in my life could be categorized as "cartoonish," but there was always the potential for serious danger to his life posed by either his euphoric feelings of invincibility or his driverless states of depression.

After I closed the door and sat on the couch across from him, his smile was still there waiting for me and was accompanied by a healthy color in his face. Given his spirited entrance, it was not difficult to determine which phase he was in.

His shoes, shirt, socks, and full tracksuit were all the color of his bright blue eyes; his eyes were visible but somewhat distorted by the thick black frames of the round glasses askew on his face.

"New glasses?" I inquired.

"You're probably wondering why I'm wearing glasses," he said quickly.

Ernest had never worn glasses into session before so I was indeed curious, but he gave me no chance to agree.

"Well, it's because of my eye dominance. I was right eye dominant before and now it's been changing. It's the strangest thing. My depth perception is completely off. I keep running into walls and tables and babies. So what I did was take these glasses. I don't know whose they are. I found them in a restaurant on someone's table…"

My mind imagined Ernest running into a restaurant, grabbing someone's glasses off their table while they ate, then running out giggling, which is quite likely to have been very close to the actual event that took place.

"The prescription was weak, but it helped. I wanted to take out one lens so I could trick my eyes into using the right eye more than the left, so I was prying out the right lens when I broke off the side here."

He took the glasses off his face to show me that the arm that should rest on his right ear was missing.

"So I got out the lens and now I wear them to keep my eye dominance to the right and not confuse things with the left." He placed them back on his face and, as before, they fell askew, right side lower than the left. "And now, no more eye dominance and depth perception problems!"

"That was very clever, Ernest, but you know that whatever is changing your eye dominance most likely will not be affected by these glasses. You should just let it happen and you'll adapt. Sometimes people's eye dominance changes over the course of their life at random, sometimes several times. Just let it happen, don't fight it."

His face showed a little trepidation, then he slowly removed his stolen and broken glasses, folded them, and put them in the left breast pocket of his tracksuit.

"It's good to see you like this," I said happily, finally out of my stupor of fatigue. "You remember the last time? You were a bit down?"

His face sprang back to uncontrollably happy. "Yeah, I do. But no problem. That was last time. Now I'm back again."

"So you think this is more the real you than who you were last week?" I asked, provoking a dialogue.

"I mean I'm literally a different person. Like two different people, seriously, like I changed my name or something." Then he paused for a moment. "I should change my name! Doctor! I know what I am going to do today!" Ernest began to stand up, but I waved him back down.

"Hold on. Do you think it's a good idea to change your name? Won't that create some legal problems and some confusion with paperwork at banks, work, et cetera?" I rarely used the word "et cetera" in normal speech and I was rather shocked that I just had.

"I suppose…" he said begrudgingly.

Ernest was a fascinating case. The source of his disorder was an easily controlled chemical imbalance. He spent months with psychiatrists trying to determine his correct dosage then suddenly decided to stop taking medication altogether. He described himself when using the medication as "not having any kind of personality" and "just blah."

He understood well that, by not taking medication, he was putting himself in danger; he could not fully control his actions during his upswings, which could lead to unintentional injury or death, and his depressive downswings could lead to intentional injury or death, but he wanted to live his life with color, not, as he put it, "in black and white."

His specific condition, his rapid upswings and downswings and the extreme degree to which he became manic and then depressive, was much more severe and frequent than that of the average person afflicted with Bipolar Disorder. Past clients afflicted felt to me like much more toned down versions of Ernest. His uniqueness, in this sense, created a great risk, but I enjoyed trying to keep him on the right track.

When he first came to me, he had been off the medication for several weeks. No other psychologist would receive him as a patient because of the liability and because he was so unpredictable. One of the first things I said to him upon hearing his story was a quote from the poet Rainer Maria Rilke. "If my devils are to leave me, I am afraid my angels will take flight as well." Rilke referred to his own hesitation at the prospect of entering psychoanalytic treatment, which was the modern day equivalent to Ernest's aversion to medication. The side effects oftentimes muted the good parts of the personality. Not only were he and I on similar philosophical pages about the medication, but I needed the income and he would prove to provide a consistent stream.

Last month, it took him one day to shop, buy, gamble, and spend his way through months of income, maxing out credit cards and emptying bank accounts. I encouraged him to lock his accounts and give the password to a family member, but he found his antics to be humorous. Then, when he fell into a downward swing, he became depressed and scared, questioning how he would survive after spending so much money.

Ernest was luckily fortunate enough to have inherited a high-end furniture store. His role as owner required little concerted intelligence or attention; both of which he very rarely was able to bring to one place. Despite his binge spending, his finances would effortlessly recover especially since he had no children to support or spouse to answer to.

Ernest's greatest characteristic was his shockingly high level of self-awareness. He always knew which stage he was going through, what to expect, and how to be relatively safe. I commended myself for teaching him how to identify and live through these swings, but it was really mostly Ernest's impressive ability to look at himself and his situation objectively that allowed him this high level of self-awareness.

"So what shenanigans have you gotten yourself into this week?" I asked jokingly, but expecting to hear an entertaining story very likely to include being jailed or fished out of the Hudson or the East River by the police.

Ernest spoke quickly and without normal breaks between his words or sentences. "Oh shenanigans!" he shouted with laughter. "I feel amazing right now. I got home late, very late, went in my bed which is so so soft because I must have put a feather bed and a down comforter under my sheets and with those down pillows and all…" He trailed off while looking through the window.

His voice then zipped back to its high volume as he tuned back in. "I haven't slept well since I was a baby! Maybe about eighteen or nineteen minutes last night. You know I can't sleep when I'm like this. No, not at all.

"I tried staying there in bed, but I couldn't so I walked around the park, not inside, but around the outside of it on the street 'cause you told me that I shouldn't do that anymore the last time I did that because it was dangerous in the park at night." He looked out at the dreary park again, giving me a chance to respond quickly.

"I'm glad you made that decision. It was a good and intelligent one, Ernest."

"Then I walked downtown to have some breakfast. Then I walked back uptown. Then I went back to bed and couldn't sleep at all that time either so I took a shower with the showerheads and water and all.

"Then I went to the kitchen and made myself some eggs and waffles with syrup and butter and strawberries and bannannannas. I was soooooooooo hungry. I scrambled six eggs and four waffles! Well, I didn't scramble the waffles. I just ate them. And so many strawberries and bannannannas. Oh and three big glasses of OJ!

"Then I turned on the TV for some laughs. It was the news. Boring, but I gave it a chance. They were talking about some shooting or car accident or weather disaster or something and all I did was laugh. I laughed hard because it was just so funny. Hard to put my finger on what about it was so funny, but it got me thinking, wouldn't it be nice to control the weather, you know? Just to be able to control the rain and the hail and sleet and snow and wind and waves and tide and the sprinklers in lawns in front of the houses in the suburbs and the rain gutters and trees and stuff? We're working on wrapping up the work week without wet weather."

Ernest stood up and began to spin around with his arms flapping in and out from his body as he sang, "Oh what a wonderful feeling so! What a wonderful morning so! Oh what a wonderful afternoon so! All of my worries go away!"

His voice backed away from a singing tone, but he still spun around. "I know I have to deal with my problems, but I'm not dreading it and it won't bother me the whole day like it does when I'm not like this. It's hard for me to truly explain to you what being sad does to me. I tried last week, but I failed. Failed. Failed..." Ernest again trailed off.

"Why don't you have a seat," I said, beginning to get dizzy just from watching him spin.

Still standing and spinning, he replied, "I need to get back to happiness and do some happy things! Enjoy your wonderful day and have a wonderful weekend." He then began to make his way toward the door. "Happy day to you, Dr. Thesiger!"

"Wait!" I shouted as his right hand reached the doorknob. I got up and walked toward the closet. "I have something for you."

"For me?" Ernest asked, sliding his hand from the doorknob to his chest in surprise.

I took a box out from the closet. "Here. Do you remember last time you were feeling a bit down and we decided you could change all of the lights in your apartment to brighter, wider spectrum lights? It's supposed to help you feel better."

"Oh, but I don't need that now," he reminded me.

"Yes, but you will need it at some point. Take the box home and put it in your closet. You can put them up when you need to. It will give you something to do. Give you a purpose, something to complete and accomplish. I got you the amount you requested."

He took the box reluctantly with a look on his face that suggested he hardly remembered the conversation that had led to a box of lightbulbs in his arms.

"Well thanks, Doc. During those times, you know, during those times, I always make my reality something sad because I like feeling sorry for myself, during those times."

"We talked about that last time, but you did not seem to agree. Do you find that statement to be true now; that, during those times, you make your reality something sad because it feels good to feel sorry for yourself?" I asked.

"Yes!" he shouted in response. "When I'm on a downward swing, it brings me some pleasure to feel sorry for myself. Makes me forget what's bringing me down. Concentrating on feeling bad for myself."

"Do you remember what was making you depressed last time? Or what you were focusing on? It wasn't necessarily the thing that was depressing you, I don't think."

I felt it important to get Ernest to think and talk about his depressed phase when he was manic and vice versa so he could see the different phases from different perspectives. I tried to make him see how capable he was of being happy when he was sad and how capable of being calm when he was too energetic and antsy. Without medication his rapidly cycling chemical imbalance could not be easily controlled, but we could help control his perception of his emotions and behaviors. I hoped it would keep him mentally and emotionally closer to center because I knew that chemically he was very much out of our control. And I was even hopeful that the literature that suggested controlling the perception also controls the chemicals on some level was true.

"Yes, yes," he said quietly and concerned. "I do remember. I took that DNA test for fun months ago and the results had come back."

"Yes, continue. Take me through it," I encouraged him.

"Yeah, and I found out I was at risk for Huntington's…" The volume of his voice again trailed off.

"What do you think about that now in comparison to how you felt before, Ernest?"

He spent a short time thinking while holding the box of lightbulbs. "I feel great now!" he shouted. "Who cares what I might get at some far off time in the future! Nothing I can do about it, right? We're all going somehow, someway, sometime."

"Okay!" I said energetically, trying my best to match Ernest's levels. "How does that compare to how you felt before about it?"

"Well, before I was sad so I thought it was really bad. Now I see it as nothing."

Ernest turned, moved the box of lightbulbs to under his left arm, and put his right hand on the doorknob, ready to go steal more pairs of glasses and shout to the sky that he controlled the weather.

"Crackle, snap, and pop! I'm out this cube, Doc!" At that, Ernest smiled and ran through the doorway before closing the door very slowly behind him.

"Oh, Doc?" I heard, muffled through the door several seconds later.

"Yes, Ernest?" I questioned as I opened it.

"There's blood on your hands," he said before skipping down the hall.

I looked down to see some drips of blood on the top of my right hand.

"Bloody nose earlier," I shouted down the hall, but Ernest had already made it into the stairwell.

———

Rather than think or reflect on the short session, I questioned aloud "Where's my pizza?" before washing my hands in the bathroom sink.

The large leather chair felt soft as I squished into it and picked up the phone from the left bottom desk drawer to find out what became of my lunch. The doorman politely informed me that nothing had arrived with my name on it and nothing had gone unclaimed, no packages, pizzas, or people other than Ernest.

"Is there anything else, Sir?" the doorman asked in a seemingly genuine tone, as if he was born to serve. Something about it sucked every bit of comfort from within me.

"No, no, thank you. Have a good day."

The doorman hung up the phone before I did. It was hard to determine what exactly about the conversation bothered me so I pushed it out and used my energy to convince my starving mind that the pizza would soon come. The next image in my mind was that of the doorman consuming it himself. Immediately I felt terrible for even considering the possibility.

My eyes moved toward the inbox on the screen ahead. Finishing the day's work then locating an adequate form of nourishment was the next short-term goal that ruled my life. One message remained.

———

Gus

"Gus" read the subject of the message. I was somewhat surprised to see an e-mail from Gus because he preferred to communicate via video sessions like our conversation two days before. I opened it hoping he had news of a completed dissertation and a thumbs-up from his advisor, but rarely did patients deliver to me the good news I hoped for. The message was long. I scrolled down to see far more words than I wanted to. I sighed then commenced reading.

—

I'm sitting here at this café. It's more of a restaurant actually. I suppose I'm considering it a café because my laptop is in front of me as if I'm saying, "Look at me; I'm a writer writing in public because I think I work best around others and I crave attention and yearn for nothing less than somebody to come up to me and ask me what I'm writing about so I can tell them all about my upcoming novel which, so far, is actually just twenty-seven pages of my name in different fonts." You only get those fools in cafés.

It's ridiculously early on in the evolution of the day. Like the earth is still covered in molten lava kind of early in evolution. Why, you ask, am I not in bed enjoying a good REM cycle? Because my idiot brother is visiting from out of town, the other side of the country actually, your neck of the woods. The three-hour time difference from East Coast to West Coast and his incessant desire to wake up early in his own time zone add up to me subtracting precious hours of sleep from my own life. Brotherly love is the only thing keeping me from strangling him to death before collapsing from fatigue on this little table separating the two of us.

He's talking, going on and on and on and on and on and… but I'm hardly paying attention. Thankfully I had the drowsy foresight to bring my laptop. "I have a ton of work to do" was my excuse. He decided to bring his too so he wouldn't look too much like a third wheel to my laptop and me, but of course mine is the only one that's open.

I'm here typing away, but he just keeps talking as if I want to hear him or as if I am somehow capable of listening while I type which nobody really is even though they think they are or pretend to be. Come on, let's be honest.

Gosh, he was up excessively early to have such a chipper tone and spunk about him. It's still kind of dark out. Who gets up when it's still dark? What is he? Some kind of farmer? He's just going on and on in his out of place peppy-person talk and I'm typing away and staring blankly, aimlessly out one of the four sets of French doors at the front wall of the restaurant, ground level.

We're here so early there's nobody else here, just us and the owners, wife and husband, mom and pop, grandma and grandpa. Every once in a while, the static picture of the exterior environment I'm blankly piercing with my half opened eyes is smeared and rearranged by someone walking through. It's few and far between for these lost souls, but they are out there and all have something in common; they all have dogs.

Walking their dogs through the streets, praying for something to clean up from their best friend, unfortunate. I remember one day you told me that you often tell patients who have problems with time management to get a dog because the dog has to be fed and walked at a particular time every single day. It forces the person into a schedule and helps them plan their day around their dog's schedule.

The problem for me is that I don't like animals. Then you told me to get a baby instead of a dog. Ha! I spent a good amount of time considering that piece of advice before realizing that it wasn't really advice at all, but a tool to make me think about why I tell myself that I don't like animals.

I couldn't use as an excuse a dislike of babies (to replace dogs in the previous suggestion) because everybody likes babies, right? This forced me to realize that I just didn't like compromising and changing my own schedule to work around somebody else's, dog or baby or sibling. Yes, big breakthrough; I know. But, I digress.

So here I sit in a restaurant at an hour in the ante meridiem that I did not know existed until now because my brother, whose schedule is quite a bit different from my own, wanted to get some early morning, very early morning, breakfast.

So good, I'm learning to compromise and not be so selfish. Steps forward and all. But I'm sitting here and I'm seeing all of these people up and walking dogs and it hits me. There are a lot of people in this area that have serious time management issues. Then I thought of everyone who ever had a baby. They too must have had time management issues at some point. Suddenly, I feel a lot better because a very large percentage of people have the same issue I do!

Needless to say (and probably assumed because of my long story to justify not feeling bad about having time management issues), my dissertation has gone almost nowhere from the last time I spoke to you. I was energetic about it for about fifteen minutes then I wasted that energy stomping around telling myself I was going to work on my dissertation. All that did was tire me out and I ended up falling asleep then waking up later, exhausted and groggy. So I got no work done for the rest of the day and most of the following one.

But then something interesting happened; I took one of my illustrious mid-day naps and, while I was sleeping, had some good ideas about how to reorganize the dissertation. When I woke up hours and hours later, it was rather shocking what I had been able to work through as I slept. Unfortunately I had no time to write anything down. I had to get to the airport to pick up my early-morning-breakfast-loving brother.

When we got back to my place, we basically just crashed then awoke at this ungodly hour for food. Assuming I will be able to keep myself awake when we return to my place, I'm going to implement some of those good ideas I had.

I'll keep you updated.

-G

—

My eyes hurt, as did my head, after reading Gus's waste of time e-mail. My response reflected my distraction as a result of my own problems. It was not a good time to return messages and guiding patients through life was probably the last thing I should have been attempting to do.

—

Gus,

"Be mindful even when you're mind's full." I read it on a shirt a couple weeks ago.

I hope you are able to focus on your dissertation and get it done with the same insight and well thought through logic you exhibit while you sleep. Here's to staying awake long enough to have something good to say about consciousness.

Good luck.

-Dr. Thesiger

—

Again, I skipped the proofreading step and sent the message unchecked. I questioned whether I should start writing e-mails in my sleep in the future then wobbled to my feet. Stricken by hunger, I walked on pins and needles to the chaise lounge like psychologist's couch near the window to sit for what I had assumed would be a moment of contemplation after a day broken by hunger-induced naps, but what turned into another one of those naps.

I woke up sore, lying in an unnatural position. It was dark in the office, lights off, but I was able to locate myself on the couch in the middle of the office; not where I remembered passing out. I determined that, in a fit of hunger, I likely stumbled over to the couch, turning off the light en route.

I made my way, almost crawling from fatigue, hunger, and poor night vision, to the computer. 7:41 p.m. In disgust, I turned to the outside, hoping to find a source of salvation.

When I first acquired the office as a young wide-eyed enthusiastic psychologist, I had this confidence that could not be shaken. I felt that I could do anything, conquer any opponent, solve any mystery. For some reason, I decided to focus my spare in-office attention out of the window, down at Fifth Avenue, left and right, attempting to discern traffic patterns. I found that it was a living thing, incapable of being pinned down into one single pattern for a set time period. There were too many variables working together and apart to determine the end result. After the long-term futile attempt, I became frustrated, but by that time my anger was less directed toward my failure to determine traffic patterns and more directed toward my failure in life.

As I looked out of the window, that frustration came rushing back. All the anger and regret over wasted time and energy. It filled my head and pushed me into the large leather chair, head in hands.

After a time I arose with a frown to empty the carafe of water into the sink. The office doorknob felt warm in my hand. For a split second, I hoped to be slapped in the face with a blazing fire as I entered the hall. However, the hallway, the elevator, even the lobby were empty. The doorman standing outside tipped his hat as I exited.

I attempted to send a smile in his direction, but it did not even move past my intention, never reaching my mouth. Ignoring the man was insensitive, but I tried, tried my best to acknowledge his existence in some way. It just never came and really never would.

En Route to the Apartment

I hailed a cab on Fifth Avenue in an attempt to shield myself from the dark of the night, from the clouds pregnant with despair. The driver, clearly a native born New Yorker, was an unpleasant surprise given that he wanted to talk to me about every little insignificant detail of my life. He represented a stark contrast to the average New York City cab experience: cabbies who speak very little English.

"Where ya comin' from?" "Where ya goin'?" "Gettin' off work?" "Visitin' a pal?" "Wha's a matta wit ya?"

Too tired and hungry to converse and suddenly hit with the remnants of my cold, I fully ignored him, not even acknowledging his existence as I walked away from the cab toward the steps of our Brownstone.

I had not even the energy to hope that the friendly cab driver assumed that I was disabled in some way and incapable of verbal communication or possibly had a problem, temporary or permanent, with my hearing. I merely swiped my card, opened the cab door, and walked away.

In my daze, I did not even close the cab door behind me. The driver may or may not have assaulted me with profanity before angrily speeding off into the darkness. My attention was so far removed from him that I remembered no detail.

The door to the building opened effortlessly, or at least the effort was not perceived. The winding stairs felt steeper and harder to execute than on a normal day. The scent and the sound in the air was that of barbecue sauce. Far too many tenants felt it appropriate to cook and play their music with their door ajar, allegedly justified because their apartments lacked adequate air circulation. The tenant committing this particular infraction on this particular evening popped his head into the hall as I slowly zombie-walked past the third floor.

"Hey! It's Dr. Nick!" Norm shouted, stopping my snail's pace. "Hi, everybody!" he said in a hard to place and clearly put-on accent. "Hi, Dr. Nick!" he responded laughing for an unknown reason.

I loosely waved at Norm's odd greeting and continued walking.

"Shut up with your hands; talk with your mouth!" he insisted.

My eyes, previously out of focus due to indifference, settled in Norm's direction. He wore an apron that read "Men at work" and what I optimistically assumed to be a small tank top and shorts, both covered fully by the apron. His dark black hair was pulled tightly back, gelled firmly in place. His mouth and chin were surrounded by the same color hair, groomed into neat straight sides and sharp edges. In a previous conversation, he referred to his facial hair as his "goat, short for goatee." He found that label to be very clever.

"Norm," I said with little inflection. "How goes it?"

"Good stuff, all good stuff, Doc. Why you didn't let me take you to lunch last week when I saw youse on the street? I was gunna treat youse to McDonald's."

Question asked, question answered, I thought.

"I had a full case load that day. I hope I didn't offend," I replied with some semblance of sincerity.

"No problem, Doc. Hey, some of my buddies from the old block is coming for dinner and poker so Sue's cookin' up a storm. Hamburgers, sausages… We got the potato salad goin', pot a beans, salad with the croutons in um. Ernie's gunna be there. Bert too."

Really? I thought sardonically. *Bert and Ernie… Those two should never be in the same room. It's too distracting.* But for once I kept my sarcasm to myself. "That all sounds like good fun," I replied.

"Julie and youse should come down. Mix it up a little, eh?"

"Oh," I said, smile-laughing at the outlandish thought. "Julie already prepared dinner, but we'll take a rain check, okay?"

"Yeah, okay," Norm said, disappointed. "Youse two have a good night and tell Julie I says hey."

"Will do, Norm. Same to you and Sue. And, Norm… don't lose too much money playing poker."

"Aahhhhh! Youse, Doc!" he said, pointing at me. "Youse…" He walked himself back into his apartment, leaving the door ajar.

Norm's appearance always gave me a smile and it was a much needed smile. Norm always struck me as painfully average. Average looking, average build, average height, average intelligence; really your average New Yorker from every angle. I had never and will never meet a man with a more appropriate name. It is just impossible.

My pace had quickened after the surprisingly rejuvenating conversation. As I rounded the corner of the fifth floor, I noticed yet another neighbor's door open. Alicia, the neighbor in question, was standing in a dimly lit doorway, no lights appeared to be on in her apartment and the weak light from the hall was a distant flicker barely illuminating her silhouette.

"Hello, Alicia. How are you doing?" I asked reluctantly.

"The night is young," she responded, tossing her long, light blond hair. "Come in for a glass of wine maybe?"

"Oh," I said awkwardly. "I couldn't. Julie made dinner and I'm starving. Long day."

"I see," she said slowly.

We stood there rather awkwardly for a moment before I said, "Okay, well thank you. I'm going to head inside now. Tell Alec and the boys that I said hello."

"Oh, they're not home. Out to dinner then a movie until ten or so."

I paused, facing our apartment door and fumbling with my keys. "Okay, thank you," I said, unsure of how to respond to that inappropriate divulgence of information.

As I juggled my keys, dropping them at least twice, Alicia walked toward me slowly.

"Naches," she whispered softly. "Do you know what it means?"

Completely uncomfortable due to her proximity, I stammered, "N-n-nooo, I'm sorry?"

"It's a Spanish word which has no direct English translation. It's like pride, joy, the pleasure we get from our children."

The door finally swung open allowing me to pull myself in as I said, "Ehh, okay. Thank you. Have a nice night, Alicia."

I closed the door quickly, relieved to be safely away from what was on the other side. The day had been trying and all I wanted was to eat, relax, and sleep without any interaction with anyone or anything.

Julie walked into the living room from the hallway. "Nick," she said, addressing me in a monotone.

"What's for dinner?" I asked quickly.

"Do you even care about my day?" she asked rhetorically, seemingly having planned which fight to start upon my arrival.

"Julie, I had a bad day, okay? I don't have the energy or the desire to deal with this right now."

"Well, I had a horrible day too," she shouted. "I hope that makes you feel better."

"Why would that make me feel better?" I asked defensively.

"Because you seem to get a lot of pleasure from my pain. At least, that's the way it seems. You cause me so much pain that I can only assume you feel better when you know I had a bad day."

Disgusted, I walked by her to the wooden chair next to the small round wooden table and began to take off my shoes as she watched, waiting for a response. As I leaned down to untie, I noticed that Michael's golf bag—an extravagant item that I had won in a contest of wits—was curiously absent, but I decided to inquire about its whereabouts some other time.

"I think you have Post-Traumatic Stress Disorder," she finally blurted out.

"You think I have *what*?" I asked, shocked.

"Because of when you saw your patient dead," she explained more calmly. "I talked to someone and she said you're probably suffering from Post-Traumatic Stress Disorder."

"What are you talking about? Who have you been talking to?" I asked, again taking a defensive position.

"No one, it's not important," she responded, clearly hiding something from me.

"Who did you speak with, Julie?" I asked as I stood up and approached her.

"No one. It's doesn't matter. Forget about it." She recoiled into the kitchen as she spoke, as if frightened of me.

Not knowing what else to do, I turned and walked back toward the wooden chair to pick up my empty shoes and place them in the closet.

"I was just trying to help," Julie said when my back was turned. "I don't know how to talk to you anymore. I don't know what to do..." She trailed off into a teary silence.

Uncomfortable with the tears, tired, hungry, angry, and feeling ambushed on several levels from several people, I responded harshly but calmly. "First of all, PTSD can't be diagnosed until at least a month after the traumatic event. Any strange behavior within that time period is considered to be a normal reaction to the traumatic event and its accompanying stress. Second, dead bodies aren't traumatic for me. I just saw another one today. I saw the guy die, right in front of me and look..." I then shouted, "I'm FINE!"

Her tears grew in volume as my words did, so I turned away to avoid my own discomfort.

"What is for dinner?" I asked again calmly.

She took a moment to compose herself before responding. "I didn't make anything." She sounded almost proud that she chose not to provide.

"What?" I inquired rhetorically. My voice had quickly turned whiny because I lacked the strength for anger. "You didn't make anything? What am I supposed to eat then?"

"We have leftovers," she offered with a bit of joy that she was able to twist the knife even deeper.

I took several steps back and fell onto the chair by the small wooden table. I could not believe that Julie and I would have leftovers again. Very few nights passed without the taste of reheated food.

Frequently the leftovers were merely scraps from what Julie had eaten for lunch. Previously I had informed her that prisoners ate better than I did; in fact, condemned men were given any meal they desired. This fact only angered her.

"Maybe leftovers with pasta? I could make pasta and put the leftovers on top?" Julie's tone implied that she was indeed enjoying the power she had over my nourishment and health, mental and physical.

"I don't want pasta. And I don't want leftovers." I pulled my phone out of my pocket to search for a restaurant that delivered.

I began to think about a patient I counseled briefly six years before. He had been going through a messy divorce: no prenuptial agreement, three children, allegations of infidelity and abuse, drug and spousal alike. He told me that the relationship was wonderful when they first married, but then, after two children, things began to go downhill. He said he could pinpoint the moment he realized things were bad.

He told me that everything was the same except for the dinners. Previously she had cooked every night, but that dwindled to five times each week, then three, then one. "The food went cold as the relationship did," he said. They started ordering out, then using the leftovers from the takeout for dinner the next day and the next.

"Every night it was either cold Chinese food or warm Chinese food." He wept openly, shamelessly in my office. A grown man reduced to tears over Chinese food.

As I scrolled down the list of restaurants that delivered, I realized that I had been eating cold Chinese food for quite a long time. I questioned when this happened, how this happened.

"Are you going to have anything?" Julie asked, no tears in sight likely due to the feeling of power she felt from her passive-aggressive lapse in food preparation.

"I'm ordering something," I said calmly.

"I hate ordering in," she responded as though she was affected by my decision. "Maybe we could go out?"

I had no desire to go out with her. It would be dangerously uncomfortable, the air thick with tension and anger, the emotions only increasing in palpability as the meal continued, but I conceded to her suggestion driven by my disdain for leftovers and the fact that ordering in for myself would only make things between us that much worse.

So I merely said, "Okay," and began to put my shoes back on.

Julie opened the laptop on the coffee table in front of the couch and directed the screen to a website to which I paid no attention. "Isabella recommended a new place in the Village," Julie started. "She was saying—"

I interrupted her. "Don't care. Let's just go."

"I was going to say, it scored an 84 with cleanliness on this restaurant review website. I know how important cleanliness is to you."

I furrowed my brow. "Eighty-four percent doesn't seem that high... If I'm eating somewhere, I'd like it to be 100 percent clean."

"That's not how the rating system works," she insisted.

"Fine, let's just go," I said, acknowledging that I was willing to eat food that was 16 percent dirty.

Julie slipped into her shoes then picked up an umbrella. No words were exchanged until we hit the sidewalk. I held my breath and stepped lightly all the way down in an attempt to not alert Alicia or Norm to our departure.

———

Dinner with Julie

"Should we take a cab?" I asked as I flung my arm up in hopes of catching the attention of a foreign-born driver.

"It's still early," Julie said. "Let's just take the subway."

I put my right arm down. *Still early?* I thought as we walked, side by side toward the subway station.

Like all New Yorkers, I bemoaned the subway system, the smell, the extremely low level of cleanliness, the old crumbling sticky surfaces, and, least enjoyable of all, the fact that we were crammed in with our fellow New Yorkers like veal calves.

But, after a lifetime of this treatment, subway riders all fell into a daze of indifference. We were indifferent to smells, urine puddles, sticky surfaces, personal boundaries. We learned to not touch, not lean, not look but only stare blankly while standing straight up. And despite the excruciatingly close proximity to our fellow commuters, eye contact was strictly forbidden.

Julie walked ahead of me as we approached the turnstile. Her metro card was ready in hand as I fumbled for mine in my pocket. On the fourth swipe, I was finally let through. People behind me scoffed and walked around to the other entrances. I could blame nothing but the inanimate machine incapable of reading my card properly so I did, loudly and with exaggerated hand gestures.

However, Julie witnessed none of my protests. I spotted her after looking both up and down the platform twice. She stood facing the tracks at the far end of the platform, looking down the black hole as if willing the glow of the train's headlights to come into view.

On a column was a sign torn in half and put back together. After the subway workers had slapped the thousandth layer of paint on the crumbling columns, they had left a sign: WET PAINT. Due to their inefficient, lazy, and careless ways, this sign was frequently left for days or weeks or months and thus disregarded by passersby. A clever vandal had torn the sign in half and literally reversed the meaning: AINT WET. The wit of the vandal brought a slight smile to my face as I made sure to maintain subway etiquette and resist my urge to check the validity of the sign by sliding my hand across the column.

There, on the platform, Julie and I stood waiting silently, tricked by the wind created by trains going in the opposite direction four times before one going our way crawled to a halt, doors opening directly in front of us.

She entered first, sitting in the seat to the right of the door. I stood in front of her holding on to the pole while making a mental note to wash my hands before eating which I, like every other person who makes that mental note, inevitably ended up forgetting about.

Skilled in the art of deliberately ignoring the presence of others, I spent the ride shaking my head in disgust at the grammatical and spelling errors riddling the subway ads plastered across the walls like wallpaper.

I threw my head up out of frustration and my squinting eyes noticed a loose screw in the overhead plastic light fixture. Rolling around and around, the head of the screw was creating countless overlapping circles in the thick layer of dust and grime which had built up in the rarely touched interior space. It drew a clear picture of how frequently the subway was cleaned and the level of workmanship and care taken when screwing parts together. I looked away before the fluorescent light increased my omnipresent headache.

Julie and I never spoke when on the subway. We had always shared a sharp disdain for the hypothetical cute bouncing couple on the subway who stand together and endlessly refer to the other as "darling" and "dear" while discussing nothing of any substance and doing it loudly enough for everyone in the vicinity to develop a loathing for their ostensibly cute repartee. But, whether words were exchanged or not, we were in no danger of becoming that hypothetical couple.

A woman holding the handles of a baby stroller stared into the black window illuminated sporadically by the passing of a light on the side of the dark tunnel. Her child appeared to be far too old and far too large to be pushed in a stroller, especially in a place as un-stroller-friendly as the New York Subway system.

She turned her head toward me unexpectedly. I looked away quickly then focused on two men holding the vertical pole in the middle of the subway car. They had assumed a stance for stability, feet spread wide and angled well. Both right hands were affixed to the vertical pole while their lefts each held a book, one thick and one very thick. They allowed the undulations, bumps, and changes of direction, determined by the subway car's movement on the tracks, to dictate their bodies' movements. Thus they rode the subway effortlessly as they read.

Then one of the readers looked up. He caught me staring, but I looked away quickly toward a man sitting across the subway car. That man, though, was unfortunately already looking at me, and did not look away when I unintentionally made eye contact with him.

"Hello," he said gleefully.

"Damn," I whispered to myself as I ignored him, looking away toward an empty corner.

"Hello," he said again, hoping to get my attention.

I decided to indulge him and see if, by some unexpected turn of events, I knew him. I looked back and did not recognize the face.

"Yes, hello!" he said, excited that I had acknowledged him. "How are you today, friend?"

"Who are you?" I asked. Julie continued to look away, pretending not to know me.

"I have no idea," he responded before pointing at himself and saying, "the name's Pillsbury McDougal."

At that point, I knew he and I had no prior connection so I stood up and wobbled awkwardly to the other side of the train leaving Julie to deal with the crazy man who was undiscriminating about those with whom he attempted to connect.

Sadly, the man ignored all others as he took up chase, following me to the end of the subway car and standing in front of me.

Despite his proximity and the fact that we were looking straight into each other's faces, I ignored him.

"You touched a dead man," he said.

With shock on my face, in my mind, in my body, I continued to ignore him, but ransacked my brain to figure out how he had been able to come to that correct conclusion. Had he been in the restaurant? Seen me helping the paramedics on the street? Did he know Courtland?

He continued. "You will be unclean for seven days. On the third and seventh days you will clean yourself, then you will be clean."

"Thank you," I said, still startled and unsure how to respond.

I then watched the man walk back in the other direction, half expecting him to disappear or walk through the side of the subway car. But he approached a woman sitting down and said the same thing to her. She stood and walked away from him. I exhaled, then walked back toward Julie as she continued to look away from me.

Without the address of the restaurant, I was forced to attempt to make eye contact with Julie each time the subway stopped to see if we should exit. My obvious impatience was ignored, just as every other attempt to engage her was, few as they were.

When our stop finally came, she ignored my silent inquiry and continued to look away as she stood and walked out. Begrudgingly I followed. I would have been more content with the night had I ridden the subway until it went to the end of the line.

Directly in front of us as we made our way aboveground were three young children, all close in age, and what appeared to be their mother, a woman jaded by a life in New York. Her clothes hung off her skinny body and her stringy dirty-blond hair appeared to be thickened by the damp polluted New York air. Her skin, pale from a life without direct sunlight as a result of dwelling in what I presumed to be a small-windowed street-level apartment in the back of her building, was weathered from long days at work and longer nights, only broken by the tiresome weekends she spent taking care of her children.

Each of their movements appeared to be a well-practiced routine. She stood in the middle holding the right hand of one and the left hand of another while the third and tallest child held on to the other hand of the first. They moved slowly in front of us, the children's little legs whipping back and forth, almost running.

As they approached the turnstile exit, each let go of the others' hands simultaneously. They passed through seamlessly and re-grasped the hands next to them without the burden of even looking. It was a neatly choreographed single motion which was simple for them, muscle memory; but, had another tried to perform the task in the same manner, they would have failed miserably. I was saddened by the routine of their lives, but impressed by the ease with which they glided through it.

We were not aboveground for more than a minute before Julie was allowing the door of the restaurant to close behind her, hitting my right shoulder in the process. She looked back, but said nothing.

The dinner at this dreary, badly lit, 16 percent dirty restaurant was the first meal in which my entire party uttered not a word to one another, even when taking into consideration the times that I dined as a party of one. We looked away, lost in thought or just lost.

The food was slow to arrive and staggeringly subpar. I ate without verbal complaint, but my face likely told an eloquent story. I had not remembered that it was the only food that I had ingested all day until my stomach twisted and contorted, expanded and contracted, moaned and groaned, as though it had forgotten how to properly digest. I ate through the pain and drank the tinny tasting, foggy water. We ordered no wine.

As the waiter lightly placed the bill on the table, I quickly handed him a credit card. I wanted to leave as quickly as possible and I cared very little about the number on the bill. Looking at it would not change the fact that I was going to pay it eventually so I attempted to expedite the process by removing the most useless of the steps.

Julie stood up as soon as the bill was returned, the receipt ready for the tip line to be filled in and a signature added. The Chef came from the kitchen and began talking to three men and two women, all professionally dressed, at a large round table. I laughed aloud at his meager appearance, not trusting his slender physique.

"A skinny chef?" I questioned quietly to myself. "That explains the terrible food."

Outside of the restaurant, I looked around for Julie, moving my focus back and forth. I decided she had likely walked down into the subway so I crossed the street to make my way underground. Before becoming subterranean, I noticed her sitting in the back of a cab so I got in. The cab drove off before I could tell the driver the cross streets.

At least she talked to the waiter and the cab driver, I thought as I sat back, looking out the window.

Her cab door opened before the driver fully stopped the car and she was up the stairs before I had completed the credit card transaction from the backseat. I used my own key to open the door to the building and, thankfully, found the door to our apartment to be unlocked.

I could hear the water running in the bathroom while she brushed her teeth. Stomach still churning uncomfortably, I lowered myself onto the couch, putting my feet up.

When the bathroom door opened, I called out to Julie, "Would you like to cast the first stone? I highly doubt that I am eligible for the honor."

"Excuse me?" she said in an angry tone. Those were the first two and the last two words she would say to me that night.

"Well, you know, God said, 'Let he who is without sin cast the first stone,'" I responded.

She glared at me with a piercing look, then walked into the bedroom, slamming the door behind her. The thin not-up-to-code wall separating the bedroom from the living room shook.

The couch supported me for hours, but did not allow slumber. The incessant napping of the day had scrambled my circadian rhythm to a state where sleep was fully unattainable.

I watched the reflection of the headlights of the cars light up one side of the room and then slide to the other as they accelerated by, up or down the slight incline, into or out of the park. I perceived very little sound. The cars, airplanes passing overhead, the vagrants shouting on the sidewalks, the low consistent hum of the city; they were all there, all present, but just not noticed.

I examined my phone at 3:23 a.m. and decided it to be an appropriate time to sneak into bed, assuming Julie to be sleeping, which she was. I set my phone to charge on the nightstand then slipped seamlessly under the covers, but still I laid there sleepless.

I sat up after an hour of attempting to get away from waking and watched the analogue clock displayed on my charging phone, its rotating arms following the same path over and over again. Simultaneously I watched its digital counterpart, displayed directly adjacent on the phone's screen, cycling through its numbers, up up up, then back to the beginning again, only to repeat the same pattern over and over. I watched, studying the meaningless journey, set, planned out, predetermined, inevitably ending in the same place it had begun, only to wonder why the clock bothered in the first place and whether it would go on now that it was fully aware of what monotony the future held.

As I sat opening and closing my eyes for extended durations, the words of Theodor Geisel slipped to the front of my mind. "You know you're in love when you can't fall asleep because reality is finally better than your dreams."

This, I knew very clearly, was not the case for me, but very likely was the case for sleeping Julie.

A Half-Marathon or Half a Marathon

[Two weeks later]

"Take it easy!" I shouted angrily as I was manhandled and pushed through the doorway by a nondescript guard, hands behind my back and cuffed around my wrists. He was nondescript because I had no intention of looking him in the face, too afraid and not wanting to further incite. I had paid little attention when previously led into the visitation room because it was a quick seamless process. This was the opposite experience so I felt it necessary to take note.

Bill was sitting on his side of the metal table on a metal chair bolted to the floor of the little room, four putrid gray walls. He looked up over his left shoulder and followed me with his eyes as the guard led me to my side and then freed my left wrist before closing the empty side of the cuffs around the ring on the table.

Several seconds of silence passed before Bill spoke. "Hi, Nick," he said pleasantly. "I was just stopping in to see how you're doing, see how things are going." His tone was far too upbeat from the point of view of the prisoner he had come to see. My own mood had steadily deteriorated since we had met the day before.

After I had interpreted his tone as bordering on insulting, several seconds were then spent in silent contemplation, pondering his enthusiastic idiocy. "You appear to be enjoying your position versus my own, Bill."

"Oh, whatever do you mean?" he asked, actually sounding unaware of the apparent mocking.

I thought for a moment and decided to accord him the benefit of the doubt given that he was not wearing his condescending white coat as he had in our first meeting. I hoped it would not return. Instead he wore what appeared to be a new suit, navy blue with faint vertical pin-striping and a white collared shirt that was covered down the middle with a tie of varying blues in a diagonal pattern; I had never seen it before on him. I looked down at my own costume; still the dark blue one-piece prison clothes. Blue appeared to be the theme of the visit.

"So how have you been?" Bill asked with a tone that still exceeded the appropriate level of enthusiasm for the situation.

"Seriously?" I asked, already disgusted.

"Yes, I'm serious. How are you handling being here?"

"Maybe dial back the joviality, okay? You're not making this any easier on me." It was a plea for my sanity, but, had I not been cuffed to the table, it would have been a warning, a threat against his well-being. My strong desire to throttle Bill during these visits was becoming a dangerous pattern.

The slight smirk, the upturning that suddenly quirked the left corner of his mouth angled my eyebrows. He noticed the stimulus-response correlation and wiped it away before verbalizing the retraction. "Sorry. I'm just trying to cheer you up a bit, raise your spirits."

"You can do that by getting me out of here," I told him.

"You're doing the important part right now. We're going to need to see every detail of that week, see your side of things."

"Well, I'm not done yet," I said to him. "Only about halfway through."

"Keep on writing then. Running half a marathon is far less impressive than running a half-marathon." Bill nodded his head and smiled at his statement.

I had to inquire, "What?"

Happy to indulge, he explained. "If you run half a marathon, it means you gave up halfway. You're a quitter, a loser. But, if you run a half-marathon, you've met your goal. You finished the race. You're a winner. The two might be the same length, the same distance, but the feeling of accomplishment that is carried with one is absent in the other. There is another half to this marathon."

"Okay," I said slowly, unsure why he felt it necessary to dole out something he probably read on an inspirational poster in a social worker's office.

I attempted to sit back in the metal chair, but found the handcuffs' chain to be too short for comfort so I leaned forward over the table instead. "I've been thinking," I began, "this whole thing is just a witch hunt."

"What exactly do you mean by that?" Bill asked, leaning back comfortably, displaying his wide range of movement, freedom.

"A witch hunt!" I shouted. "You know what I mean. They're looking for something that doesn't exist, something that isn't there. All they want is someone to blame and their method of proving my guilt is fixed; it either convicts me or drowns me to death, metaphorically. Their accusations became fact in their minds and soon to be in the minds of the jury. In the end, no one cares about what really happened. They just want someone to blame and I'm the fall guy."

"Oh! I thought you were trying to tell me you had converted to Wicca in here!" Bill exclaimed.

Again, I was dismayed by his idiocy, this time shaking my head in his direction. "Please stop trying to cheer me up," I asked of him.

Laughing as he spoke, he said, "Sorry, sorry. I just think smiling might help you out a bit. You really don't look too well. You might have lost weight from yesterday. Maybe I can bake you a cake and put a file in it or something?"

"Please just stop," I pleaded.

He scrunched his face and nodded at my request, but mostly ignored it. "I can see cheering you up will be like going through the eye of the needle."

"What does that even mean?" I asked, rolling my eyes.

"Oh, I have a story for you!" he suddenly remembered.

Knowing there was little I could do, I gave up. "Go ahead, Bill."

"I killed a fly earlier," he began, pointing toward the closed door, guarded by the guard. "It was buzzing around my head when I was sitting at my desk and I smacked it down to the floor with my bare hands. It continued fluttering across the floor so I got up and walked over. Before stepping on it, I said, 'This is a no fly zone.' Then I smushed it under my shoe." He laughed at the recollection of his play on words. "It was great!"

"Is that supposed to be relevant in some way?" I asked, having little faith in the direction of the conversation.

"No, I suppose not. Just something funny that happened earlier," he replied.

"Then please keep your irrelevant stories to yourself," I said, wanting to shout, but seeing no point in it.

Again he scrunched his face and nodded.

"Did you meet with the lawyers?" I asked, hoping to reroute the conversation. "What have they been saying? When are they going to come in and meet with me?"

"We'll get to that in a moment. Tell me how you're doing. I want to make sure you're all right."

I dropped my head to my left hand, resting on the metal table, and groaned at my futile battle with a fool.

"I can see your grouchy mood isn't going away," Bill said in a quiet voice.

My head remained in my hand on the table as I spoke. "Try to put yourself in my position. Maybe then you'll see why I'm not quite enjoying your non sequitur stories and stupid jokes."

Bill said nothing for a while so I picked up my head to see what his facial expression could tell me about what was going on inside. He was clearly pondering something, his chin resting in his right hand and his right elbow resting in his left hand, but I could not figure out what. "What are you thinking?" I finally asked.

"I'm trying to figure out a clever way to allude to the thought of you living in a garbage can and reiterate your grouchy mood so I can equate you to Oscar the Grouch from *Sesame Street*. It will be a funny joke once I come up with it."

Again, my head found my left hand on the metal table. "Do you know what a Mexican Standoff is?" I asked him, then responded before he could make another stupid joke. "In the old westerns, those movies with a bunch of tough guys riding horses and wearing cowboy hats and cowboy boots in the desert, they always find themselves in a bar fight and they're never sure who is on their side. Four or five guys end up standing in a circle holding a six-shooter revolver in each hand pointed at a different guy. That's a Mexican Standoff. And, you know, I always felt like, if that had been us, we would be back-to-back pointing our guns at the other guys and not at each other. Now, I'm not so sure."

"What are you saying?" Bill asked, knowing well what I meant.

"Let's put it this way: I wouldn't trust you to shoot an apple off my head right now, but it seems like I have no other choice."

Bill thought for a moment before saying, "We're not so different, you and I…"

"Now that's a terrible thing to say," I said, cutting him off and making my first verbal joke in a day.

Bill's resulting laughter at his own expense brought a small smile to my lips.

"Now doesn't that feel better?" he asked, still chuckling a bit. "You're not fully dressed until you're wearing a smile!"

Smiling and shaking my head at his idiocy, I said, "Please spare me the platitudes."

"A smile confuses an approaching frown!" he exclaimed with a big smile.

"Can we talk about the trial?" I said more seriously, mounting disgust beginning to erase the sliver of a smile from my face.

Bill, ignoring me and, still smiling, asked, "How are you sleeping in here? Maybe you're losing weight because you're not sleeping."

Knowing I would have to answer his questions sooner or later, I decided to pick sooner in an attempt to speed up the process. "Sleeping is quite difficult."

He responded whimsically with, "Hmm, well sleep is for the dreamers. Do you think maybe you're scared of something happening to you while you sleep?"

"No. I have my own cell. It's just loud; it's like nobody else around here sleeps at night."

Bill pondered for a moment before saying, "Well, experience shows that the thing people fear the most is silence."

"Who said that? Bob Dylan?" I asked before shaking my head at Bill for suckering me into the game of trying to name the source of a quote. "No. There's no fear. I'm not fearing anything. I just need quiet to sleep."

Again, Bill pondered for a moment before speaking. "I noticed it before, but it's much stronger now. Your voice sounds different than it did before you came here. It sounds a little like it did when we first met, freshman year of college. A bit deeper, more baritone, a grumbly undertone of a raspy rumble; you sound more like the sardonic street-smart hustler you used to be."

"I don't know what to say to that," I told him. "Maybe I'm changing who I am a little so I can fit in here, so no one bothers me about not being a hardened criminal."

"I see," Bill responded, clearly not seeing. "Is this the first time you've done something like this?"

"What are you getting at?" I asked.

"Well, nothing specifically. Just that maybe you did the same thing, changed yourself to fit in, when you made it to college, then continued to wear that façade through graduate school, and thereafter. Life has been a bit of a lie and maybe it's finally catching up to you."

I shook my head and rolled my eyes then tried to cross my arms, but failed. "This isn't a therapy session," I informed Bill. "Plus you're completely off base and, not to mention, bordering on insulting. Can we just talk about this trial please?"

"Okay, okay. I can see you might want to think about this for a while before we talk about it."

Overcome with frustration, I then shouted, "We're not talking about anything except this trial!"

Bill nodded his head for a while before saying, "Let's discuss your writing."

"Finally!" I exclaimed, feeling as though we were getting somewhere. "What do you want to know?"

"How is it going?" he asked.

"It's moving along," I told him. "How is it going on your end?"

"Well, I haven't quite had a chance to read through what you've completed so far."

"Is this another one of your jokes to cheer me up?" I asked. "You told me yesterday you were putting it at the *top of your list.*"

"Yes," he said. "And I did, but I didn't do anything else on my list since yesterday either."

"I'm guessing you didn't meet with the lawyers then," I said, knowing well the impending answer.

Bill shook his head to confirm his negligence.

I thought for a moment before informing him, "I have no intention of discussing how I'm doing. You haven't yet read what I've written or met with the lawyers. You and I, we have *nothing* to talk about."

I started to stand but was jerked low by the cuff attached to the table and, to my surprise, Bill began to do the same, calling my bluff.

"Where do you think you're going?" I asked him, having no intention of allowing him to leave such an unproductive and short meeting before I had a chance to storm out.

"Back to the office," he said. "Why? Where are you going?" He broke into a light chuckle, knowing well that I had only one place I could go.

Quite perturbed, to say the least, and with my brow furrowed, I asked "If you're content to leave so soon and you came with nothing to report, why did you even come at all?"

"Just to make sure you were doing okay," he said as he buttoned his jacket.

"So there really wasn't anything for us to talk about here?"

Bill smiled and responded, "No, not really. Just wanted to make sure you were doing okay and maybe try to cheer you up a bit."

"You could have just sent me a note or called me," I said as I motioned to the guard that we were finished.

"Don't be mad, Nick. How could I not come by and visit—"

I cut him off and said, "For less than five minutes at a time? It was the same thing yesterday only I had to wait an hour first. You had no reason to come here and you spent less than five minutes. How much do I owe you for that, Doctor?"

As the guard uncuffed me from the metal table and then recuffed my left hand to my right behind my back, Bill ignored my angry inquiry and said, "Make sure to focus on Courtland's potential connection to everything, like I asked you to do yesterday. I think it's important. Oh, and also don't forget to write about this meeting. Just to keep a record."

I looked at him, glared at him, enraged by his idiocy once again, only to see his face smiling a smile of genuine hope; however his eyes told a different story. Their depths showed concern and uncertainty, possibly even pessimism for the future. Still, though, he smiled. It took me a moment of peering into his eyes to understand that he was scared, scared for me, scared of what might happen, scared that he could not help me and that I would spend the rest of my life in here. But still he smiled, attempting to cheer me up and assure me that everything was going to be okay. Despite my perception of a condescending subtext, he was truly trying to help me.

As the guard led me out of the room, manhandling me all the way, I stopped beside Bill and muttered, "Thanks, I guess."

"I'll come back tomorrow and I'll be sure to read what you have written so far," he said before leaning toward me and attempting to give me a hug.

I pulled back aggressively and shouted, "Get off me! Are you serious? What's wrong with you? I'm in prison! Too much, Bill! Too much!"

He appeared stunned at my outburst and uncertain how to respond while the guard pushed me out of the room and down the hall.

"I look forward to reading about the week," he said when the words finally came to him.

I turned my head and shouted over my right shoulder, past the guard, "I'm not done yet!"

Thursday Morning

I opened my eyes, somewhat startled to be aware, then wrenched my neck right, toward the nightstand, toward the phone; the phone which was not there.

Julie must have moved it, I thought.

And so I went that morning without the knowledge of the exact moment of waking; a rarity, but without the phone, I knew no time. After several excruciating seconds, I rotated my head left, eyes shut tight in agony; I was unsurprised to see Julie's side of the bed absent of Julie's resting body.

"Awake," her voice rang out, startling me as she stood in the doorway. My head moved quickly in her direction which, for a sharp, painful moment, increased my agony.

"Yes," I sputtered out in a weak battered voice. "I was awake most of the night actually."

"It was a declarative statement referring to my state of consciousness, not an interrogative question inquiring about yours," she snapped back. "I saw you looking at my side of the bed."

"What?" I mumbled unclearly. Due to my early stage of waking, my brain was not yet functioning fast enough to fully comprehend and effectively respond to her condescension; not even conscious enough to inform her that "declarative statement" and "interrogative question" are both redundant.

"Where did you go last night?" she asked, a thin veil over her accusations.

"What are you talking about? I didn't go anywhere," I mumbled, more to the pillow than to her.

"I heard the front door, then you came in here at 3:30 a.m.…."

"I didn't go outside. I was on the couch until then."

"I don't believe you. And what about Tuesday night? I heard you leave and come back in a while later."

I shook my head and frowned, offering no further explanation.

"Your phone's buzzing in the living room," she said as she turned to walk away, leaving me lying in bed, assuming she had left to retrieve the phone.

As time passed and I progressed through the stages of wakefulness, it became increasingly clear to me that Julie had no intention of delivering my phone.

My feet tingled as I stumbled my way into the living room, mentally questioning how long she had been standing in the doorway waiting for me to open my eyes and turn my head so she could execute her well planned, if poorly phrased, attack.

In the kitchen cutting up fruit, she paid me no attention as I looked at her angrily. The phone's screen read, "Home Visit—11 a.m." The current time was 10:21 a.m.

"Why is it you told me my phone was buzzing, but you didn't bring it to me? One would think that would be the logical next step if the person you're telling is in bed, no?" I spoke in a perturbed tone.

Julie continued to ignore me as she cut up apples and grapes and strawberries. I stumbled my way back down the hall and into the shower, but I emerged as fatigued as I was when I had entered.

I found it difficult to determine if it was my eyes' inability to adjust properly or if it was the weather that grayed the light in the bedroom. The colors of my clothes were hard to determine. While I held my best educated guesses up to the window, Julie swung open the door.

"Where is the blue bowl?" she shouted as she began wildly throwing pillows from the unmade bed onto the floor, searching for her elusive blue bowl.

"Get out of here!" I shouted back. "I'm trying to get dressed! Have you ever heard of knocking?"

"What?" she asked, hardly paying any attention to me.

"Knocking: when you form your hand into a ball and hit it against the door to make sound alerting those on the other side of your impending arrival?"

She looked at me angrily, seemingly ready to start a shouting match, then thought better of getting into a battle that she would inevitably lose and walked out.

"What ever happened to privacy, decorum?" I asked, door still wide open.

After dressing, I noticed that the couch in the living room felt several degrees softer than it had the previous night. The shower had thankfully loosened my back, giving me no trouble while I bent to tie the laces of my left then right shoes.

Unexpectedly, a sharp ringing tore through my head, right to left. Inches away on the coffee table, the apartment phone rang with the intensity of what had to have been its loudest setting.

"Can you pick that up?" Julie asked in an unconvincingly sweet tone.

"You're already standing," I said, voice strained from bending.

"You're sitting next to the phone," she informed me, as if the ringing in my ears due to my proximity to the phone had not already conveyed that bit of information.

"But you are already standing," I insisted again.

By that time, the phone stopped ringing. I could actually feel her glaring at me, but I continued on, leisurely tying my shoes, being sure to generate equal pressure on each foot. Her cellular phone then began buzzing itself around the kitchen counter.

"Look," I snapped, "now it's closer to you *and* you're already standing."

Julie glared at me, opening her mouth to respond with a long string of premeditated complaints when she and I both witnessed her phone buzzing its way off the edge of the counter. All we could do was watch as it plummeted, breaking into five or six pieces on impact.

The silence that followed was broken only by the faint sound of a woman's voice. "Hello?" The voice was shrunken by the dismembered phone. "Honey, are you okay? This connection is terrible," the voice said. "Hello? I'm calling the apartment again. Hello?"

Seconds later, the apartment phone again began to ring. This time I was leaned back into the couch, head farther from its piercing ring.

"I think it's for you," I said with a smile.

After more glaring in my direction, she walked over and picked up the phone then began a conversation by explaining that the phone difficulties were due to "Nick's incompetence."

As she spoke, I walked over to the kitchen and checked the refrigerator for something resembling food. Yogurt was the closest match.

The sink felt like the right place to leave the two empty yogurt containers and spoon. The feasting had been mildly enjoyable given that Julie's phone conversation had been unintentionally drowned out by the hum of the mutual morning disdain that bounced back and forth silently between the two of us.

"That was Mother," she said happily after she hung up. "Everyone's there now; they want us to come early!"

"Absolutely not!" I shouted angrily. "I refuse to go to your parents' house with the rest of your family for a single hour more than I already committed to."

"But they're all there having a wonderful time. If we leave now—"

"I'm not going today!" I shouted before she could finish her sentence. "I have to work! My patients depend on me."

"Then why don't I drive out by myself? I can leave now and you can meet me at the house later," Julie suggested reasonably.

I opened my mouth to agree with what seemed like a perfect solution, then I began to think deeper about her *generous* suggestion. Of course this was what she wanted, a two-day head start on the Poor Julie routine. Then I could either arrive to face a crowd of in-laws primed against me or back out of the visit altogether and be subjected to weeks of the silent treatment once my wife was back home.

I readjusted before responding. "You're always complaining that we don't do anything together so I kill myself to rearrange my schedule so we can spend the weekend with your family, and now you want to go without me? That hardly seems right."

"But, Nick, I only wanted—"

"We made plans, Julie, and I am sticking to them. So are you."

"Please stop interrupting me and putting words in my mouth, Nick," she barked back.

"For the record, I wasn't putting words in your mouth, but I know what you're going to say anyway so why don't *I* just say it? I know you well enough to know what you're thinking, Julie."

"Then I'm sorry you had to hear that," she said before picking up her blue bowl of fruit and turning on the TV.

I wanted to glare at her just as she had done to me earlier, but I found myself smiling instead. *Clever girl...* I thought as my phone vibrated my leg.

"Home Visit Now, 11 a.m.," the screen flashed.

I closed the door lightly behind me and walked quickly across the hall.

"What are you doing?" Julie asked from our doorway just as I began to thrust my arm, hand in a loose fist, toward the neighbor's door.

Startled, I turned around quickly before answering, "Knocking. It's that thing I was trying to explain to you earlier."

"Are you having an affair?" she asked point blank, confident, serious, and suspicious.

"No, no, Julie. Just close the door. I can't tell you what I'm doing, okay?"

But Julie just stood there looking at me. She was not glaring like she had been for most of the morning. She was just looking at me, the look of a wife who has given up, just completely given up on her husband. And I looked back at her, but angrily, silently willing her to get back inside, close the door, forget it ever happened, and she did.

I could only begin to imagine what I was putting her through emotionally; this was abuse, psychological abuse, but I knew no other way. She needed to understand that my job and thus my personality was that of a private person with secrets that she could never know.

I exhaled my dissatisfaction with life, but no relief came in on inhale, just the hollow emptiness I knew Julie had felt for years and years.

Home Visit

The door was soft on my knuckles encouraging me to knock several more times than one might on an average door, old worn wood. The excess of knocking did not, however, expedite the answering process.

There I stood for a hundred or so seconds thinking about Alec, Alicia's cuckold of a husband, paying the man his wife desired to determine if his children's psychological development was on track.

"Paranoid by nature" was how Alec described himself to people. Before his boys were born, he came to me terrified that one of his children might be afflicted with a developmental problem or disability with which the child or he was ill-prepared to cope.

His shaky trembling words flashed through my mind as I stared at the public side of their door. Alec had been struck with the uncertainty of raising children, twins, and was focusing on the most recent estimate of the prevalence of children that have developmental disabilities.

"One in six isn't just a statistic when your wife is pregnant; it's a real human being, maybe one of my children. And when they start to think about their existence… They'll know that one of them was not planned, or rather one half of each of them. How can they reconcile something like that? Isn't there something you can do? Some kind of screening process? Some kind of monitoring? Check up on them every week or something? I'll pay you. You have to help me right? You took an oath?"

I complied more for the check he sent every month than to ensure the normal development of his sons. Regardless of my reasons, my presence each month in his children's lives kept his mind at ease.

Just as I was about to begin another bout of knocking, the door was pulled open.

"Nicholas!" Alicia said joyfully. "I'm so glad you're here! Please take them off my hands for an hour." She draped herself onto me, presumably for physical and emotional support.

"You seem a little hassled," I responded somewhat uncomfortably, as she rubbed her face on my chest.

"I have two three-year-old boys. What do you think?"

"Children can be a handful," I agreed as I attempted to maneuver my way into their apartment and down the hall to the living room while politely repositioning her away from my body.

"Where are the boys?" I asked, hoping they were in the next room and not with their babysitter on a walk; a concern I had each month after Alicia had once executed that simple and devious yet effective plan.

Malcolm then rushed in fully naked, waving his little arms straight up and shouting "aaaaaahhhhhh" as if he was riding an imaginary roller coaster around and around the room. He was followed by his identical twin, also naked, but Darren's preferred mode of imaginary transportation was a plane to his brother's roller coaster, arms straight out at each side guiding his turns with an "eeeerrrrrrr" sound effect mimicking, I assumed, the plane engine.

"The boys are in their naked phase," Alicia said, offering an explanation. "Instead of putting on clothes after they've woken up, they take off their pajamas and run around the apartment for a while."

I nodded my head and smiled instead of straining my voice over their sounds.

"That's normal, right?" she asked, concerned by the absence of a verbal response from the person employed to assure that her children were developing properly.

"Yes! Of course!" I said loudly. "Totally normal."

Alicia smiled and let out a deep breath of air as she moved closer. "Oh my; you scared me for a moment there."

"Nothing to worry about," I assured her. "I do the same thing every Tuesday morning. Completely normal."

She let out a laugh and put her right hand on my slightly sore left shoulder. "Wouldn't that be a sight?" she asked rhetorically. "Come on, boys." This she directed toward her sons. "Let's go put on some clothes so you can play with the doctor."

I sat on the couch in the living room as Alicia walked into their bedroom followed by two noisy naked boys.

Their long curly dirty-blond hair and dark brown eyes were identical, but thankfully, Alicia was not the clichéd mother of twins who dressed her children in matching clothing. Telling them apart was never an issue as long as she indicated which one was which at some point during my visit.

Three or four minutes later, the boys both bounced into the living room at the same time and rolled their way onto the floor. They ignored my presence, paying all their attention to the bright colors and rapid scene changes of the cartoons on their large TV.

The show quickly lost my interest, however, so I allowed my eyes to wander around the room, noticing the childproofing techniques. Rubber bands on the kitchen cabinet doors closest to the floor. Rubber pads on top of the electric stove burners. Soft plastic covers on the corners of tables and counters.

Their apartment always struck me as improbably clean for the home of three-year-old twins, but the unforgettable smell of children was ever present.

I left the boys in a TV induced daze and walked to the only messy room in the apartment, theirs. Two miniature beds that looked like they could be bunked, but were not for obvious reasons, were at joining sides of the square room. There were crayons, pencils, an assortment of different sized pieces of paper, and toys were everywhere. Action figures and little plastic cars, blocks, and Legos. I always feared the Legos presented some kind of choking hazard, but there was never an incident as far as I knew. A pile of books occupied one corner of the room and did not appear to be very popular. There had clearly been a party with all the toys and the books had not been invited.

A miniature table and four miniature chairs occupied the center of the space. I had a strong urge to test the capacity of one of the miniature chairs, but quickly realized that I would likely crush it.

I went back into the living room to find the boys in the same positions they were in when I left them; disinterested in the guest in their home and fascinated by their cartoons. I asked if I could watch TV with them and interpreted their absence of a response to be an affirmative. Again I sat on the couch behind the coffee table behind their posts on the floor and we all stared at the giant screen.

During my visits, I generally watched them play together before asking some questions to each of them separately or sometimes asking them together. Since I could not force them to play, I decided to wait until their program was over to address them further. Unfortunately, the cartoons were designed to keep children watching all day. As soon as one ended, another began. No breaks in between whatsoever.

Fifteen minutes of fast-paced, headache-inducing cartoons later, I went to the hall and said loudly, "Alicia, can you help me with something?"

She came and took the remote from the floor, changing the channel unintentionally before turning the power off. The boys protested for two or three seconds before realizing it was their mother who ended the fun. She went back down the hall without even being asked to. Three years of my requests to not be disturbed when viewing the boys finally had sunk in.

The two of them began to spin around while practicing some jumps which appeared to mimic the cartoon before Malcolm got bored and walked to a closed laptop on a desk in the corner of the room, their father's work computer. Darren followed him shortly thereafter.

As it teetered back and forth, they climbed up to the thick cushy wheeled chair and quite willingly shared it. No pushing, no exchange of words, just sharing. They worked together to open the laptop quickly, silently, effortlessly.

Seconds later, Darren turned to me and said, "Help!" He pointed straight at me and waved his hands over his face. Malcolm seemed not to know what Darren was trying to communicate, but sat quietly, only repositioning himself to find a better line of sight to view the commotion on the other side of his brother.

"What can I do for you, Darren?" I asked in a slightly higher pitched voice than what I normally used.

"The thing you showed us before," he responded.

I thought for a second before recalling the events of the last visit. Then I opened the computer camera program and Darren pushed my hand away when he saw himself on the screen.

The boys spent the next fifteen or twenty minutes entertaining themselves with the functions of the program: replacing their background with one of palm trees and a beach or outer space with stars and a spaceship, distorting the images of their faces, changing the color scheme, and using different filters.

Malcolm became overwhelmed or frightened by what he saw on the computer several times and was forced to cover his face with his hands. When this happened, Darren hugged his brother, comforting him, then pulled him to the middle of the screen. The two played together quite well and with no real indication of one dominating the other and with no attempts to control the other.

Darren became bored first again and flung himself off the chair, hitting the wooden floor with a thud. Malcolm copied his brother's method of dismounting seconds later. This was not the first time I had witnessed this display of efficient travel, so I barely flinched at the potentially harmful behavior.

I called for Alicia again and asked her to occupy Malcolm while I asked Darren some questions. She turned the TV back on and left the room.

"Darren, can we go play in your room?" I asked quietly so that his brother did not hear, but luckily Malcolm was already lost in the TV so there was no danger he might wish to join us.

"Yeehhh!!" Darren shouted as he ran to his bedroom, forgetting me in the process. I followed slowly behind.

When I poked my head into the room, Darren was sitting comfortably on his miniature chair at his miniature table, playing with one of the toy cars. He laughed at my head suddenly appearing in the doorway.

After sitting on the floor across the table from him, I began with some easy questions (What's your name?), but had a lot of trouble getting useful responses out of him. He was always shy for the first few moments without his brother. He repeatedly hid his face as if the notion of "if I can't see him, he can't see me" were true.

I allowed him some time to play with his toys and become more comfortable before continuing with my list of multiple choice questions, but, instead of putting any meaningful thought into his answers, Darren seemed only to repeat the last option that I offered him.

Playing with his juice box and looking away while he answered, it was quite obvious that he was not thinking about the answer when I asked him if he or his brother was named Darren.

"My brother," he answered confidently.

"Who is taller, you or your brother?"

"My brother."

"Who is shorter, you or your brother?"

"My brother."

Realizing quickly that we were getting nowhere, I began asking him questions with the options first. He still chose the second option every time. I then tried to not give him any options, instead asking open-ended questions. He responded with silence then continued to play with his beloved juice box, rotating it in his tiny hands and chewing on the straw.

"Darren, what did you do yesterday?" I asked him for a second time, pushing him to answer.

"I don't know." He appeared to be getting a bit restless, captive in his bedroom without his brother with whom he did everything.

His head then perked up when he heard a recognizable cartoon laugh through the silence in the room.

"Can I go watch TV?" he asked in a miniature hopeful voice.

I decided to let him go because I was not getting much out of him at that point anyway. I followed Darren out and asked his brother if he wanted to play with his toys in the bedroom.

"No!" he shouted happily before laughing at his own defiance.

"Please, Malcolm…" I said, elongating the words.

"Hhmmmmmm," he verbally pondered, then after some deep thought he shouted, "Oookkkay!"

Alicia had told me the previous month that Malcolm was about an inch taller than his brother, but I was unable to see any difference. I was, however, able to see that he was consistently noticeably more rambunctious, jumping up and down while moving forward as opposed to a standard walk into the room. He also consistently appeared less intimidated by me and was less uncomfortable without his brother.

Malcolm plopped down where his brother had been sitting just moments before without any instruction, as if Darren told him exactly what to do. I said hello and asked Malcolm if I might ask him some questions. He suddenly began to behave just as shyly as his brother before him.

After a correct answer to "What is your name?" I quickly jumped into the harder open-ended questions in hopes of more thoughtful answers than those of his brother.

"Who has more friends, you or your brother, and why?" In retrospect, starting with a hard question may have scared him away from putting any thought into the rest of the questions.

He showed silent discomfort, playing with his hands for a while, before saying, "No?"

"How old are you?" was my next question, getting back to easy.

He held up three fingers.

I decided to take what I could get. He was, of course, correct, but I wanted him to use words.

"Do you and your brother fight?"

He shook his head and crossed his arms.

At that point, I knew he was not going to use many words during our session, but at least he appeared to be listening to the questions and thinking about the answers.

"Do you have a lot of friends?" I asked.

He shrugged his shoulders, cocked his head, and put up his palms in a perplexed manner.

"Does your brother have a lot of friends?"

Same response as before.

"What do you like to do? Use your words this time, Malcolm."

Malcolm forced out, "Watch TV."

"Good answer," I said excited. "What does your brother like to do?"

"Watch TV," he said again.

"Alright!" I said enthusiastically. I was happy to hear words, any words.

These were not the answers I was looking for, but they were something. I had always hoped that one of them would tell me about how the other dominated him in every aspect of his being and his resulting thoughts of inadequacy were pushing him to act out in the form of wetting the bed and throwing toys into the garbage, but that dream quickly slipped away when I realized I would only get one or two word answers out of them.

Three years earlier, I had convinced myself that this could turn out to be an interesting project. Maybe one of the boys would be a genius while the other was a born athlete and their constant rivalry for their parents' and my approval would bind them together in some respects while ultimately tearing them apart. I would counsel them, bringing them together as partners. I would receive all the credit for their success in life and rightfully so. But, after three years, as I sat there, my mind could only acknowledge that I had definitively determined that these boys were normal. I disdain that word when used to describe individuals; normal. What is normal? My mind only used it to adequately display my dissatisfaction with the situation.

"Do you like your brother?" I asked in an attempt to uncover some controversy.

Malcolm thought for a moment before darting toward me and hiding his face between my arm and torso. I hoped that he had realized the answer was uncomfortable for him. He did not want to admit that he hated his brother because of how his brother dominated him so he decided to literally hide from the question.

I probed deeper. "Do you not like your brother?"

He left his head stuffed under my armpit and shouted, "NO!"

I thought that maybe my question was worded too confusingly and what he meant was that he "did not" like his brother rather than he "did not not" like his brother. I forced him to sit normally, placing him back into his seat, then asked him again, "Malcolm, do you like your brother?"

"Yes," he answered.

"Why?" I asked, still hoping he was mistaken on some level.

He shrugged his shoulders then his head found its way back to my armpit.

These were the last words I was able to get out of him because he seemed to have noticed that his absence of words was frustrating me. Seizing his advantage, he then played the game of silence to his great amusement. When I finally told him that he could go, he ran out of the room and back in front of the TV.

Slowly I got up and followed him into the living room where he and his brother sat next to each other on the floor in front of the TV. One show had just ended and another was starting, but the boys did not like the new program so they began to search for the remote to change the channel. Theirs was a system that lacked voice or gesture control.

I was always amused to see children behaving like adults. They easily could have taken two steps forward and changed the channel on the TV or box, but they decided to search for the remote instead.

They looked under and on the coffee table, under and on the couches and all around the TV and box. They searched only their silently assigned area; each somehow knowing where the other had been and in no place double searching or overlapping.

Malcolm then began to take the couch cushions off and Darren, seeing his brother struggling, went to help him. The cushions were held in place by Velcro, too strong a bond to break for one, but easily conquered by two. They worked together and pulled every cushion off the two couches. They then headed toward their bedroom to continue the search, leaving the couch cushions all over the living room.

I had seen the remote on the kitchen counter earlier, but said nothing. I enjoyed watching the boys work together on a task. But on their way to their bedroom Darren spotted the remote, ending my entertainment.

"Can you give me the remote?" he asked in his tiny voice. He pointed at it, straining his arm and wiggling his little fingers.

His sentence was the most consecutive words he had said to me that day so I rewarded him with the remote.

"Thank you," he said before they returned their attention to the TV, settling on the previously rejected program after a fruitless channel surfing session revealed that nothing better was on; again, adult-like behavior.

After several minutes of losing myself in the bright colors on the large TV screen, I pulled out my phone to see that it was time to go. 11:49 a.m. I called to Alicia that I was done and she immediately sashayed down the hall.

"Can I offer you a glass of wine?" she said smiling. "I meant to offer you something when you came in, but you threw me off with your dashing appearance and that thought of your Tuesday morning naked dance."

Had she been anyone else, her inappropriate banter would have shocked me, but I had grown quite accustomed to it by that point. "Oh, no, no. Thank you, but I should really be heading off to the office. I have a patient coming in a little while and I want to go over some files beforehand."

"Oh," she said, noticeably disappointed. "Maybe next time? Or *anytime?*" She put her left hand on my right shoulder and her right hand on my left shoulder, before sliding them down to my waist.

I pulled back respectfully. "I should really be going. Tell your husband that I said hello."

I then turned to struggle with the door, unable to open it. Alicia came over slowly, leaned in, and unlocked the deadbolt with a loud click, a click which I had not noticed when I entered the apartment.

"I'll send you an e-mail with the report by next week," I said as I made my desperate escape.

I then turned to see her standing in the doorway, her tousled blond hair grazing her shoulders as she smiled with a sultry satisfaction. "I'll be looking forward to that e-mail and any other kinds of contact with you." The door closed slowly as she spoke.

―――

En Route to the Bar

I shook my head before turning to regard our own apartment. From the outside, our door looked painfully sad, as naked as the boys after a good night's sleep. I disliked looking at it from that angle, leaving another person's apartment, but there I stood, spotting my faint reflection in the peephole, pondering my next move; to knock and apologize to Julie, for this, for everything; or to cowardly do nothing.

As I descended the steps, the sound of a piano playing a slow tempo-less jazz was muffled only by the air between me and it because tenants believe *open* to be an appropriate position for a door. The sound increased in intensity as I passed the fourth floor then decreased as I descended farther.

Moving that piano years before was an experience that I have made sure to never repeat. Six hours of trial and error accompanied by the largest quantity and quality of profanity I had ever heard or helped produce in my entire life. Jacob, the owner of the unnecessarily large instrument, along with the man who sold it to him, and I strained our bodies and minds lifting this oddly shaped wooden percussive piece. The legs came off after much deliberation. So did the top, pedals, and several pieces from inside which I did not recognize as necessary for the production of sound.

When we finally finished the job, Jacob treated us to a hefty meal of pasta with his "special homemade sauce." I was not one to attend or enjoy impromptu gatherings, so I initially declined his offer.

"No, no, thank you. I should get back upstairs so I can watch a little TV and unwind before going off to bed," I told him.

"Do you listen to Jazz?" he asked me.

"I've heard some jazz before," I said.

"But do you *listen to Jazz*?" he asked again before telling me, "If the answer is anything but 'yes,' the answer is 'no.' " He then went on to explain why Jazz was not just a form of music, but a way a life; a way of life that I, apparently, should look into. I will never forget his words.

"Jazz," he began, "is all about improvisation. You know, improvise, don't follow the rules. Most people, when they make a song, when they're at the point where someone tells them that it's good, it sounds okay, they stop. That's it. They move on to the next song or whatever. They're happy with that. Those people, they need that security of being told it's fine. That's where they want to be; that's where they need to be; that comfort zone, that zone of comfort.

"That's not it though. They don't realize, but that's not it. They need to get out of that comfort zone, that zone of comfort, go way beyond into something they never saw coming. That's where the really good stuff is. That's where you want to live. That's Jazz.

"Miles Davis once told Herbie Hancock, 'I'm paying you to practice onstage…you can go and practice in your room, but don't go bringing that onstage.' Miles didn't want the stuff that was already made up, he wanted the making up of the stuff! You got me?

"The preconceived, the already created, that's not Jazz. And that's not life; reading music, reciting notes, following the rules and patterns. Guidelines: you're not living life, you're not a real person, not a real human being. You're just going through the motions. There's nothing inside, nothing behind it. It's empty, hollow."

That night, Jacob invited two other friends and we ate his amazing pasta, his homemade sauce, had some wine, talked art, music, philosophy, and anything else that came to mind, all right there in his apartment. I had one of the best nights of my life. We, the five of us, were such different people on every level. It almost felt cliché, like we were members of a platoon in a World War II movie. Our differences were what brought us together and made for a dynamic conversation.

That night, I saw my life through the eyes of others. My past, my present, my goals, my seemingly inevitable future. I saw what my life could have been, should have been, but, the next day, despite my vehement promises to the contrary in Jacob's apartment, I fell uncontrollably back into the routine of the life I had been living and I forgot about the knowledge of the fleeting potential that had the chance of changing who I was.

The Jazz faded away.

Just as the previous one, the day was severely overcast, intense sun rays beating through the clouds, but the sun was still darkened by those same clouds. My eyes immediately ached from the simultaneous contradiction of wide iris and abundant rays. My brain followed in the wave of pain, feeling like it was expanding and contracting two inches every second.

I attended to very little as I allowed myself to be pulled along toward the restaurant. Life was beginning to lose its detail. Departing and arriving were becoming one in the same.

A child wearing all green grabbed my memory as he rode his cherry red tricycle. He pedaled with great effort up the minimal incline of Manhattan. Adults walked around him, but ignored him in every other way. I scanned the scene for his parents, but saw no person with any visible connection to the little green boy riding red.

"Where are they?" I said aloud. "What kind of parents would let their child wander off in New York City like this? I should kidnap him to teach the parents a lesson," I snickered.

I took out my phone and looked at the screen. 11:58 a.m. "No time," I said as I sped my pace away from the lost child.

The phone was flashing "1 NEW VOICEMAIL." I pressed to listen and held it to my left ear. As it connected, I thought about how I had read three weeks earlier that the middle of the week, Wednesday, was statistically the most likely day for suicides. I froze in place for a moment, then relaxed into slight annoyance as I identified the speaker.

Julie's voice quietly and calmly conveyed her message. "Please don't forget that tonight is The Martins' party. It starts at 5 so we should probably leave here around 4:45. I told you about this two weeks ago and three times last week. I also mentioned it on Sunday. You promised you would go so please don't stand me up again, okay, Nick? I will see you at the apartment at 4:30."

"I hate life," I said aloud.

The remainder of the trip was spent in an attentionless daze.

Thursday's Drinks

As I turned the corner onto the restaurant's street, I saw Bill standing outside paying particular attention to the door. I barely looked at him, glancing only briefly in his direction then returning to my daze. Bill's silhouette, reminiscent of Alfred Hitchcock at the beginning of his old show, was all I needed to identify him.

The closer I walked, the more information I gathered about the situation. He was reading a small sign taped on the glass of the door.

—

Closed this Thursday for bereavement purposes

Open Friday normal hours

—

"Great," I said from behind Bill, startling him. "That idiot can still ruin the rest of this week's drinks even after he's dead." I felt filthy and crass as soon as the words left my mouth.

"Nick Thesiger! How are you doing? Looks like they're open tomorrow. You want to meet here then? Have a drink…"

I interrupted Bill. "Oh, tomorrow… I'm going to the in-laws tomorrow, remember?"

"Oh," he said, clearly not remembering because I had not told him.

"Sorry, buddy. So what's the plan?" Not giving him a chance to respond I suggested, "Get a cup of coffee? Change things up a little?"

"Sure, I'm free. Don't mind changing things up. Which one? We're in New York City; there's coffee on every corner!" Bill laughed at his slight exaggeration as we walked down the street and past a man who I momentarily mistook for Courtland with a slow double take.

The closest café, literally just as far as the end of the block, looked much less crowded from the outside than it did after the closed door was to our backs. The small space was stuffed with several dozen people, far exceeding the legal capacity for such a small footprint. Astonishingly, three of the four minuscule but tall tables were free. The vast majority wanted to get in and out and back to their lives, not sit and observe or attempt to relax. Our out of place desire to loiter made me feel old or unemployed.

"I'll leave my jacket here," Bill said, pointing at the stool closest to the window at the table.

"Good thinking," I commended sarcastically.

Assuming his jacket would be stolen by the first passerby, I scanned the immediate vicinity so I could identify and describe accurately to the police the people who were missing when we returned to the table.

My eyes met those of a middle aged man who sat at the table closest to ours. His fitted dark leather jacket suggested he was not interested in Bill's. The stool on the other side of his minuscule but tall table supported a black full-head motorcycle helmet. I nodded at him before making my way to the back of the rapidly shortening line. By this time another patron was separating Bill and me. The two of us shared a quick glance of acknowledgement.

As the line dwindled down, my eyes spent the duration squinting to read the tiny letters on the menu posted on the wall behind the counter. My headache, which never fully left, increased in intensity.

When it came to his turn, the sharply dressed speed talker ahead of me ordered for his entire office in what sounded like some language that vaguely resembled Italian or Portuguese. To my surprise, the cashier seemed to have no problem deciphering his order. The man stepped to the side within seconds while I stood squinting.

"Can I help you, Sir?" the cashier said in a direction in which no one was standing.

I gave up attempting to understand the menu and stood there silently, waiting for the transaction ahead of me to complete.

"Excuse me, Sir? Can I help you?" the cashier asked, her voice quickly jumping past insistent to rude, almost obnoxious. The intonation of the word "Sir" was familiar to me given that I have taken flights with perturbed flight attendants who were, as they all are, experts at conveying superiority, resentment, contempt, and impatience all in a seemingly polite three letter swear word.

I attempted to respond without retaliation. "Oh, I'm sorry. I didn't realize you were talking to me."

"Sir, can I help you?" she asked again, ignoring my apology.

"Can I have a cup of tea, please?"

"What kind of tea?" she asked with a tone of disgust that my order was not, by her measure, exotic enough.

"Plain tea, please," I responded, still brushing off the cashier's rude tone.

"We don't have plain tea."

"Regular tea, then?"

"I just told you, Sir, we don't have regular tea," she snapped back.

At that point of the day, of the week, of my life, I did not believe I possessed the patience for the idiotic back and forth that we were fighting through, but I calmed myself with an extra five seconds of breathing in and out and, in this seemingly short time, I learned that she possessed even less patience than I did.

"Sir, if you can't make a decision, I'm going to have to ask you to step aside so I can help the next person in line."

I looked at her for a moment, not stepping aside and not flinching. "I have already made my decision…" I paused to look at her nametag. "Margaret, but it appears that you are having just the slightest bit of trouble understanding my request. I am asking you for regular tea or plain tea or the closest thing you sell to whichever one of those two identical teas that I have already politely requested."

Margaret looked at me with both brown eyes, rotating her head slightly to face me directly, her black hair shifting under her visor. She knew well the childish challenge that stood before her, but decided to back down after glancing then glaring at the lengthening line which would only become more difficult to deal with if our conversation was further extended.

"So, Earl Grey, then?" she asked.

"That, Margaret, sounds delightful," I said victoriously.

"What size?" she asked, pressing on the screen in front of her.

"Large."

"We don't have large, Sir."

I looked at her with a blank stare. *How could they not have large as a size?*

"We have a large-equivalent…" she continued.

"That would be just fine."

"For here or to go?" she asked, needlessly adding yet another step on to the process.

"Really?" I asked. "Does it really matter? Doesn't it come in the same container either way?"

Then, as I looked at her, I saw something that I was not expecting. I saw, actually saw, the cashier. Late twenties, medium height, medium build, dark hair partially hidden beneath a silly looking visor even though she was inside where the visor's sun blocking abilities were rendered useless. Equally silly was the script writing on her black collared shirt: *Coffee Café*. The shirt had clearly been washed countless times, evident by its faded appearance in comparison to the other workers. She had worked there for a while. Her pretty face was as worn and tired as her shirt. Day in and day out dealing with people like my ignorant self had taken its toll. I was willing to walk all over her, dominating her to satisfy my own need to feel superior, so that I could feel more in control, so that I could feel more powerful, so that I could be victorious, but, most importantly, so that she would lose. I preferred to ruin her day than to allow her to take my order in the way management forced her to.

Disgusted at myself after spending those few seconds looking at her, I apologized and said, "For here."

As she tapped the screen in front of her, going through the mandated process which management frustratingly forced upon her

179

and subsequently upon me, I reached into my pocket and pulled out a number of bills.

"Fifteen ninety-five," Margaret announced.

Inside I was perplexed and infuriated by the fact that the painful process of attempting to have this establishment oblige me with a cup of hot water and an extremely small bag of leaves could possibly cost so much. On the surface, I remained stoic and handed over the inappropriately large quantity of cash.

"Ma'am, can I help you?" she asked of the next person before she had even finished placing my money in the register, the store's money now.

Receipt? I asked silently. Then I realized that there would likely never be a scenario in which I would have to verify that I was indeed here and buying this beverage for this astronomical sum of money.

I squeezed my way past the two dozen people in line behind me and picked up my large-equivalent cup of regular/plain tea-equivalent. The cup was twice the size I expected which came slightly closer to justifying the ridiculous cost, but still not close at all.

Bill was sitting at the stool closest to the window where he had left his jacket which was, surprisingly, resting on a shelf next to the tall table and not stolen.

I glanced over at the biker across from us as I sat. Tattoos covered his arms, exposed by his empty jacket under his helmet and by his loose sleeveless black shirt.

He nodded to me then turned his energy back to his muffin which he was eating in the most peculiar way; meticulously, with a fork and knife, as if he was performing surgery. He gently placed each perfectly sliced piece into his mouth with visible enjoyment physically exuding from his entire body as he twitched in pleasure.

Bill noticed that I was watching the man enjoy his food and remembered he too wanted to enjoy a snack.

"Oh! I meant to get a muffin!" he said before sliding off the stool and rejoining the long line.

As I waited for Bill's return, I continued to watch the biker's methodical consumption. After he completed his muffin, he tore fully open a bag of potato chips, poured the contents onto a napkin, arranged them in descending order of size, then began to consume it in a manner equally as peculiar as that used with his muffin. For each singular chip, the man stuck his tongue out as far as it would go then very gently placed the chip at his tongue's tip before retracting it quickly and dramatically, allowing his head to snap back and forth.

I watched him perform this odd ritual over and over, from largest chip to smallest, until all the chips were gone. This was my entertainment until Bill finally returned with his muffin.

He again settled in on his stool and I realized that I had not looked at Bill, truly looked at him, for years. I saw him five times each week, but we spent that time sitting at a bar and facing a brick wall in the back of a dimly lit restaurant. Our positions at the café forced environmental observation rather than a tête-à-tête.

Bill was never a beautiful man, but he had been much better looking in college. He had not aged well; his balding head was an odd oval shape, hair clinging to the lower half for dear life.

"Look at this place," he said, "there must be over seventy-five people in here."

"I know! They must be doing amazingly. Do you know how much I paid for this tea?"

"It's ridiculous," he agreed. "How can they charge like this for nothing?"

Nodding, I took a tentative sip of my scalding tea which proved my prudence to be wise. I removed the lid from the cup to expedite the cooling process.

"That muffin looks pretty good," I said, smiling toward Bill.

"It is," he responded, some of it in his mouth, bitten off like an apple. "I'm quite fond of it."

"Well, I too am beginning to feel somewhat of a fondness toward it…"

Bill cut me off. "Well, you're not getting half of it, King Solomon…" He laughed at his muddled reference as I frowned.

"Nick? Is that you?" I heard from behind Bill. "Yes, yes, it is! What are you doing here, old boy?"

I did not recognize the man who seemed to recognize me but I smiled and stuck out my right hand to meet his anyway.

"Jon Pu!" Bill shouted. Suddenly I recognized the shadow of a strikingly familiar face from college, but aged almost as badly as Bill's.

"Bill? Is that you?" Jon asked.

Jon Pu was a man whose name accurately conveyed the olfactory experience of anyone in his immediate vicinity. Back in college, his perpetually disheveled appearance and long greasy, unwashed hair fit him perfectly. It appeared that his grooming had improved, but the odor had not dissipated.

Shocked to see us both, Jon ignored my extended hand and bent down to hug the two of us simultaneously in one awkward swoop of his short arms.

"What are you two doing here together? You're still friends after all this time? Do you both live in the city?"

"Yes!" Bill responded. "We're…" he paused before continuing, "colleagues actually."

"Really?" Jon responded quickly. "Well, I suppose we all knew it back in school."

"Yes," I interjected. "Bill and I were on the same track; same major, same interests."

"Well, this is just wonderful," Jon said, right hand on my slightly sore left shoulder, left hand on Bill's right. "Gosh, Nick, you know I was always chasing you in that Econ class we had together. You were a mark on the bench, if there ever was one. I'm donating twenty grand a year to that department now! And you know what they give me? A lousy calendar!"

I smiled and confessed, "I donate $20 a year and they give me a calendar too. I always thought it was a bad deal. Now I see the deal is a lot better than I thought. I guess that Econ class paid off, eh?" I said of my ability to receive the same item as Jon by donating one-thousandth of the amount he did.

"We should all catch up sometime soon," he said enthusiastically. "I'm in town this week for meetings. I'm doing real-estate development now." He pulled his card out of his right inside pocket with his left hand and spun it around twice before handing it to Bill. "Oh gosh," he said, looking at his shiny silver wristwatch but moving it too quickly for an accurate identification of the brand or authenticity. "I have to run, but give me a call. We can all do the dinner thing."

"We'll call," Bill responded in a happy tone, clenching the card with his left hand while shaking it in the air.

Then Jon said, "It was great to see you two together. You know, I've been keeping up with the obituaries in the school newsletter, crossing off people's names and writing 'deceased' with a pencil next to their pictures in the yearbook. I thought you guys were dead."

"Why not use a pen?" I asked, somewhat stunned by Jon's strange confession, but his right hand had already allowed the door to close behind him. He was apparently in such a hurry that he had time to walk into cafés, but not enough time to order coffee.

"Jon Pu…" Bill said slowly after his exit. "That reminds me of a story."

"Go ahead," I encouraged.

"In the 1960s, American astronauts found that their pens wouldn't work in space. Because of the zero-gravity thing. Intelligent as they all were, NASA decided to design a pen that would suit their needs and work in those conditions.

"Millions were spent in the research and development of this little pen. Finally, when it was complete, the astronauts had something they could use to write with in space. Then someone, after all the time and money and man-hours, asked, 'Why not use a pencil?' "

Bill waited for my response for a moment before informing me, "It's a classic case of looking at a problem and trying to solve it rather than trying to find a solution."

"What reminded you of this?" I finally asked.

"Pu using a pencil to cross off people in the yearbook."

I shook my head before telling Bill, "You know that story is completely fictitious? A guy name Fisher designed and produced that 'space pen' in the '60s with no connection whatsoever to NASA. It wasn't until years later that NASA even started using those pens because they conveniently happened to write in zero gravity."

"Is that true?" Bill asked, knowing what my answer would be.

I merely nodded before my right hand reached into my right pocket, sliding out my phone. 12:23 p.m. and two new messages in the inbox.

"What's that?" Bill asked. "Patient calling or e-mailing or something?"

"Yeah," I answered, not wanting to delve into the topic before reaching the office.

"Do you ever feel like you're too available to them? They can call you or e-mail you or have a video chat pretty much anytime. That's the model you predominantly follow in your practice, right? Wouldn't they become dependent? Maybe you're hurting, not helping, some of them?" Bill's words may have been insulting, but I felt that they were designed merely to make conversation.

I responded with honesty. "I know it's not necessarily healthy for my clients, but it's the only way I can make a living, Bill. And I *am* helping them. I'm providing a service that is making their lives better."

"Fair enough," he responded, apparently sensing that I was not up for an argument on ethics.

Bill and I sat for a while, not talking, but what made this silent interlude dissimilar to others was that it was awkward. When staring at a brick wall, not talking was easy and comfortable. But, while sitting across from one another, not talking felt antisocial, almost rude in a way. Our eyes kept meeting as we looked at each other for the first time in years. I tried looking by him, staring over his right shoulder, through the window, at the red brick building across the busy street.

The building was an average height for the area, six aboveground levels. In a window on the fourth floor was a lone infant. It sat pushing its hands and feet up against the glass. I again thought about the significance of the middle of the week for the taking of one's life, but luckily the closed window prevented the infant from becoming just another part of the statistic.

In the window directly beneath was an elderly man. He stood observing the same streetscape as the baby. The man was very old, so old that standing was a feat accomplished by leaning and swaying. His severely wrinkled skin made it difficult to gauge his mood, but I assumed he was as gleeful as the suicidal infant above.

These two, standing a floor apart, did not and could not see the other, yet they saw exactly the same thing. They may have never met, but they were two parts of the same story, the first chapter and the last. But the first chapter seemingly craved the proximity to the story's end that the other longed to push further away from.

A woman with a large blue hat walking in front of the café momentarily blocked my line of sight. When I regained my view, the elderly man was gone. I questioned whether he had walked away from the window or if he had collapsed.

The baby was still in its window, still alive, but banging as it enjoyed its vantage point more and more and more. I questioned whether the dead man lying beneath would begin to create a malodorous environment and disturb the baby at some point. How long would it take? I pictured his old lifeless body lying there in front of the window, sadly unable to see out.

I started to count the windows on the side of the building so I could estimate how many different apartments there were. The smell would likely seep into the apartments next door before it made its way up through the ceiling and floor above, or would it? The question bounced around in my head as I counted eleven windows before coming to the infant's window, the infant's empty window. I jumped off the stool, unable to see clearly if the window was open or broken or still closed. I ran outside to get a better look, petrified of what I might find.

No baby, no broken glass, nothing; just people walking by without a concern for anything or anyone around them. Umbrellas, mostly black, opened as the sky opened up, allowing water to trickle down in a light mist. The ground was still bone dry.

I looked up and down the street and watched the umbrellas open in a wave of indifference. Still nothing in the infant's window; I stared and stared. Nothing in the elderly man's window; I stared and stared. And below, people passed by briskly, faceless.

Realizing that I was overreacting, I turned around to return to the café. I found myself face-to-face with Bill who had exited, concerned.

"Everything alright?" he asked.

"Yes, fine, fine. Sorry. I thought I saw somebody," I said, lying convincingly.

Bill and I went back inside, I passed as he held the door for me.

"Can't enjoy a sunny day without some rainy ones, I suppose," Bill commented as we mounted the stools. "How's work? How's the wife?" he asked.

I put my hands together and forearms onto the small tall table separating the two of us. Both hands slid my large cup of tea to my right.

"Same… we had a bit of a fight last night. We have a bit of a fight all the time and then I walk away or she walks away. I don't even know what any of them are about anymore; we just fight and then walk away. It all just stopped making sense."

"Oh. Sorry to hear that. Julie always struck me as a nice girl, never wanting to argue with anybody," Bill offered.

"Well, yes. She's great, but I only see that when she's happy and she's never happy anymore. It's like putting your favorite candy on the highest shelf in the kitchen. You can't even reach it so it's as good as not there. You end up forgetting about it as if it never existed. Then, when you finally do remember it, it's gone bad, all rotten and inedible." My words hurt as I spoke them because they rang too true; words I wish never occurred to me.

"Nice," Bill congratulated my metaphor.

"Thanks," I said, but this time it was not some competition of who could think up a sly way of seamlessly working some premeditated forgettable metaphor into our conversation. This time, it was all too true and all too painful.

"You know," Bill started, "I've been working on a theory about marital disputes."

Begrudgingly, I encouraged him to continue with a slight nod.

"Do you know what the Fibonacci Sequence is?" he asked, unintentionally insulting my intelligence.

"I think you've known me long enough to know that there is a one in a million chance that I won't know any given piece of information so, I ask you, what do you think?"

"Sorry, Nick. Well, I was thinking that arguments often progress, escalate in the same manner of the numbers in the sequence."

188

Indulging him further I said, "Explain, please."

"Well, the sequence consists of numbers starting with 0 and 1, followed by another 1 and then a 2…"

"Yes!" I interrupted before regurgitating the first dozen numbers in the Sequence. "0, 1, 1, 2, 3, 5, 8, 13, 21, 34, 55, 89."

"Hey, you asked *me* to explain it," Bill said, beginning to get a bit perturbed at my interruptions.

"Sorry, please continue."

"Each number is the result of adding together the previous two numbers. One is 0 plus 1, 2 is 1 plus 1, 3 is 2 plus 1, 5 is 3 plus 2…" I allowed him to continue with the monotony of this simple addition because he was writing the numbers down on a napkin as he spoke them. He stopped at 89, just as I had, and continued.

"So," he said, "the numbers represent the level of anger in your speech on each side of the argument. So the 0 is no anger and the 89 is a lot of anger, okay?"

"Yes," I said, having no trouble understanding what Bill assumed to be a complex idea.

"My theory assigns every second number to one of two people in the fight." He then wrote a "J" then an "N" above each number in sequence as he read it aloud. "The 0 is J, then the 1 is N, then the next 1 is J, then the 2 is N, then the 3 is J, then the 5 is N…" Again Bill went through the dozen numbers, assigning to each either a "J" or an "N." I watched the rain fall behind him beyond the café window as he droned on.

"Then," he said, "at some point the argument comes to a crescendo and the numbers start to come down in the reverse sequence."

I interrupted him to avoid going through the dozen numbers again. "So 89, 55, 34, 21, 13, 8, 5, 3, 2, 1, 1, 0?"

"Yes!" he responded excitedly. "And with that top number, that 89, instead of an N above it like the 89 right before it, we put a J because we just continue with the J's and N's." Bill quickly jotted down the mirror image of the sequence, assigning a "J" or an "N" to each.

"This is your theory?" I asked mockingly.

"Yes, but let me explain." Bill adjusted on the stool, leaning in so no one could hear then steal his idea and publish it themselves, selfishly protecting his pending Nobel Prize. "The switching at the top of the sequence, in the middle, that's the key! The one who repeats the other person's level of anger in their speech is the one who turns the argument around. The other person is preprogrammed to then speak with less anger when their previous level of anger was matched instead of exceeded. It's all subconscious. It all follows the sequence."

"Okay," I said slowly. "How does this relate to me other than your N's stand for Nick and your J's stand for Julie?"

The look on Bill's face conveyed his shock that I had broken his cryptic code. He quickly shook off his astonishment, however, and looked me dead in the eye and said, "You keep the argument going and, even when Julie matches your anger level, or responds with a lower anger level, you continue to raise yours."

I sat there and looked at Bill. He looked back at me, forcing me to think about it all, everything. Was everything really my own fault? Had I been destroying our relationship or was it the fact that Julie had changed, her aspirations, expectations, desires, what she wanted out of our relationship, out of life?

Bill added to his theory. "And in every fight, it sounds like one of you walks away when tempers are still high, never allowing the anger to come down, never to reconcile. Time does not heal all wounds, only the sequence does; talking down the levels. It's the only healthy way."

I was silent for a while. Bill's theories had always been predictable, strictly by the book; but this was a huge deviation for him. Bill was thinking outside of the box for the first time that I had ever noticed.

I thought for several minutes, half looking at Bill, half staring out through the rain, before allowing, "Even a broken clock is right twice each day."

Bill nodded at the successful debut of his theory.

"This is a lot like that great idea you had in college," I added, moving mentally and verbally to something completely different.

"You mean Responsibly Beer?" he asked, knowing well to what I was referring; the bane of his existence, the one thing that he constantly looked back at and regretted. This was what Bill believed would have changed it all. He would be a different, better person had he just gone a different way and this one thing represented the fork at which he took the wrong direction.

"That's the one," I replied.

"You know, I would be rich now if I just ran with that. To start a beer brand with the name of Responsibly. It would immediately be the most well-known beer around. Other beer companies would literally do advertising for me in their own advertisement, even on their beverages' bottles and cans."

Then Bill looked at me and said, "Drink Responsibly," while shaking his head.

"Genius," I added.

"I could even add another flavor called In Moderation."

I smiled and said sadly, "If only…" and allowed my voice to trail off.

Bill sat, shaking his head with a slight smirk. Years earlier, the anger was much more prevalent when Responsibly Beer came up in conversation. But, the years of anger and regret had allowed Bill to see and accept that his life will never be what he had hoped. Trying to pinpoint where things had gone wrong was useless; dwelling on the past served no purpose for the present or future. It was a realization that we all come to at some point and, judging by that slight smirk, he had reached it.

" 'The dangerous man is the one who has only one idea, because then he'll fight and die for it,' " I said, quoting Francis Crick.

After a bit of thought, Bill, completely defeated, responded with, "And it's true."

"We've been here too long," I said as I looked around at a whole new set of dozens of people from the set I had most recently noticed. "Let's get out of here. This place is getting old."

We dropped our refuse in the garbage hole at the end of the counter and exited into the wet city. Bill opened his black umbrella, twisted and broken, but still functional.

I pointed and laughed.

"Thanks," he said disingenuously.

The fat raindrops slid down Bill's mangled vinyl umbrella and directly onto me. He smiled as I would be soaked regardless. I smiled back, accepting the inevitable.

"So, want to get together next week?" he asked.

"Obviously, I'm away tomorrow and for the weekend," I responded before we parted ways, walking slowly in opposite directions.

"Oh, Bill!" I shouted when we had separated a number of steps. "I meant to ask you how you are doing? How work has been treating you?"

"Eh, you know," he shouted through the rain, "they all think they're God."

"What?" I shouted, cars passing, drowning out his voice, the sounds of engines and tires against the wet street.

"They all think they're God," he repeated. "The schizophrenics, the temporal lobe epileptics, the bipolars, the severe narcissistics, the antisocials. Nick, day in and day out, I talk directly to God and, to be honest, I don't like what I hear…"

I smiled, responding with a wave above and behind my head, then I turned to continue on my way as he turned to continue on his; our separate paths to intersect again the following week.

―――

En Route to the Office

I knew I would get just as wet if I ran, but I ignored logic and physics. Faster and faster through the rain I ran, running toward my office.

I asked myself what I was running from. I asked myself if I could outrun it or if it was as impossible as outrunning the bulbous raindrops. I asked myself if I was getting anywhere, if I would ever get anywhere, or if I was just lost and would only get more and more so if I continued, potentially–inevitably–making circle after circle. Had it not been for the street signs, I would have ended up nowhere or not ended up anywhere.

From the back of a cab, out of his slightly open window, a man shouted, "It doesn't matter how fast you go as long as you're headed in the right direction!"

For some reason, it made me smile, laugh even.

"It's really comin' down out there, eh?" said the bone-dry doorman as he opened the door protected from the splatter and splash by the large awning.

Soaking wet, I looked at him grimly. The only dry thing about me was my affect.

Alone on the elevator, I depressed the button for my floor and waited. As the doors slowly approached one another, a spry twenty-year-old slipped in and, judging by his shorts, loose sweaty tank top, and the earphones jammed in his ears, he was coming from the gym on the ground floor. He ignored my presence while I stared at him in disbelief when he depressed the "4" button; due to the vagaries of numbering in upscale real estate, the fourth floor was the floor directly above the lobby from whence he had just entered the elevator.

I stared at him for the entirety of his disgustingly short vertical trip. His presence and then quick absence angered me to an absurd degree as I began to tense up. The anger shook my body and mind until I required two steady hands to transport the carafe filled with filtered water from the small refrigerator to the coffee table. I needed to sit down.

Thursday at the Office

The large leather chair stuck to my clothes just as my clothes stuck to my body so I found a small fan in the closet and positioned it on the desk, directing air across the dampness.

I caught a quick glimpse of myself in the black computer screen before it flickered to life. The image was blurred and fleeting, unrecognizable.

My schedule showed no in-office sessions and no scheduled video sessions. The corner of the screen suggested the time to be 1:10 p.m. Only two messages graced my inbox, but I was sadly certain more would come. I leaned back, sticky, and closed my tired eyes; dry when they opened an hour later, as dry as my lips and tongue; I had slept directly in the path of the quickly moving air from the fan with my mouth wide open.

After sucking on my tongue and wetting my lips for two or three minutes, I stood up slowly, bracing myself on the arms of the large leather chair. The points of contact between the chair and myself were still wet and stuck together so I turned toward the park, back in the path of the rapidly moving air.

After my backside's two minute drying session, a tapping, quietly building in intensity, turned my head toward the computer to confirm my current understanding that today's schedule held no in-office sessions.

Pizza? The thought brought a smile to my face.

Kristin

I tiptoed toward the door then peered out of the peephole to see Kristin leaning most of her weight to her left side, legs and head positioned to accommodate for her lopsided stance, creating a tall "C" shape with her slender body. I looked at her for slightly longer than necessary before she looked directly into the peephole, smiled, then knocked again, eyes fixed right at me. My heart skipped a beat before resuming double-time.

Was she looking at her reflection? Could she see me?

I opened the door and pretended to be surprised to see her. I was pretending, but I was surprised. Her next scheduled appointment was Tuesday.

"Kristin? Do we have a session?"

"Dr. Thesiger! I wasn't sure you were in. Are you busy?" she asked, peering beyond my body to see the empty couch.

"Ah, no, no. It's just me here. Come in," I invited, stepping aside.

She walked in, wet from the rain, but not as wet as someone who had been running in it umbrellaless. Her dark hair clumped together in large long bunches, while her makeup remained oddly flawless. Judging from her hair, she had forgotten that she had a hood on the same thin red long-sleeved sweatshirt that she had worn to our session two days before, but now with jean shorts rolled up, shortening them further. I focused on her upper half and ignored what deviated from two days before, imagining that the time that separated our last meeting never occurred, that we had remained together.

I closed the door then turned to find her arms around my torso holding tight.

"Everything okay, Kristin?" I asked, startled and concerned, sensing everything to not be okay. Kristin's emotions were always visible to me, right there on the surface as though she was some kind of human mood ring. I scoffed at the cliché thought after thinking it. I was glad I had not said "mood ring" aloud. I remembered a patient once gave me one as a gift; it was meant to be ironic.

She said nothing for a while, holding on for dear life then, "Everything is fine. I just wanted to come and see you."

She let go and walked slowly to the couch then, in several fluid movements, pulled her red hooded sweatshirt over her head to reveal a green and red tank top with muted floral designs, slid herself onto the couch, rested the hooded sweatshirt beside her, slid off her sandals, pulled her feet up, then turned and leaned back, head resting comfortably on the small pillow at the end of the couch.

"I had a dream," she confessed.

"About what?" I walked over to the desk to turn off the fan, then sat across from her, admiring her proportionally long limbs.

She looked at the ceiling as she spoke. "I was in the living room at one of my parents' off-base apartments, but I was my age now, not six or five like I was when I lived there. No one was home; it was just me. And it wasn't empty or anything; all of our stuff was there."

Kristin said nothing and continued to stare at the ceiling, never to continue her telling of the dream. For almost ten minutes, we sat there in silence until she began to openly weep.

"Kristin, what's wrong?"

"I did something bad," she sobbed.

"What? Is everything okay?"

She continued to cry before responding, "I don't want to say…"

For a moment, I considered the possibility that she had murdered her ex-boyfriend like she did in her dream described in our session two days earlier. I wiped the thought from my mind quickly. "Now, Kristin," I said taking the role of the adult. "If you tell the truth, your mistake becomes part of your past. If you lie, it becomes part of your future."

"That's the nerdiest thing I've ever heard!" she said smiling, laughing, and crying all at once.

"Well, I have a reputation for doling out nerdy advice… It's my only talent. What can I say?"

Again, she laughed through the tears. "I just like to cry sometimes; I like the way it feels… Good, sometimes it feels good. That's what I need."

When Kristin cried, I rarely tried to stop her. As the tears again consumed her, I got up and sat on the edge of the couch next to her and began patting, then stroking her wet hair to calm her. Kristin's tears never made me feel uncomfortable like others' did. When other patients cried, I would slide the tissue box to them as quickly as possible. When Kristin cried, I wanted nothing more than to console her, to be the one she ran to for help, to get her through her hard time, our hard time.

Strongly feeling her emotions, I questioned whether I should allow myself to cry with her. Would it bring us closer? It was the only way I could show her that I was feeling her sadness, that we had a deeper connection than what appeared on the surface. But I knew she would lose respect for me. She would think I was incapable of staying strong. She needed me to stay strong. It was the only way things would remain right. I knew I could not cross the line. But, despite what I knew not to be right, what I knew needed not to happen, I began to tear up as she cried harder and harder.

Fortunately she hid her face in the couch just missing the tears welling in my eyes. I walked over to the desk and took out the box of tissues, using one for myself before putting them on the coffee table in reach of beautiful crying Kristin.

She sat up and attempted to pull herself together, dabbing the edges of her eyes with a tissue and looking everywhere but at me.

"I went to the doctor earlier today," she said.

My mind immediately went to the worst case scenarios, but I waited for her to continue before physically reacting. Holding my breath, I listened as intently as possible.

"I thought maybe Jason would like me better if I changed."

"What do you mean? What are you saying, Kristin? And I thought you broke up with Jason weeks ago."

"I just wanted to check it out, see how much it would cost."

"See how much what costs?" I asked frantically.

"Cosmetic surgery…" she admitted.

Relieved, I leaned back. "That's what you're crying about?" I asked, not considering how insulting it was for a therapist to belittle the reason for a patient's tears.

"Yes!" she shouted. "I wanted to change myself so somebody else would be happy. You always told me never to do that; to only do things for myself, not for someone else. You always told me to be myself."

Still in a daze of relief I smiled and said, "No reason to cry, Kristin. So you had a little lapse in judgment. As long as you realized it to be a quick little bout of weakness and you stopped yourself from changing to suit somebody else, then you're perfectly fine!"

She sat for a duration of silence, thinking. "Oh," she said finally. "I guess everything *is* okay then."

"Yes!" I shouted. "Of course it is! You're being too hard on yourself. We all have a slip or two once in a while. You should be proud of yourself for catching it before it became a permanent mistake."

"I guess you're right," she said slowly, assessing the validity of her words as she spoke them.

With a smile and a laugh, I crossed my legs, left ankle on right knee, and said, "There is nothing wrong with cosmetic surgery, of course, as long as it's done for the right reasons. And, as you pointed out, pleasing somebody else is not a good reason."

"You know what the doctor told me?" she asked.

"No, what?"

"He told me that he could do a job on me that would be really hard to spot. No one would be able to tell I had anything done." Then she mimicked the doctor by pushing her elbows out away from her body and talking in a deep voice. "He said, 'People won't be able to tell if it's Splenda or just splendid!'"

I laughed immediately despite the fact that it took me a handful of seconds to fully understand how fake sugar related to the conversation. "Regardless," I joked, "it would be a pretty sweet deal, am I right?"

Kristin laughed and laughed, guilt completely out of her heart.

"The forecast said rain, but it's certainly not raining in here," I quipped, convinced I was on a roll.

She laughed harder, this time at me as opposed to with me, but I was happy to see her smiling and laughing anyway.

"You know, Kristin, I generally find that girls your age who live in the city are really quite a bit boring. They're all the same, dress the same, talk the same, walk the same... You're just... different. It's refreshing."

"Oh, well thank you, Dr. Thesiger," she responded confidently, flattered but not bashful. "I think it's just the city."

"How so?" I asked.

"Well, I've been thinking about this and, when you've lived here for a while, people just seem to turn into emotionless robots, kind of following mindlessly along with what everybody else is doing or wearing or saying.

"You wake up, go to school or work, then back home to the internet and sleep. Then you repeat it all the next day. Maybe you deviate a bit on the weekends, but that's the exception that proves the rule.

"In between you see millions of people, and the vast majority you have no connection to whatsoever. You kind of lose the ability to properly connect with others. Everyone just becomes another random person so you end up not even understanding your friends are people, your family are people. Then you don't have a chance to cultivate who you are as an individual so you just act like whoever is around. I agree. No one is an original around here. Everyone is fake and phony and boring. I feel like I'm getting off track here. Sorry."

"No, no. That sounds about right," I agreed. "But you're different; you really are. You still have that emotion about you and you don't mind showing it. Sad, happy, guilty, whatever; it's all there and you're not hiding from it. That's really wonderful. Don't lose that quality, okay? Promise me that."

"I promise!" she shouted happily.

We sat there smiling at one another for a while when suddenly her face reflected her realization that she had popped in unannounced and that I may have had work to do, so she asked, "When is your next patient coming? Should I head out?"

"Oh, no," I insisted. "I don't have any in-office sessions today. Just e-mails and videos to watch and respond to, maybe a video session, but none are scheduled."

"Do you watch movies or TV when you're doing video sessions?" she asked.

Suddenly, my face became angry, eyebrows arching and upper lip tightening up. "No, of course not!" I shouted. "I hate people who turn on a movie for background while they're doing something else. Then they think they've miraculously earned the right to have a meaningful opinion on the movie without even giving it the attention it deserves, the respect it deserves? Ahh! I hate people like that; absolutely hate them!"

Kristin laughed at the extremely deep disgust and anger she had provoked when indirectly equating me to a self-important fool who believed his uneducated opinions to be valuable in some way.

"Sorry, that's one of my pet peeves, I suppose," I said, somewhat bashful.

"So, I'm guessing you wouldn't let me stick around for a while then? I kind of want to watch you in action… with someone other than me, that is."

I thought about her request before realizing how unethical it would be to comply. "Sorry, Kristin, doctor-patient confidentiality. You can't read any e-mails or watch or hear any videos from other patients. It would be a bit of an invasion of privacy."

"I guess I knew that," she said as she smiled then slipped her feet back into her sandals, tank-topped torso back into her thin red hooded long-sleeved sweatshirt. "So I should head out then?" she asked.

"I think I would prefer for you to leave me with your presence," I responded.

Kristin paused and thought for a moment, stood up slowly, took some steps toward the door, stopped, turned back around, took one step back toward the couch, thought some more, then turned and continued to walk away, stopped once more, turned around, came back to the couch, then finally asked, "What?"

"Ha!" I laughed. "Ambiguity…"

I stood and she followed as, without words, we walked toward the door slowly, swaying our limbs to elongate our movements. When the door was a foot away, she hugged me for some unknown duration, her arms wrapping around me for as long as they desired.

"Thank you," she whispered lovingly when she released me.

I rocked back and forth, weak at the knees, then remembered. "Oh, wait," I said, running to my desk and pulling open the top drawer to extract a stunning self-portrait she had effortlessly sketched in our last session, but forgot to take with her. "Your picture!" I ran back to her and extended it gently.

She took it, looked at it, then glided through the open doorway, smiling.

"Keep that, okay?" I said. "It will probably come in handy at some point."

Still smiling she pulled her hood over her head, covering her dark damp clumped hair, and waved with her right hand before walking quietly down the hall toward the elevator. The plastic sequins on her sandals sparkled like the twinkling in her eyes. I waved with my left hand and closed the door slowly with the right.

My head felt light, as if it was in danger of floating away. I watched the door shrink as I took several backward steps ending with my heels hitting the bottom of the couch. There I lay where she had just been, staring at the ceiling and thinking of nothing at all.

"Transference...countertransference..." I said as I shook my head.

When my eyes started to close under the increasing weight of my forgotten fatigue, I made the quick decision to pull myself to the large leather chair and start reading and returning messages. I wanted to finish early enough to take a substantial nap before being forced to accompany Julie to the cocktail party at her family friend's Brownstone across town.

Losing Kristin's joyous presence in addition to moving the reality of my day to the front of my mind revealed then exacerbated the pain which riddled my body. Inverse to the morning, my neck was the only part of me that did not ache in some way, throbbing, tightening, sore...

On my journey from one side of the room to the other, I moved the tissue box onto the desk then moved the e-mail program over and opened the billing program onto the computer screen.

If there was ever a patient I felt bad about billing, it was her. Our time together was consistently enjoyable; the way a roller coaster is enjoyable, pulls you every different way, makes you feel things you thought you forgot how to feel, things you never knew you could, always ending just when you're shouting for more, leaving you tingling and smiling.

"Thank you," I said, repeating her last words to me. Very few patients had said that. Even fewer actually meant it. Kristin was genuinely beautifully honest and when she thanked me, I knew I had done something worth the gratitude. I billed her with a swift tap on the screen, reconciling my conflict of interest with the knowledge that I was in fact billing her father.

I then reached to replace the tissue box in its customary drawer, but noticed I had left the top drawer open in my haste to return to Kristin her drawing. I glanced down to see the picture of Courtland, faced obscured and arms spread wide as he looked out over the Grand Canyon. I closed the drawer and looked up past the computer screens and onto the couch where he sat, not looking at me, but looking across to the chair in which I habitually sat during our sessions.

I left the large leather chair and settled in across from him, in his direct line of sight on the chair across from the couch. He was previously just staring, looking at the wall, through the wall, but then he looked at me, into my eyes. He nodded, face expressionless, before fading away from sight, mind.

———

Emily

My heavy head hit my left hand and I rubbed my eyes before rising as I walked several paces only to collapse once again into the large leather chair behind the desk. The first message in my inbox was from Emily, a twenty-one-year-old college junior. Her sessions with me were not mandatory, but strongly suggested by her college.

"At approximately 1:30 a.m. on Saturday, January 19th, Emily's roommate brought a friend into their shared room to continue studying." When I first read that sentence on the report the school had sent to me, prior to my first session with Emily, I had immediately assumed it to be misinformation. More likely the roommate and the *friend* were drunk and had met at some bar or frat house. Very little studying, I assumed, was involved.

The report from the school's disciplinary department went on to explain that the roommate's guest picked up and began roughly playing with and manhandling a stuffed teddy bear that belonged to Emily. Allegedly, Emily reacted in an inappropriate manner, punching and clawing at the guest. She continued this attack long after the guest had released the teddy bear. The roommate eventually had to enlist two neighboring male students to tear her off the guest.

Emily was unimpressed and fully dissatisfied with the college psychologists and college-recommended psychologists. In three months, she wasted her time with seven of them, hating each one more than the previous. The college, however, "strongly suggested" that she go through counseling. If she did not, then she would not be permitted in her dormitory. Since the school was unable to provide the appropriate counseling, they allowed her to find a psychologist on her own, but required monthly confirmation of continued treatment.

I never learned why she chose me. One day I received a call from the college psychological services office with a request to bring Emily on as a patient; they would cover all costs.

I initially questioned to myself why they would not just expel her, why they were working with someone who was clearly difficult to handle and hard to please. The rest of the report, which was sent to me after I agreed to see her, answered my questions.

Emily had had an unfortunate childhood, almost echoing the plot of some clichéd movie. Abandoned by her single father at a very young age, she "bounced from orphanage to orphanage." I had been surprised to see the word "orphanage" used in the report, as I was certain that, in the field, the word was considered archaic and derogatory.

The report went on to divulge the details of her schooling and her relative success, earning her a full scholarship to the college. She participated in the student government and played an undisclosed sport. At this point, I started to question the validity of the report as it became vague and rather uselessly wordy.

When summarizing the incident, they suggested the teddy bear to be a "meaningless item" and Emily's act of defending it, "disproportionately intense." What they failed to recognize was that "meaningless item" was actually the most important item Emily possessed.

Emily's past consisted of moving around, never making lasting friends, and the absence of any consistent environment; she never got the chance to attach to a place or a person, this forced her to push all of that need to emotionally connect onto the one thing that followed her from place to place, the one constant in her life, her teddy bear. When it was in danger, her reaction was completely normal. How the college psychologists missed this obvious fact was beyond my comprehension. I supposed they were mostly very busy and saw hundreds of different students, but this was clear to me from the beginning.

Emily had admitted to me in an e-mail three weeks before that she was unsure of how to think of herself. She knew well that she was an orphan by definition, and had been almost her entire life, but she did not identify with what was commonly thought of as an orphan. Like many college students, she was having trouble defining herself.

In our in-office session the week before, we began to talk about her past, allowing her to remember, even relive her life through the memories of her journey.

The first lines in her e-mail quoted my words from our previous session.

—

"Maybe travel back in time mentally to try to track yourself; learn who you were. It might help you define who you are and maybe who you'll be."

When I was young, just like a normal kid, I had dreams I thought I could reach. Every day, month, year those dreams became more and more narrow, more and more realistic, more and more of a letdown, and less and less like dreams. Astronaut, professional athlete, doctor, lawyer, career woman, having a job with a future, having any job…

I held each one of those dreams until I came to the realization that they were too hard to attain because of my circumstances, then I shifted down a level, down the scale; the cycle repeats. I got into the grind of it all—the lazy autopilot of life you were talking about—and never tried to accomplish or chase anything, let alone one of my *dreams*.

Even now, I'm so drenched in what I call life that I have no idea what it is that I actually am. I never really took a metaphorical step back and looked at what I've become or where I came from. I did the opposite; I tried to forget about the things that hurt and just keep moving forward.

But, I've given it some thought, and do I even want to know who I was or about my past? If I thought about it all, I'd realize that what I am is so far off from what I wanted to be, so far off from those dreams that I once had. I don't know if I can take that right now.

Where did it go, the ambition? I know I no longer have it so why should I mentally travel back in time to watch it slowly degrade? What really matters is that I know who I am, what I am, and that I realize that I am who I am and this is me. I need to accept it, whatever it is…

—

Kristin's visit seemed to have had a lasting effect of empathy within me. I was so saddened by Emily's message that, had I not been paying attention to my quickly changing emotional state, I may have cried.

I started to write without filter about society, our culture, and its effect on us all.

—

Hello Emily,

It hurts to live in a meritocratic society, doesn't it? "People are at the level that they should be." That's pretty much what we're led to believe. Work hard, you become successful. Don't work hard, you don't become successful. It makes you feel good when you're at the top, but when you're at the bottom (or really anywhere other than the top), you feel pretty bad. You're told your whole life that you are what you're supposed to be; in the case of the bottom, a failure.

But this theory is not the reality. It is hardly applicable to the real world because there are so many uncontrollable random factors (race, gender, parents' socioeconomic status, etc.) and events (health issues, emotional issues, pregnancy, etc.) that control or change the direction of your success.

So you should just wait for something random to happen to you to bring you success, right?

Well… the answer is right and wrong. You can't expect something to happen to you, for success to fall into your lap, but you also can't get down on yourself when you work your hardest and you end up getting seemingly nowhere.

—

I stopped myself and read over what I had just written and realized that my oddly fragile emotional state was affecting my words. What I was writing had very little, if anything, to do with Emily. And there was no direction in the message. I deleted what I had written and started over, but only after thinking about what needed to be addressed. I decided to fabricate a story about my past which outlined the importance of defining one's self.

—

Hello Emily,

Allow me, for a moment, to tell you a story about being yourself.

Gender Neutral Housing

A guiding principle behind room-draw is the ability of an individual to select their own room and roommate(s). Gender neutral housing is an additional option provided by the College, one not limited by the traditional gender binary. It allows for same-gender, opposite-gender, or other-gender identities to live together

regardless of biological sex. Two gender neutral housing options are available:
Apartments and Suites.

Above is a description of a rooming option added to the existing standard options (quiet, no specified sound limit, alcohol, no alcohol, etc.). First let me attempt to explain the backward way in which my undergrad college forced us to choose our rooms and roommates after pre-assigning rooms/roommates freshman year.

All members of the sophomore, junior, and senior classes crammed their way into an inordinately small (for the number of people) room. Each student had been previously sent a card with their "randomly generated number" on it. Those numbers ranked each student's ability to get a good room, bad room, or no room at all on campus.

Twenty or so large boards graced the front of the room displaying on them in small, hard to read letters the building names and the room numbers of the available rooms. There were all combinations of rooms with living rooms, rooms without living rooms, rooms with bathrooms, rooms without bathrooms, rooms of all sizes, and suites with between one and six bedrooms.

Students were expected to get together with friends and pick several rooms that would suit them. The lowest and thus best number held by the members of the group was used to get closer to the front of the line making it more likely that the group would get the room they desired.

However, each student was a part of at least five different groups of students, often committing to competing and conflicting groups. If your option for a four-bedroom room got crossed off the large board in the front before that group made it to the front of the line, you would go off with another group to get a five-bedroom or a smaller three-bedroom leaving the other group members to find their own other options.

People were constantly being pulled into other people's room plans or cut from the room plan they thought was ironclad. Each time a room was crossed off the board, friends were made and friends were lost, enemies reconciled and secret alliances emerged. The result was a dizzying bloodbath as what were once considered to be lifelong friendships were unceremoniously terminated. It was like a gigantic, cruel, and unusual mathematical, social, and psychological experiment, all in one small room.

Each student was double-, triple-, quadruple-timing their "first choice" roommates and rooms. Students ran from one end of the room to the other, pushing through people to find someone, anyone, that could be "the fourth" in the four-bedroom suite that was next on their list of available rooms.

Those who held the lowest numbers were kings, wielding their power to drop people from room plans and pull in others, commanding respect, humbling even the most popular students, and even, on some occasions, procuring monetary compensation.

It was the worst day of the year at college. Some scars from that battle of room-draw would never heal.

The year that gender neutral housing was introduced, it made this process even more complex, adding another level of confusion and betrayal.

I guess it's actually really good for those people who are more sexually ambiguous. One may have laughed about it though. And one did (and by "one," I mean many), but students also tried to take advantage of the amazing rooms and suites in prime locations set aside for the gender neutral. Dating couples that want to live together were the most common group trying to sneak in through the gender neutral passageway, but there was another group, one that will live on in infamy.

212

A number of football and baseball players who possessed bad numbers for the room-draw process tried to use the gender neutral option in an attempt to obtain good rooms. This, of course, blew up in their faces. Athletes were not necessarily unintelligent, but they, like many other members of the student population, did not fully understand what "gender neutral" actually meant in this context because it was never actually explained to anyone. The best they could come up with was "homosexual." It was a different time, a long time ago, so they came to the room-draw night dressed like and acting like what they presumed to be the stereotypical homosexual of the time, exaggerating specific mannerisms and walking in a particular way. In reality they were mocking an entire demographic for a plan that had been doomed from the start.

When they were interviewed; a process everyone interested in gender neutral housing had to go through; they answered questions completely inappropriately and without any consistency. After the mandated DNA testing and physical examinations were conducted, each one of them was suspended for an entire academic term and they all ended up losing their athletic scholarships and their positions on their sports teams. And they were also, not to mention, ridiculed for the rest of their time at college.

The point of this story is that you shouldn't pretend that you are something that you are not, especially when you do not fully understand what it is that you are impersonating. As you said, Emily, "what really matters is that you know who you are and what you are and you accept it." That is the most important thing; knowing who you are and embracing it and never compromising yourself, your identity, for anything.

Maybe next week we can try to start thinking about who it is that is you? Come ready for some discovery! Have a fantastic week, Emily.

-Dr. Thesiger

I quickly checked the spelling and grammar before sending the message. I was much happier with this version than the first; I hoped that it would bring a smile to Emily's face. For a moment I questioned if she would be able to check the veracity of my tale, but I wiped the thought from my mind, not wanting to worry myself.

———

Al

I wasted no time or momentum, moving quickly to the next message, but just before opening it, the speakers began to ring lightly and the smiling face of a patient who had been with me for a few months, Al, was displayed on the screen to my left. I sighed loudly and stretched before pulling Al's window to the screen in front of me and answering.

"Al!" I said loudly.

His face had a look of shock. "Dr. Thesiger! I didn't think you were going to be there. I figured you had patients or something. I was just sitting around not doing anything and I thought I would try you."

"Oh, well you got me! How's everything going?"

"Everything's good, good. Not a lot going on really. Same old, same old."

"Hey, I have two quick questions," I began. "I was looking at your paperwork a couple days ago and you didn't fill in your height. How tall are you?"

"Depends on what convenience store I'm leaving. Anywhere from 5'9 to 6'2."

"Not very good at hanging those measuring stickers, are they?" I asked.

"It's like they're not even trying…" he responded. "Like they don't really care about accurately identifying robbers."

"Eh, they wouldn't catch them anyway. Also, I noticed your real name, your given name, is Eliza? Is that right?"

"Yes," he said dryly. "I go by Al."

"That makes sense," I said. "Eliza. That's a girl's name, right?"

"Yes, yes, it is. Thank you for asking." Again, his affect was dry.

I laughed at his deadpan humor, assuming it was that and not disgust that prompted him to respond with a monotone expressionless gaze. "Were your parents expecting a girl?" I asked, pushing for an explanation.

"They were certainly hoping for one," he said as he adjusted his seating position then flipped his longer than average hair from his face with a slight head movement. "They decided naming me a girl's name would be the next best thing."

"Wow." I laughed. "Parents…"

Al was one of my out of town patients and he was still getting used to the flow of therapy from afar. He had still not designated a specific time of the week to claim as his own, but it was no problem. He caught me at least once in any seven day stretch and he seemed to be benefiting from sessions.

"How is the weather in Colorado?" I asked. "It's raining here."

"Clear skies over here. No rain in the forecast, just clear skies." He spoke proudly of his hometown. He was born and raised there and had considered himself fortunate to be admitted to one of the state's best colleges. He then took a job in a law firm as a paralegal to build up his resume and save money before he applied to law school.

"That's good to hear…" I told him, then said nothing more, waiting for him to guide the conversation as he saw fit.

The short silence was awkward on his end, evidenced by his shuffling and looking away from the screen and camera. Finally he admitted, "I had a little fight with my family last night. It felt like a great plan to move back home after college; get a job, save some money, not pay rent, Mom does my laundry. That sounds to you like a good plan, right?"

"Yes, of course. I thought it was a good plan and it was going well. What about it isn't working out the way you had hoped?"

"I don't know. I mean, it's hard to explain. I've just been having so much trouble communicating with them. Before I went to college, it was fine, but now that I'm back after those four years, it's like impossible. They just don't get what I'm saying and I don't get them."

"Go on," I encouraged, nodding my head.

"Well, last night, I was trying to explain that I had a long day and I was revising someone's note on a case and they just couldn't understand what I was trying to tell them."

He stopped talking to regain his thoughts.

"So what exactly was the issue, Al? How did you get into a fight?" I asked.

Al's screen began to break up and then the window went black.

"Al?" I said three times. "Are you there? What happened?"

There was no answer except a black window. The connection was either lost or the "end" button had been mistakenly pressed. I considered the possibility that Al was at work, given the time of day, and that his boss walked in so he abruptly ended the session.

While I waited for him to reconnect, I pushed myself back deep into my large leather chair and spun around watching the walls surrounding me. I stopped myself facing the wall which displayed my precariously hung diplomas.

When decorating the office, I made it a point not to plaster my walls with my accomplishments. I always felt that dishonest people surrounded themselves with awards and diplomas and certificates of excellence in an attempt to mask their true selves, to convince others they were good people; "See, I'm a good person. Look at what I've done." Or maybe they do it just to convince themselves.

I continued my rotation after nodding politely to my accomplishments which were displayed, I told myself, on a mandatory basis only. Had I not been required to have them in plain sight by the state, they would be in storage, in a folder, in the basement of the Brownstone, forgotten like all else that was down there.

It had stopped raining in the park, water dripping off everything but the sky, finding its way into every crack and crevice in the exposed city, drowning the saturated pavement.

I decided that, while I waited for Al, I would continue answering messages. There was only one more message in the inbox and it was from Winston, my patient seemingly having some self-identified and probably self-induced OCD issues. I groaned loudly, knowing whatever lay within was going to give me a headache and likely strain my eyes with strange capitalization or odd punctuation used for the sole purpose of convincing himself that he was indeed afflicted with Obsessive-Compulsive Disorder.

I stood up, stretched, and shook my limbs, hoping the increased blood flow would help ease the chore of dealing with Winston's hypochondria of psychological disorders.

———

Rachel

As I sat back down, I noticed the screen on the left flashing. *Al,* I thought, but then saw the window filled not with the picture of Al but that of Rachel. I looked closely at the picture to be sure that it was her. I had not seen her for months and months. I hardly recognized her. If her name was not flashing above the live feed from her camera, I would have guessed incorrectly.

Creating a symmetry, there was a window behind her on each side, a large tree trunk occupying the one to her left. I assumed her position in vertical space to be on the second or third floor. Her hair was straight, but I remembered it to be curly. She wore no glasses, but I remembered them always blocking the view of a third of her face. And her face looked more chiseled than I recalled; somewhere she had found cheekbones.

She was one of my consistent in-office weekly patients through her high school years. We then switched to video sessions when she went off to college, but their frequency decreased while her e-mails increased. Then the e-mails decreased to one every month or two. It had come to the point where I had not heard from her in almost four months.

I touched the "answer" button. "Rachel?!" I said both enthusiastically and inquisitively. "It's been quite a while! To what do I owe the pleasure?"

"Oh, Dr. Thesiger! I'm sorry I haven't been contacting you that often. Things've been getting really busy for me. You know, college and all."

"Oh, course, of course. Well, how has everything been?"

"Oh, fine," she said, smiling as she gazed off camera, obviously envisioning all that she loved about life. "Actually, everything is absolutely amazing!"

"Wow! Okay! That's great to hear. That makes me really happy. What have you been up to? How has school been? How are your parents?"

"Oh, it's all amazing. I've actually been talking to my parents every couple of days for, like, hours."

"Really? Fantastic!" I responded. The central reason Rachel's parents had her in sessions with me through her high school years was their inability to connect with her. They thought a psychologist could brainwash her into being more compatible with them, to make her a better daughter.

"Yeah, well, we talk much much more than we did when I was in high school living with them. It's weird; you leave home then you start to see and appreciate your parents as people instead of just as your parents. They're actually really good people. Who would've guessed, huh?"

I laughed aloud, a jovial laugh, one that was unexpected in its genuine glee. "That, Rachel, is probably the nicest thing you have ever said about your parents to me. I hope you let them know you feel that way. They would be ecstatic."

"They know how I feel," she said, twisting happily in her seat back and forth. "It's taken some time, but I'm really able to look back at how I used to treat them and see how stupid and juvenile I used to be."

"Oh," I said fully shocked. "Who am I talking to? Where did this new grown-up, mature Rachel come from? When did all this happen?"

It took years, but Rachel seemed finally capable of looking at her past as her past and not a part of her that should heavily influence her behaviors. I had been attempting for years to show her that she could change how she acted and her beliefs without being hypocritical or untrue to who she used to be.

"I guess life happened to me," she responded. "I've been doing a lot here. Meeting people, learning; you know, college stuff."

"They grow up so fast," I said tearfully, but still smiling wide.

Rachel looked at the screen for several seconds before saying, "Ahh… I feel like I'm breaking up with you." She covered her face with her hands and growled, "Eerrrrrr."

"Breaking up?" I questioned quite confused.

"Yeah, I think we shouldn't see each other anymore. I mean, not like we're dating or something, but as a psychologist and patient. I just feel like I've been in sessions for a really long time and, no offense or anything, but I don't feel like I'm getting enough out of it."

I leaned back, away from the screen, away from Rachel, distancing myself in retaliation for her dumping me. "When did you start feeling this way?" I asked her in a voice transparent enough for her to determine that I was deeply hurt.

"Listen, Dr. Thesiger, it's me, it's not you," she said before pausing then laughing at what sounded too much like a line from a messy and silly teenage breakup. "What I mean is that I've really changed a lot in the past year or two and I just feel like our relationship was more suitable for me as a young girl, not as the more mature person I am now."

"I can see that," I snapped back, looking away from the camera. After I said it, I realized that I was allowing my pride and emotions to color my behavior and words. "It's understandable. It's actually quite commendable, the fact that you're growing up; that you've grown up, rather; and that you can see that you no longer need me and my services."

"Well, yes, but I don't want to trivialize our relationship too much. You were more to me than just a psychologist. You were a really good friend."

Each time she used a verb in the past tense, I cringed, but I knew that she was right. Even the way she was speaking was completely different from the little girl I remembered.

"Well, I'm very happy to hear that," I said, nodding.

"It's not just you, Dr. Thesiger. I found that I've outgrown my friends from high school too. It's like I've changed and none of them have. They're still all the same old immature kids, and I'm just not anymore."

"Do you still talk to them a lot and see them?" I asked in an attempt to act as her therapist, likely for the last time.

"Not really. They still message me and everything, but I pretty much just ignore most of them or tell them that I'm busy. I just don't want to talk to them anymore. Things are different now. But, I'm not here to talk about them. I can figure all that out on my own. I'm here to tell you that I think we've run our course."

I was truly amazed at how focused and attentive Rachel had become over the years. As far as I was concerned, it happened overnight.

"Yes," I said. "You're right. Well, I have to say that I am very impressed with your progress over the years. And I am very happy, elated, with the fact that you're able to see that you need to move on and grow. I want you to know that you are always welcome to contact me, anytime, okay?"

"Well, thank you, Doctor. It's been fun."

I looked at the screen filled with this grown-up girl who I had tried my best to help, but what she had taught me was that the thing she really needed was life, not a psychologist. She was a different, better, more aware person; she had learned much more than I ever could have imparted. I sighed aloud without realizing it.

"That's it?" Rachel asked, appearing to feel jilted.

"What do you mean, 'that's it?' "

"No cliché inspirational words to leave me with?" she asked smiling.

"Oh, Rachel." I laughed. "You know me too well. I held back so as to not sound too sappy. I'm trying to change too, you see?"

"Oh, come on! That's one of the things I loved most about our little arrangement. Please!"

"Well, I suppose I could leave you with a little something…"

"Alright!" she shouted enthusiastically, cheering with her waving arms.

I thought hard about what I could say. It was likely the last thing I was going to say to Rachel, the words by which she would remember me. Our memories are based on single occurrences, not some accurate amalgamation of all of the relevant experiences. It had to be special.

"I am confident that we will all end up where we are supposed to be; it may take some time and there may be some bumps along the way, but, knowing that we'll eventually get there, I say, 'Let's enjoy the ride.' "

"Seriously?" she asked, disappointed.

I looked at the screen, uncomfortable after receiving a failing mark. "How about this?" I remarked. "History was yesterday so today is your present to the future. Make the most of it and make a difference."

"What does that have to do with anything?" she asked, laughing. "I know you can do better than that."

Now fully on the spot, placed there by a woman who I knew only as a girl, I was stumped. My mind froze and I was no longer capable of putting words together in an appropriate manner so I sputtered out the first relevant thing that came to mind...

"Twenty years from now you will be more disappointed by the things that you didn't do than by the ones you did do. So throw off the bowlines. Sail away from the safe harbor. Catch the trade winds in your sails. Explore. Dream. Discover."

"Wow," she replied, nodding. "That was pretty good."

As she sat there, smiling at my words, I thought about whether or not I should tell her that they were not my own, but those of Mark Twain. Was it worth risking her learning later that I was indeed a fraud or did I want to own up to it before she learned the truth elsewhere?

"Yes, it is beautiful," I said, "I'm sure Mark Twain would appreciate your accolade."

Rachel laughed and clapped at my performance. "Thank you, Dr. Thesiger, for all that you have done for me over the years."

"You are more than welcome, Rachel. And here is one last quote with which I would like to leave you."

"Go ahead."

"Maya Angelou said, 'I've learned that people will forget what you said, people will forget what you did, but people will never forget how you made them feel.' I hope that I've helped, in some way, make you feel well, Rachel. That is all that I hope for any and all of those who I call friend."

"You have surpassed your goal with me, Doctor."

"One last thing, Rachel," I said. "Make mistakes. No one ever gives that as advice, but it's something to consider. Make mistakes, lots of them."

Rachel smiled, nodding. "Bye, Dr. Thesiger." And with that, it was over, years and years of counseling her, years and years of being her therapist, her friend. I lost something then that I did not know I had, but it left me feeling even more empty than I had been.

Most of all, at that moment, it pained me that so little was me. So few words, phrases, sentences… So few pieces of advice or statements of encouragement. I used the word "quote" to describe it, over and over, but, over and over, I lost myself, more and more of myself each time I stole from the more intelligent, those whose words will last the test of time, a test I was failing.

I stole so often, with such frequency, because I had nothing of my own, no inner wellspring from which to take inspiration. Others' words were always superior to my own. I quoted because I had nothing valuable to say on my own…

———

Winston

After sitting, staring at the blank computer screen, I opened what I knew would be a draining message from Winston.

There was no subject to the message. Inside I found a mostly blank screen with nine numbers occupying the third line.

—

1 3 6 10 15 21 28 36 45

—

I sat back in my large leather chair and looked at the numbers from afar. "He must have been talking to Bill," I said aloud.

The pattern was an obvious one; the difference between one number and the next number in the sequence is added to the second number. One is then added to that sum and that yields the next number in the sequence. The difference between 1 and 3 is 2. Two is added to 3 which equals 5. One is added to 5 to get the next number in the sequence; 6. And so on. But I knew Winston therefore I knew there had to be much more to it than just that. What was it that he was trying to show me?

My mind went toward my time working in the clinic when I was just out of graduate school. I spent countless hours attempting to decipher the cryptic messages of patients with Schizophrenia. I was convinced that those with disorganized speech were attempting to communicate something and that it was somehow hidden in the mash-up of words and phrases, inflections and emphases.

But I never found anything meaningful. It was a futile search and I questioned whether trying to decipher Winston's simple pattern of numbers would be futile as well. I then questioned if attempting to decipher the speech of my patient diagnosed with Schizophrenia, Harry, was a similarly futile endeavor. Maybe I was convincing myself there was something there when there was not. Maybe he just liked riddles.

I closed my eyes and visualized the numbers interacting, moving around, the differences between them mingling and exchanging parts and potential meanings. I turned them into all combinations of proper and improper fractions. I multiplied, divided, added, and subtracted them. I tried representing each number with a letter and then attempted to create words, but nothing of any relevance emerged.

It was not until I imagined the numbers as their simplest terms, as mere quantities, as mere dots, that I found meaning. When I rearranged the dots, each number of dots from each individual number created a perfect triangle. The next triangle in the sequence had sides of one dot longer than the previous triangle. I assumed the triangles' three sides corresponded to Obsessive, Compulsive, and Disorder. The fact that the triangles increased in size in the pattern suggested that Winston believed his condition to be worsening.

Triangles made perfect sense. Symmetrical, simple, easy to check and recheck. They can be rotated several ways and still get the point across. They were perfect for someone who had, or thought they had, OCD.

"Triangles!" I shouted.

I leaned in toward the computer and typed a response.

—

Winston,

I am really quite a bit concerned. Please call me or send me a number at which I can reach you. I think you may need to seek counseling with your school psychologist. And, yes, I get it; triangles.

-Dr. Thesiger

—

I knew mentioning the triangles was unnecessary, but I was proud to have broken the code. I wanted Winston to know I was smart enough. I wanted to know I was smart enough. After being dumped by Rachel, I felt that I had to prove myself.

I skipped my standard check of the spelling and grammar and touched the "send" button.

Empty; the inbox felt right. I momentarily wished I would see it that way more frequently, but sadly realized I did see it that way frequently, an indication of my continuously dwindling practice.

I opened a folder of standard messages I had written and saved over the years. To Rachel's parents, I sent the one that informs parents of patients that their child decided to terminate counseling. Then I turned my attention to more pressing matters.

Chinese, Italian, Greek, Japanese, Mexican, French, Indian, Southern, Vietnamese, Cuban, Dominican, Jamaican, Korean... the list went on and on and on. For a reason not immediately obvious to me, I had decided to choose food from a list of countless restaurants organized by country. The list went on and on, with subcategories and fusions multiplying the possibilities.

The task felt daunting so giving up felt appropriate. Pizza was the default upon which I fell. I was sure to select a different pizzeria from the previous day's no-show.

Several screen taps later and assuming that fifteen minutes meant fifteen minutes, I laid down comfortably on the couch for a nap. My intention was to wake for a late lunch, enjoy it, then take a leisurely walk through the park before returning to the apartment so I could begrudgingly accompany Julie to her cocktail party.

———

Courtland

Eyes covered by lids, my mind wandered, and, against my fight for it not to, it wandered toward Courtland. He sat across from me, sitting where I sat when he was in session, on the chair across from the couch, watching me as I attempted to drift away. He kept me awake for an unknown duration; it was difficult to determine with no reference of time.

"It's chemical," I heard myself say to him, trying to explain his depression. "Don't get down on yourself for it. You aren't doing anything wrong. You never did anything wrong. You didn't do anything to deserve it so, yes, you're right; it's not fair."

After I pushed him and pushed him to find an emotion—he was trying to express verbally his dissatisfaction with life—the best we could muster was only three monotone words.

"It's not fair," Courtland said. He feared he was alienating people with his flattened, detached demeanor so he decided to seclude himself.

He told me that, because he was so numb to the world, his facial expressions and physical reactions during conversation never matched what they should; never smiling or laughing or frowning or anything, just an expressionless face. He tried compensating by approximating what he believed were the appropriate facial expressions and physical reactions.

"But, approximations are just that, *approximate*," he said. His resulting affect was off-putting and people became less and less comfortable around him, so, with others in mind, he withdrew.

"Humiliating," he called it. "It's not fair," I heard him say again.

After the conversation, still he sat there, just watching me as I shut my eyes tighter and tighter. Then finally, he spoke. "It's hard to explain it all. I wish I could just get up and do something about it, but I can't. Everything looks, feels, like it's in shades of gray; that's not how I'm *seeing* it, just how I'm *experiencing* it. All the colors are still there, just muted. It's like seeing through lenses; everything looks worse if you've got the wrong prescription.

"It's not fair," he said again. "It makes you want to kill yourself, you know?"

I opened my eyes and turned toward the chair, but nothing. The room was a silent hue of a mixed monochromatic pallet just like he explained it. It was as though I had lost the ability to perceive colors, but not quite completely. I rubbed my left shoulder and frowned.

———

Delivery

The knocking at the door was soft, but relentless. Instead of pausing for a rest, it continued on and on and on at a steady pace. After walking myself to the door, whole body tingling from tired muscles, I opened it quickly to stop the sound sooner.

"Delivery," the old dark-haired delivery woman said much louder than necessary.

I rubbed my right eye with the back of my right hand before grabbing the small box and opening it, ensuring its accuracy and good condition. I wanted, in no way, to be surprised by some exotic and uncalled for topping on my plain slices.

"Thank you," I said after the inspection was complete.

"Tip?" she requested, hand out.

"I put in a tip when I ordered it… on the card," I said as I closed the door. "Thank you."

The open pizza box felt appropriate on the low coffee table for some reason. I had trouble determining why so I gave up thinking and just ate mindlessly. I poured myself a glass of filtered water, room-temperature after several hours of sitting there out in the open.

In need of a napkin for which I intended to substitute a tissue, I walked over to the desk and opened the drawer as I checked the time on the screen. 4:32 p.m. The delivery had taken over an hour.

"At least I slept," I said to myself, but I hardly slept at all.

No in-office sessions were scheduled for Friday, Saturday, or Sunday and I very rarely received more than one or two messages during that time so I considered the end of Thursday as the end of my workweek. This moment of completion brought on a surge of energy to accomplish something, but nothing ever came of it.

I felt that I needed to make lasting changes in my life at the end of most weeks, but the thoughts were always vague. I came to the quick conclusion that the most appropriate place to start was right in front of me, lunch. I decided that the pizza sitting on the coffee table would be the last lackluster lunch of my life.

This feeling of determination and drive was fleeting, lasting only until I remembered that it would all repeat itself the following week; there would be no change, it was too difficult to step away from the cycle.

As I ate, my mind wandered toward the weekend and what it normally held. Friday was spent in the office checking that all my clients had been charged properly. It took up less than an hour of the day, but still I stayed, hiding from the apartment and Julie, from life, watching movies and shows on the computer and reading news and academic articles.

Fridays were days to forget or days to never remember. Little ever happened so little went into memory. Sadly, the same was true for most, if not all, of each weekend. Friday, Saturday, Sunday, all spent the same way, in the office not remembering.

My weekend schedule, however, was quite busy according to what I told Julie. I used my fabricated busy Friday, Saturday, and Sunday schedule as an excuse to not accompany her to parties, to her parents' estate, or on vacation anywhere, not that we could afford a vacation.

Julie knew nothing of my actual schedule, only that I left in the morning and returned in the evening. Naturally she at first assumed I was working. Skepticism, at some point, replaced trust in our relationship, which preceded accusations of affairs. I did little to dispel them. Selfishly, I felt that she deserved to wonder, to be in the dark, to never know for certain what the truth was; it was how I retaliated to the accusations themselves, with nothing.

The pizza tasted terrible, but I knew it would not be the last time I tasted it.

I poured out the rest of the filtered water in the carafe then refilled it from the small refrigerator before placing it inside and closing the small door. All the computer programs had already been closed, so I guided the screen to blackness. The room looked both clean and tidy, so I backed out quietly, turning off the light with the back of my right hand.

————

En Route Back to the Apartment

The elevator felt larger than it did on the way up and it moved much quicker, quieter. The lobby itself was also silent, absent of residents and doormen. I questioned if there was a fire and everyone had been evacuated without my knowledge.

Get the rich out before notifying the poor, I thought before saying aloud, *"Fuego."*

As I opened the door to walk out, my fears of fire were dispelled by a little old woman, slowly walking in with a closed but wet umbrella in her left hand. She acknowledged that I was not a doorman by thanking me.

"Thank you, young man," she said politely.

"You are quite welcome, Ma'am," I responded. "Have a good day."

"Have a good always," she said as she continued slowly toward the elevator.

It was and is hard to put into words how angry her response made me feel. For some inexplicable reason, her one-upmanship in gracious pleasantries was so antagonistic that I had an almost overwhelming desire to shove her forcefully into the golden elevator and grasp her tightly around the neck until that elevator became her coffin.

My immediate disgust with myself for having that passing impulse kept me from performing the act. She turned around in the elevator and smiled at me as I remained in the doorway watching her infuriatingly polite aura disappear from sight when the elevator doors slid together.

The rain had stopped hours earlier, but it had effectively saturated the outdoors. I walked slowly to ensure my tardy status. I may have been protecting myself from another spill. Or I may have been passively punishing Julie, but for what?

Details were increasingly escaping me. Depth in all directions was dwindling away. Color was practically gone, bringing my mind to Courtland who I thought I spotted crossing the street, but it was nothing, no one.

Halfway through the short commute, my phone vibrated in my pocket. I knew it was Julie because hers were the only calls I ever received. I ignored it until her third separate attempt.

"Good afternoon, Julie," I said reluctantly after pressing the "answer" button.

"Come back to the apartment," she shouted toward the phone, her faraway voice suggesting I was on speakerphone. "We have to be at The Martins' soon!"

"I'll be back there in a few minutes," I told her.

"Oh," she responded. "And I'm mad at you. I just had an awkward conversation with our neighbor, Alicia. I handed her a condolence card for Chip's death. I gave her a reassuring hug. She laughed at me and said Chip was a bird they found on the street. You told me Chip was her father."

I thought for a moment and then burst into laughter. I had completely forgotten about the seed of mistruth I had planted earlier in the week, only to have it come back to me as a fully formed plant. "You took her a card? That's great!"

"You're an idiot. Just get back here," she told me before the call ended abruptly.

I continued to laugh before telling myself, *I'm hilarious.*

Suddenly rejuvenated by the knowledge that my joke had run through its intended path to its end, I danced up the slippery steps in front of our Brownstone then slid in through the doorway behind a non-tenant middle-aged man on his way out.

He smiled at my dancing ways as I thought, *I could be a murderer, a very happy murderer, which he just let into this building.*

I jogged up the stairs quickly, hoping there were no young children around each bend of the winding blind corners. The door to our apartment was unlocked; fortunate because I did not want to break my stride to find the right key.

"You're late," Julie shouted from the bedroom, alerted to my presence by the squeaky old wood floors.

"Slow and steady wins the race," I answered.

"Yes, if you're a turtle racing a mentally incompetent rabbit. Now get ready so we can go!"

I stopped in my delightfully light tracks as Julie brought me right back to reality, then sat at the small wooden table in the small wooden chair waiting to leave. I had not anticipated waiting for the length of time which I did because I assumed that Julie was hurrying me on the phone because she was ready to go. I was quite incorrect.

Dozens of minutes passed by as I watched Julie frantically run to and from the bedroom and bathroom, then halfway down the hall, then she would turn around to repeat the same path which appeared to have no apparent direction.

Finally, visibly announcing the completion of her process she stood before me wearing a long black dress that looked like every other and the bracelet that represented several months of rent in both our apartment and my office; she looked me up and down and said, "The least you could do is to put on a jacket."

"I don't need one. Come on, Julie. It's not a wedding or something. Just a small get-together, right?"

"Put on a jacket, okay? We don't want you getting sick. It's going to get cold tonight."

"It's not the cold that makes me sick, it's you," I responded, smiling.

After she spent some time glaring at me, trying to keep a stern face, she walked into the bedroom and returned with the matching jacket for my pants. "Put it on," she ordered.

I complied.

As I walked behind her, I watched Julie slowly click and clank down the uneven centuries old worn steps in her shoes which looked far more uncomfortable than I could see a reason for. When we reached the street, I put my hand up to hail a cab despite my belief that one would likely not stop for the likes of me.

"No!" Julie shouted as I attempted the impossible. "We'll be too early."

"What do you mean, 'we'll be too *early*'? When does it start?" I asked.

"Five."

I took out my phone. "You know it's 5:39 p.m., right?"

"Yes," she responded. "But we can't get there that early. Let's walk. That'll get us there at a good time."

"Are you kidding?" I asked shocked and angry. "Can't we just go back upstairs? Or even ride around in the cab for a while?"

"We're walking, Nick," she said as she clicked and clanked up the sidewalk.

"Through the park?" I asked concerned. "It's going to get dark… and you're in heels. I am not going to carry you!"

As we argued in the street, a group of teenage girls walked between us. Julie and I looked at them angrily then to each other, bound for a fleeting moment by our disgust for the rude and impolite youth of the city. We shook our heads and, for just a second, understood one another.

The park was damp. She and I both spent the majority of our time looking down at the ground in front ourselves, carefully avoiding uneven ground or puddles. Not a word was uttered. The trip was unmemorable.

When we finally emerged onto the concrete, I noticed that we were further south than we should have been. Julie too appeared to have noticed it, but the path in which she attempted to guide us made little sense to me.

"Why are we going this way?" I asked.

"This is the way to get there," she responded.

"We should go straight here on Broadway, it's faster," I said, pointing straight ahead.

"No," she shouted.

"This is completely out of the way," I insisted, still pointing forward as we stood at the corner. "The shortest distance between two points is a straight line. With your way we're walking up and then over instead of diagonally. We're walking the legs of the triangle instead of the hypotenuse. Why do you walk so inefficiently?" I allowed my frustration to raise my voice.

"I walk perfectly fine," Julie responded, insulted. "This is a very efficient way to walk."

"No, it's not! We're walking straight then making a left then walking some more when we could have just walked straight without any turns."

She turned her nose up, so I simplified it with an example. "If we walked 3 blocks up and then 2 blocks over, we just walked 5 blocks instead of the 3.6 blocks we would walk if we had walked straight in the first place."

"How do you know it's 3.6? You just made that up," she said, doubting my mathematical abilities.

"It's trigonometry!" I shouted. "I know the turn we make is 90 degrees and, since the legs we walked are 3 and 2, I can figure out the angles at the ends. Then figuring out the hypotenuse is a simple equation."

"I know trig. You don't need to explain it to me," she informed me with a tone of disdain.

"If you knew, you wouldn't have asked," I responded, as proud as I would have been had I invented trigonometry myself.

"I do know," Julie insisted as she crossed the street obeying the sign that changed from the *don't walk* picture to the *walk* picture. "Ask me a trig question."

"Okay, what were the other two angles of the triangle?" I asked, knowing she would not be able to figure it out.

"Well, it has to add up to 180, right? And the turn was 90, so they must be 45 and 45."

I was impressed by her basic knowledge of how a triangle worked, but she was incorrect and I felt it necessary to inform her in the most delicate of manners.

"Eeehhhhh!" I shouted into her ear, mimicking the wrong buzzer from a game show. "Wrong answer! And, for future reference, that would be algebra you just used, not trigonometry."

"Whatever, I know more than you give me credit for."

"Ha! Whatever you say. Hey, why don't you give me an address, any address? I'll tell you the quickest way to get there, but I'm sure you'll still go the least efficient way."

"Please stop belittling me," she asked sincerely.

"Maybe if you acted a little more intelligently, there wouldn't be any reason to belittle you." I knew I was pushing too hard, but it was difficult to stop.

"Why don't you just go to hell, Nick?"

"Because, if I go with you, it would take us forever to get there." I smiled, as proud of myself as I had ever been.

"You're such a jerk. Why don't you just go back home?"

"We're too far along and I wouldn't want you to get mugged and murdered. Who would not clean the apartment? Who would not cook dinner? Who would not make the bed every morning?"

"Just go back," she said, sounding close to tears.

"No, no, we're going to this party and we're going to have a *wonderful* time," I said maniacally.

When we turned the 90 degree left turn at the edge of the triangle, we faced the sun setting over the west side of the island. I found it hard to agree with anyone who preached that pollution had only changed the world for the worse. Over any major city each clear day at dusk is a breathtaking display of the splendor that is pollution. Absolute and unquestionable beauty.

When we were slightly past the halfway point of the next block, I informed Julie that, had we followed my directions, we would have already been there. She ignored me as if she were alone. I wished she had been.

With their staggered heights and the slight hills beneath, the assortment of buildings in the city made for a broken, inconsistent, and often quick dusk. Mellow yellow and orange fingers of dwindling sunlight which caused an enchanting glow when they caressed most items beamed me in the eyes, momentarily blinding me. I attempted not to squint, but my body overpowered my mind.

Cocktail Party

When I regained clear sight, there it was, the six stories' high, two-townhouse wide, breathtaking Martin Townhouse lined with large columns of what appeared to be marble, but to my mind could not possibly be. Meticulously manicured miniature specimen trees, shrubs, and bushes guided us from the street, up the front stairs, and between the magnificent columns to the front door.

With my mouth still open in awe, I touched the column to my right, soft, smooth. On the ground, between Julie's and my feet and centered to the symmetry of the building, was a large script "M" formed with tiny mosaic tiles.

" 'M' doesn't stand for 'modest,' does it?" I remarked to Julie.

She looked at me sideways, silent, then pressed the doorbell. As we waited, she quietly informed me, "They just completed a big renovation, so don't make any silly comments."

The door suddenly swung open, giving me no time to verbally decline Julie's orders.

"Sorry we're late," I said to the man standing in the doorway. "Magellan here was in charge of the directions."

Julie's right elbow dug deep into the ribs on the left side of my torso in one swift jabbing movement.

"*Bonjour, Monsieur, Madame. Entre-vous, s'il vous plaît.* Please come in." The man bent over, gestured for us to enter, and quickly tiptoed backward. His accent was French, and sounded fully authentic.

"Seriously?" I whispered to Julie. "A French butler?"

Again her elbow found its way deep into my side.

"May I take your jacket, Madame?" he asked to Julie.

"Yes, of course," she responded before turning around and allowing him to help her with her useless mesh shawl.

The butler wore a black suit with the bottom corners of the jacket elongated in the back. An impeccable white collared shirt underneath was accompanied by an equally white bow tie and equally white gloves. After folding Julie's mesh shawl over his right arm, he bowed and hurried himself off.

"Why didn't he ask me?" I asked Julie aloud.

"Because it would be inappropriate for you not to have your jacket on," Julie responded as she walked away from me.

"Hey, don't leave me," I said loudly, not afraid to admit my fear and increasing discomfort.

I quickly stepped after her. She, moving swiftly, had emerged into a brightly lit, breathtaking ballroom by the time I caught her left arm in my right hand. Almost forgetting my place, I stood motionless as I gazed around the room in awe. The -walls were lined with fine paintings, many instantly recognizable as works by historically significant and well-known masters of the art. The light from the four chandeliers—surely made of the finest crystal, gold, and silver— reflected off the tin ceiling stamped with floral and geometrically symmetrical patterns. A magnificent Steinway grand piano lived in one corner and was manned by a gentleman dressed the same as the man who had answered the door.

Probably also French, I thought.

He sat motionless, merely guarding his post, while delightful classical music echoed around the space from what I assumed to be hidden speakers. Three of the four walls of the room were marked by archways, gateways through which I could see snapshots into beautifully designed rooms with several windows and carefully chosen antique furniture suited perfectly for its surroundings.

All of the colors in all of the rooms were concertedly incorporated in each detail of the spaces and felt antique and worn, but in a deliberate manner. In the large center room in which I found myself, all of the moldings, arches, ceiling details, even frames for the paintings, contained a bit of gold. Above the thick, tall, tan-colored wainscoting, the walls were an off-white that approached a pinkish hue, but only when the wall was a background contrast to the bow ties of the French butlers. The color was not uniform, but was whimsically rubbed on to create the feeling of a worn, old, plaster wall.

It was several minutes of admiring the room before I noticed that it was filled with people. To me, they were all stick figures. None were significantly underweight; I just felt that there was nothing to them. Their simplistic façades were all that I saw and I, in no way, had the desire to learn the intricacies of their separate lives. My disinterest was likely due to jealously of their ease in life as a result of familial wealth, but I effectively convinced myself that they were all a bore.

I had made this blanket judgment about all of Julie's peers after only a few years of marriage. Initially, I attempted to learn about them in an attempt to become them, but all I gained was the realization that I had almost nothing in common with any of them because they and I were from completely different worlds. Common ground existed in no way and I felt as though they were too closed-minded to attempt to create any. In reality, it was I who had been too closed-minded; it was I who was incapable of seeing them as anything outside of the confined boxes in which I had placed them. Each was unique in their own right, but my decision to remain indifferent had been made far before I learned that fact. To me, they were all stick figures.

After quickly identifying the few to whom I had been introduced on prior occasions, I started to notice that there were many more people there with whom I had not been acquainted. My discomfort grew. I turned to find Julie, whose arm I had released inadvertently when I was struck by the vibrancy of the space.

I started to shake slightly in my suit. *It had probably already been identified several times as not a top brand,* I thought, unnerved.

At that moment, I heard two people in a group laughing so I naturally assumed they were laughing at me, standing there uncomfortably, beginning to sweat and noticeably shake.

These are the kind of people who use "winter" as a verb, I thought.

I heard words from many of the romance languages waft across the room. These polyglots made use of their knowledge of foreign languages as frequently as they did English, another measuring stick. I had studied French, but was sure I would not be capable of keeping up.

Someone suggested Louvre Pyramid to be "an architectural disaster, an expletive directed to history." I was shaken, having never seen it outside of a computer screen.

Their words brought to mind a conversation I had several years before with one of Julie's friends. He told me that, at any one of these cocktail parties, the boards of every major prestigious New York City museum, library, ballet, and opera house were represented. "Tens, maybe hundreds of millions spent to attain and maintain their seats," he told me. The thought of those gross quantities shook me further.

My ear was caught by a nearby conversation. Someone was complaining about the conductor at the opera several days prior. The woman knew each singer and their character and she spoke degradingly about all. Her criticisms were harsh, referring to the director as a "hack" and a "dullard." How was I to stand confidently with individuals with such high standards?

A butler holding a round silver tray approached me from behind.

"Pardon me, Sir. May I bring to you a glass of wine?" His accent was also French, but sounded slightly inauthentic.

"Oh no, thank you," I said politely. "I don't drink."

He nodded, then bowed away.

After watching him tiptoe backward through an archway, I turned my head to see two people with whom I wished I was not acquainted, walking in my direction. Ivan Lloyd Morris, a drone of a man whose annoyingly droll demeanor was matched only by that of his wife, Debra Robertson-Morris. Julie and I disdained them to the same level, a rarity among her acquaintances.

"Nicholas!" they both droned in an enthusiastic monotone, tainted by a cultivated and constant disinterest.

For a reason which I was unable to identify, I had the urge to pretend that I did not remember them. Maybe I did it because I wanted to appear too hassled by the countless parties I attended and people I met to remember each and every one of them. Maybe I just wanted them to feel insulted and leave me be. Maybe I wanted to have them stand around me for longer, playing the jog-my-memory-game.

I cocked my head to the right and stuck out my left hand to shake Ivan's. "Sorry. I am really bad with faces and names."

"Are you?" Ivan replied. "I'm amazing with names."

The first time I had met Ivan, it was painfully obvious that he was terrible at remembering names. He had to fall back on what he had learned in Business School; while we spoke, he repeated my name over and over and over in seemingly appropriate places, at the beginning or the end of a sentence, but ad nauseam. Only a fool, terrible with remembering names, needs to repeat something one hundred times for it to sink in. Unfortunately, the party at which we met was a fund-raiser put on by some of his Business School classmates. The night was a long hum of an amalgamation of business industry buzzwords peppered with repeated nomenclature.

"Are you?" I asked, knowingly suspicious.

"You don't remember?" Debra said, putting her left hand on my right shoulder. "We met at the Livingstons'." She pointed to herself then her husband. "Debra and Ivan. You remember," she insisted.

At this point, I would have been willing to admit that I knew them had she not been completely incorrect about where we met. I bulked at the audacity; calling my bluff before one-upping my lie.

"Take no offense," I said. "I come into contact with more people than I can comfortably count."

Then, as I looked around appearing disinterested, Julie caught my eye. She stood in her black dress speaking with an older couple, The Martins, owners of the home and hosts for the night.

Ivan laughed a droll laugh. "You are a funny one, Nicholas," he remarked, incapable of accepting that someone did not remember him. "You should come on the boat with us. Have you ever boated around the island, Nicholas?"

I knew Ivan and Debra had no intention of actually having me aboard their boat, but he was occupying my time so I allowed him the opportunity to continue.

"Which island?" I asked.

"Manhattan," he responded confidently. "You know it's an island, don't you?"

"Oh well, I'm afraid I haven't been around the island in a boat," I confessed.

"Oh, you must join us," he began. "We dock at a private pier on the Hudson. It's absolutely magnificent; the vitality of the city from a nautical perspective. Gives you a renewed understanding and appreciation of the island." His tone deviated in almost no way throughout the conversation, a dazed dreary monotone.

"Is that right?" I inquired.

"Oh yes!" he responded while Debra nodded along, but still looking disinterested. "Going under those bridges is like nothing you've experienced. We've all gone over them a million times, but to be dwarfed by them as you pass beneath is an entirely different perspective."

Julie had parted from The Martins and was walking slowly toward us.

"Did you hear that, Julie?" I called to her. "We have an invitation to boat around the island."

"Oh," Julie said nervously, unsure if it was a legitimate invitation or a hollow one used surreptitiously for conversational purposes. "That would be wonderful. We'll be in touch about that."

She smiled with half a heart and half of her mouth. Then she lovingly put her left hand on my right elbow. "Can I just steal my husband away for a second?"

"Of course," Debra droned. "We'll catch up later on. You'll be here for a while longer?"

"Yes, of course," Julie responded as she led me away. Then, when out of audible range of the Morrises, she whispered powerfully to me, "Stop doing that!"

"Stop what?" I asked.

"Stop making fun of everyone."

"I'm not making fun of anyone." I laughed.

Julie looked at me silently for ten seconds then whispered, "I know what you're doing and I want you to know that I don't like it." She began to walk away then took a step back and held on to my elbow again, guiding me with her. "Come, husband," she said aloud so that everyone could see all was well.

———

The Martins

As we approached the older couple with whom I had previously seen Julie speaking, the owners of the home and our hosts for the night, I noticed that the husband, Edward, appeared to be holding a short wide thick glass filled with scotch. When ordering, he likely told his butlers to skip the ice and fill the glass completely. He took a large gulp as he stood there with his wife, Elisabeth.

Goes down quicker when it's room temperature, I thought.

Edward and Elisabeth had been friends to Julie's family since she was young. She and their children played and attended school together from an early age.

I had met them several times over the years, but the last time I had seen them was at their property in East Hampton. They had been gracious enough to extend an invitation to "Julie and her husband" for their Seder. I had embarrassed myself greatly when I showed up late, saw no seat for myself next to Julie, then decided to slip quietly into the empty seat that was, unbeknownst to me, "left empty for the deceased relatives of Judaism."

Guests were shocked, Julie was horrified at my ignorance, and I, oblivious, was greatly relieved to have avoided looking foolish by arriving late to a religious ceremony and then having to ask for a seat. I went uninformed until after the ceremony and dinner when Julie explained to me my misstep in great and belittling detail once she was able to pull me aside.

Faux pas in mind and cocktail in hand, I began to mentally panic and attempted to right my social wrong by doing what I always did when I was nervous and uncomfortable; I tried crafting thoughtful jokes. The strong recollection of the religious origins of the dinner fresh in my mind and my penchant for inappropriate jokes led me in inappropriate directions; fortunately my internal filter, for once performing optimally, stopped all the jokes that had lined up in my mental queue.

The halted jokes were never voiced, but unfortunately my mind was still on those topics that should not have been introduced into conversation. Eventually, inevitably, my extemporaneous speaking brought those topics to the surface. More than once, I said *gesundheit* when someone sneezed. And, still ignorantly blundering on, I later questioned several guests if there was an origin to the homonymic connection between the name for the most prevalent bread at the table (Hallah) and the deplorable mass murder against their people and others during World War II (Holocaust).

When word of my unfortunate and completely inappropriate small talk reach Julie, she rightfully sent me back to the apartment in the city alone while she stayed an extra week at her parents' estate on Long Island. She was embarrassed, as she should have been, but luckily my disgraceful behavior did not leave any lasting marks.

"Nicholas!" Edward shouted as we approached. "It's amazing to see you. We heard you weren't coming."

"Oh, I made him come," Julie interjected quickly.

Edward and Elisabeth gave each other a knowing look which I ignored.

"Mr. Edward Rooney Martin III!" I said enthusiastically as I extended my right hand to shake his. "I see they let you out of prison!" I continued jokingly.

Edward bellowed out a strong bout of laughter which lasted longer than I had anticipated. He put his half empty glass of scotch on an adjacent table and shook my right hand with his, covering them both with his left and caressing them gently.

Edward was the kind of man who felt as though he needed to be in contact with the person with whom he was speaking. And he did not merely touch his audience like a benevolent pope, he felt them with a pulsating old hand that moved around as if he were blind and trying to gather as much tactile information as possible to transpose into a mental picture. There is a significant difference between touching and feeling and Edward fell squarely on the latter. The man appeared to have never learned about personal space or personal boundaries and his scotch did nothing to help the situation.

After the five- or six-second long handshake, he needlessly stepped in to hug me for an unnecessarily lengthy duration before caressing both of my cheeks with his hands as I pulled away.

Ignoring his touchy ways, I turned to his wife. "And Ms. Elisabeth Vivian Martin." I pulled her right hand toward me with my left, bending down to kiss it softly.

"Always the gentleman," Elisabeth said as she turned toward Julie.

Julie smiled with her mouth and frowned with her heart.

"I was looking around and I noticed a number of magnificent people whom I remember from past gatherings," I said. "It always amazes me how everybody knows everybody."

"Well, everyone is here!" Elisabeth said proudly. "We socialize with only New York City's finest."

I thought about making a joke about fraternizing with the police, but decided against it.

"Dionysus would be proud!" I said as I nodded.

"He would indeed," Edward agreed.

There was a short pause in which all members of the group thought quickly about where to steer the conversation.

"Martins," I began, "I love what you've done with the place. Julie told me on the way over that you did some renovations."

"Oh, it was a nightmare!" Edward exclaimed.

Elisabeth elaborated. "When you renovate, where do you live? You have to move all of your things. Feeling unsettled, ungrounded for months!"

"Is that right?" I asked with an almost sarcastic tone detected only by Julie who shot me a quick angry look.

"Indeed," Edward responded. "We set out to rent a place, but couldn't locate anything suitable. We ended up buying in a co-op downtown. Exclusive."

"Oh, but the dogs," Elisabeth exclaimed. "Co-ops don't like dogs. This one only allowed one per apartment and you know we have two dogs."

"Oh no!" Julie chimed in, sounding concerned.

"Yes, yes. Even though they're small little things, the co-op wouldn't allow it." Elisabeth sounded defeated as she spoke.

Then Edward added, "That was until I reminded them that the apartment we were buying was actually three apartments combined by the previous owner. That shut them up!" His tone showed the pride he had for his victory over the co-op board.

"Well done!" I said happily, genuinely pleased for the two of them. Julie, however, did not hear the authenticity in my voice and assumed I was making a joke. She gave me another quick, but searing look.

"Jolly good!" Edward agreed.

"It felt like an extended vacation right here in the city," Elisabeth said of their new co-op. "I became fond of downtown. The little lively restaurants and the bohemian lifestyle."

Then Edward added, "Now we go down there twice each week, sometimes thrice."

"Are you thinking of moving there permanently or just keeping it as a pied-à-terre?" Julie asked.

"The latter, of course, my dear!" Edward shouted. "We will be moving out of here soon enough, but feet first!"

"Soon enough," Elisabeth repeated. "At our age, we don't buy green bananas."

"Oh no, no! You're a spring chicken," I said, laughing inside because I had used the term "spring chicken" in polite company. My internal laughter was echoed outside by The Martins but not by Julie who, again, appeared to think I was making a joke of them which, this time, I may have been.

"But who *would* want to leave this beautiful place," Julie said as she looked around the room.

"Nicholas," Edward said. "Did you know this Townhouse has been in our family for well over one hundred years?"

I mentally questioned the validity of his statement as he continued.

"Most of our friends have sold their family mansions and now reside far above Central Park. The terraces, the views, the windows, the light. Who can blame them? But we like this old house. More problems and more to deal with, but that's why you have help!"

I tried to interject that my office was on the park, but he continued before I had an appropriate opportunity.

"We kept it all original during the remodel," he insisted. "Everything in the house is original and authentic. The furniture, the fixtures, all the materials were repurposed, everything."

The irony of his words; spoken as he stood next to a wafer thin but gargantuan TV, diagonally much longer than he was tall, with a fire burning in extremely high definition on screen; gave me a headache almost as strong as the headache I was developing from gazing into the extremely clear fire.

252

"Most of the furniture is over a hundred years old as well," Elisabeth added.

"Yes," Julie said. "We love the older furniture. They're all legs, better to showcase the carpets and the magnificent floors beneath. Newer furniture hides it, makes the place look smaller, closed-in."

"Quite right!" exclaimed Edward. "Take a look at this one," he said, pointing down at a large decorative carpet with what appeared to be every color in the earth-toned rainbow incorporated. "This put us back four hundred thousand dollars. Elisabeth just *had* to have it. Don't want to hide something like that, do we?" Edward asked rhetorically.

"What?" I shouted, questioning the price. "Are you serious? Does it fly? It must fly. Can I take it for a ride around the block? You wouldn't mind, would you?"

Julie was somewhat embarrassed as I spoke and even more embarrassed when I plopped down on the carpet, grasped the edges and began to thrust myself forward in hopes that it would levitate and take off.

Finding my antics delightful, The Martins laughed and laughed.

Julie, embarrassed, helped me up after I had definitively determined that the carpet was indeed not magical.

When the laughter slowed, Edward said, "Why you don't kick out your tenants and renovate your Brownstone into a beautiful piece of art like ours is beyond me."

I then did what I always did when someone questioned us about our Brownstone. I defended it as though it actually did belong to us and was not just an embarrassing lie which we had maintained for years and years.

"Edward," I began, "in these times, charitable donations are nowhere near what they need to be to sufficiently support the increasing number of people who are in need of aid. It is my belief that anyone who makes more money than that of the expenses of their chosen lifestyle should do their best to get those extra funds to those in dire need, whether it be through direct donation or indirectly through a certified nonprofit organization. We decided to purchase a Brownstone and convert it into low-income housing. That is our way of giving back."

As I spoke, I could see Julie looking up at me and smiling, almost lovingly, at the thought of a potentially generous philanthropic husband.

"Oh, a martyr in our midst!" Edward snapped humorously.

"No, no!" I laughed. "It's a pretty nice tax write-off. And you've seen my car; I'm no martyr."

Edward, Elisabeth, and Julie all laughed. It was the first time I had seen Julie laugh at something I had said for a long time. I took some pride while ignoring that she only laughed because others were around. That or she laughed at the irony.

"But you speak blasphemy," Elisabeth added. "Simply giving your money away and to get nothing back? Your hard earned money? Julie's family's hard earned money? It simply should not be done. It simply cannot be done!"

I glanced at Julie out of the side of my eye. Her expression changed in no way. The thought of me having any manner of access to her family's money was laughable, but she allowed the assumption to live.

"You know what George Bernard Shaw said, don't you?" I asked the group to no response. " 'People who say it cannot be done should not interrupt those who are doing it.' "

Julie quickly interjected after my rather awkward, rather rude remark, only augmenting my fictitious philanthropic lie. "Why should poorer people be penalized if they chose not to be super-capitalists? Many of them are contributing more to society than most of us, are they not? Our doormen, our janitors, our schoolteachers, police, firemen, and so on. They should be able to live near their places of work. Their children should be able to go to good public schools."

The uncomfortable silence that followed quickly informed Julie that her attempt at smoothing over my rude remark may have been alienating her very wealthy audience so she added, "And it's just the two of us there. We don't know what we would do with all the space. We've always liked small spaces. And the things you can do in a small place are infinitely entertaining as far as decorating and making certain art pieces work with others and with the space. Everything needs to match because you see everything at the same time."

Edward added, "And you can do all the more and the better with more space! It's like having several small spaces. "

Then Elisabeth added, "And where do you put all of your art?" As she spoke, her hands rose with her arms above her head, each the mirror image of the other, as they rotated 180 degrees up and then down to draw our eyes to the art that was conveniently and prominently present on the wall directly behind her.

Oblivious to the fact that it was our place to compliment her collection, I said, "Oh, Julie likes to pick and choose which pieces to showcase. It's what we see every day and, since it's just us, we put up only what we like. And we allow for new pieces to rotate in and out frequently; it's not just a showcase of what we know will impress others."

"These are beautiful," Julie added quickly as she pointed at a piece at the far end of the wall. She and Elisabeth moved in that direction leaving Edward and me alone.

I put my right hand on Edward's feeble left shoulder. "So how's business?" I asked, knowing Edward had no trouble speaking for hours on the topic.

His great-grandfather had started a bank and gave Edward's grandfather a job there and then his father. These were the times when nepotism was nothing more than getting an entry-level job through family connections. Both Edward's grandfather and father worked his way up the ladder until each was, in his own day, a top man in the bank. Each, separated by forty or so years, then inherited the bank when his own father passed.

What nepotism became in his day was exemplified by Edward; he inherited the bank after merely sitting on the board while serving no purpose whatsoever for years. He had not lifted a finger or worked for anything in his entire life as a result of familial connections and assets. Substantial contributions and legacy status ensured his admission at a prestigious private college-preparatory school then Ivy League institution. And, from what I understood, his son and his grandson were following the same beaten gold path, nepotism.

"Business is great!" he exclaimed enthusiastically. "You know Einstein said that compound interest is the most powerful force in the universe?"

"No, I didn't know that," I said despite knowing very well that Einstein was rumored to have said something similar to that, but the mangled and massaged pseudo-quote had never been substantiated.

"Why you don't have an account with us, I don't know. We bring huge returns to our investors, Nicholas! Give me a dollar today and I'll give you ten by the end of the quarter. Exponential growth!"

"Actually," I responded quickly, "there is no quantity that the number one can be raised to that will yield a higher number than one, therefore any growth from the number one to a higher number cannot be defined as exponential."

There was a short and awkward silence that I very quickly filled with, "I read somewhere that Andy Warhol once said the way he prefers to carry his money is 'messy, in crumpled wads in a paper bag.' "

"Yes, of course!" Edward remarked, seemingly ignoring my previous comment about the definition of exponential and excited to speak about Warhol, an artist of whose work he owned quite a few pieces. "He also said he would throw money into the East River, down by the Staten Island ferry, just to see it float…"

I replied, "Warhol also said he didn't think everybody should have money. He said, 'You wouldn't know who was important… how boring!' "

"Haha!" Edward laughed. "*Il est très vrai, Monsieur!* [That is very true, Sir!] I still think you should put your money with us though. We added a new vault last year. State of the art."

"I hadn't known that banks still had vaults," I said.

"Oh, not for money, but for personal belongings, jewelry, precious metals, deeds, priceless art, that type of thing."

Edward then went on about his new vault for some time, all of which I spent staring at the huge crackling fire not a meter from his backside. He then stopped mid-sentence; a sentence to which I was paying no attention.

"Elisabeth, Elisabeth!" Edward shouted. "Fix the music! The music has stopped!"

Elisabeth quickly left Julie and shuffled over to an antique armoire with a muscular stance, wide shoulders and taut sides creating a v-shaped torso. She opened the mirrored doors to uncover several levels of home entertainment controls in the form of knobs and buttons and screens sensitive to touch and gesture and probably voice judging by the way Elisabeth was barking directions at it.

"State of the art," Edward said to me as he nudged me with his right elbow, noticing that I was admiring.

The music continued.

"Ahh," Elisabeth sighed in relief before informing us, "according to Beethoven, 'music can change the world!' "

As she closed the doors to the armoire, I noticed a small crystal statue on the top shelf.

"That's a beautiful piece, there on top," I said to Elisabeth. "Why hide it?"

"Oh!" she exclaimed. "I had forgotten that was up there. You have a good eye, Nicholas. We brought that years and years ago from Murano, a small island off Venice. Those were the days when Venice was romantic and beautiful. Now it's full of tourists, constantly flooding, and the dirty murky water smells of rotten eggs."

"It's a unicorn," Edward added. "Beautiful. Majestic. A very rare and unique animal, just like the love I have for my wife, rare and unique." He reached out for Elisabeth's hand then put his arm around her waist.

Julie smiled and graciously responded with, "Your love, still strong after all these years, beautiful."

I could only push out a fake smile while holding in my laughter. I had decided it inappropriate to inform them that unicorns are not rare animals; they do not and never have existed. Instead I told a lie so that I could be a contender.

"My birthday was last month, you know? I had a long day at work. I came home and there she was; Julie had baked me a chocolate cake, chocolate frosting, my favorite. It was dark, lights set to a low dim and the candles on the cake flickered luminance around the room. Julie wore a beautiful long red dress. She told me to blow out my candles and make a wish. I told her I wouldn't be able to blow out the candles because she took my breath away, but, luckily, my wish had already come true."

"Aww," our hosts said in unison.

"Do you know what I do on each of my birthdays?" I added. "I ask, as a present from my friends and family, that they do something nice for themselves. That is the only gift I want to receive, happiness for those I love."

"That is a beautiful idea, Nicholas," Elisabeth said softly.

I could see Julie out of the corner of my eye rolling hers. I smiled at her without looking in her direction, acknowledging my foolishness.

"Do you know what the two of you should do?" Edward began.

"No, tell me," I answered.

"Last month, for our fiftieth anniversary, we renewed our wedding vows in the South of France on a private beach. It was an amazing place. It can only bring the two of you closer."

I was mildly insulted that Edward's insistence on competing with our façade of love brought him to tacitly suggest a hidden problem with our relationship, that we needed to be brought closer; but I ignored it and responded politely.

"Renewing your long-term lease? I prefer to rent month-to-month," I responded. "And I don't get to travel much. My work keeps me very busy."

"You don't travel?" The Martins said in unison, the pitch of their voices rising in disbelief.

Edward continued after the two of them looked inquisitively at one another. "You must be doing quite well then, not taking any time off like that. The money is too good; you can't pull yourself away from it!"

"Well, my intention is to do good; if I do well in the process... well, good."

Edward smiled and nodded his head while Elisabeth shook hers, still not satisfied. "You can take *some* time off, can't you?" she continued. "*We* just *have* to fill *all* the pages in *our* passports!"

"And trust me, Nicholas," Edward said as he leaned in close and gave me an elbow, "taking a trip with the wife to an exotic place is worth the money." He pulled away after quite a duration of occupying my personal space then winked before turning to Julie with a smile.

Julie heard everything given that our elderly host was, as many elderly people are, incapable of discerning the volume of his own speech which frequently led him to speak significantly louder or significantly quieter than he intended. In our case, significantly louder was the unintentionally chosen volume.

"I don't think it's just right for me," I replied. "For one, I hate the small talk people try to make while they're traveling. If one more idiot sitting next to me on a plane turns to me and says, 'So where you going?' I swear I'm just going to kill them. 'Same place you are, jackass... we're on a plane.'"

Julie jumped in before my crudeness could be processed by our hosts. "And it's too late for us this year anyway. Our anniversary was actually yesterday, a milestone one as well. Nick bought me this bracelet."

I took a step back mentally to fully comprehend what Julie had just revealed. *Is she lying to The Martins just to continue the conversation or had I actually forgotten the most important day of our lives together? And which milestone? Did I forget our twentieth anniversary?* I wondered.

Edward and Elisabeth admired the bracelet with "oohs" and "aahs" while I attempted to read Julie's face. She smiled with such an obvious and strenuous effort that it was clear that she spoke nothing less than the truth.

"Good choice," Edward said to me with a rub on the back which lingered for far too long and low.

Visibly unfazed, I said, "It's my job to be the best husband in the world and it's Julie's job to keep my humble. But, if you ask me, I'm succeeding more than she is."

The Martins let out a simultaneous laugh, powerful enough for heads to be thrown back and eyes to close.

As the laughing dwindled to a chuckle, Julie said to our hosts, "Well, we've taken enough of your time. We'll let you converse with the rest of your guests."

"Mingle, mingle, mingle," Elisabeth suggested to us with her words and her shooing hands.

Edward then grasped both of my hands with his and pulled me, again, uncomfortably close and smiled for several seconds before I was able to shake myself loose from his unexpectedly strong grip.

"Sample the roof deck," he suggested loudly as we parted ways. "The garden will overpower your senses!"

"Yes," Elisabeth added. "Take the elevator to the top floor. You'll simply love it, Julie."

"Onward and Upward," I replied, but to brows only unfurrowed due to politeness as they did not understand my subtle reference.

"Thank you," Julie said as I waved us off.

She turned to me when The Martins were out of hearing range, which was not very far given their age, and said, "What are you doing? Stop making a mockery of this."

"Of what?" I asked.

"Of everything!" She then started to walk away.

I stopped her by gently grasping her right arm with my right hand. With a dramatic flair, she swung around as though she was about to swing a limb in my direction, but all she did was stare.

"Listen, Julie, all I want to do is walk around with you. That's all," I said in a conciliatory tone.

She thought for a while before obliging with a slight nod and fading frown.

I wanted nothing less than to confess to her how sorry I was—for yesterday, for everything—but all I was able to say was, "Let's take the pulse of the party, shall we? Determine whether it's half full or half empty." I then extended my right arm for her to hold on to, but she ignored it.

Discomfort

My intention was for the two of us to glide around the room smiling and nodding at everyone, maybe shaking a hand or two, a short "How are you?" "Oh, fine" with those Julie was more closely acquainted. Then, assuming that would satisfy, we would leave.

As we circumnavigated the room, I heard bits and pieces from different conversations. "Staying in the Hamptons past Labor Day is wearing white shoes after Labor Day; you just don't do it."

Responses of "hhmmmm" and "aahhh" were all around me; those and other monosyllabic expressions of arrogance and superiority.

Physical articulations of words, mannerisms, and gesticulations all seemed put on and exaggerated, as if they were posing for a "candid" photo or acting on the Broadway stage.

The word "adore" was used here and there to refer to inanimate objects and places and almost never to people.

"Look at that guy," I said to Julie as I placed my left hand on her right elbow. I pointed to a skinny man with a large mustache covering his upper lip, extending about two inches away from his face on either side of his mouth and ending in neatly curled points. His suspenders held his loose light beige pants high above his waist exposing his white socks as the suspenders pressed his shirt, two sizes too large, tightly to his torso. His right hand held a cane, but his walk appeared healthy without it. In his other hand, he swung a pocket watch despite the fact that his cell phone surely told time, as did the gaudy gold old-fashioned watch he wore on the same wrist which he rotated to swing the pocket watch. As with his other accoutrements, his tall black top hat also appeared useless. Completing his costume, worn intentionally or incidentally, was a red bow tie that one would assume to either shoot water or spin in a circle at the touch of a button.

"That's Popeye," Julie responded.

I could not help but laugh at the walking sight gag that was Popeye; the oddly disproportionate skinny little man with no hope of ever having muscles no matter how much spinach he ingested.

The floor felt soft under my feet, so soft that I felt it necessary to inspect. I looked down to see large brown and tan marble tiles with a tinge of a pinkish hue arranged with smaller darker diamond patterned tiles weaving in and out of each other around them.

Marble is a relatively soft stone, I commented to myself. I knew well that this specific marble was likely quite hard; the harder the marble, the more valuable. So said the interior designer for my office while planning the renovations all those years before. On closer inspection, the marble floors were confirmed to be quite hard with small calcites tightly crystalized within the rock and with very few impurities visible.

Impressive, I said in my head. I had learned far too much about decorative material during my ill-fated renovation.

My eyes then went up to the beautiful tall curtains which were pulled away from the antique-looking glass windows, forming a passageway for the eyes of the pedestrian passersby to gaze briefly upon their dreams.

"What am I doing here?" I whispered to myself.

The space radiated a consistent attention to detail in its lavish appointments. Surrounding all edges of each room, corner, hallway, doorway, or archway were hand carved moldings with floral designs or beautifully complex geometric shapes.

I became so mesmerized by the opulence of the home that I did not notice that I had again lost Julie. Attempting to mingle with the guests was unappealing to me, so I made my way up the stairs to the second floor to see what treasures lay there.

Upon ascending, there was a beautiful long room to my right. As I entered, one of the home's many magnificent luminescent chandeliers lit up above an expansive antique mahogany table which supported six tall vases, each with a long stemmed floral arrangement. Lights resembling candlesticks had been carefully placed all around the room, bathing everything in a dim glow.

"Motion detecting lights in the dining room," I said to myself.

Four large cabinets grazed the exposed brick walls, each showcasing ornately painted plates, likely a rare collection from some far-off exotic location.

"Hello, Nicholas," I heard from the top of the steps.

Startled, I swung around quickly.

"I'm sorry," the woman said. "I didn't mean to scare you. I saw you come up here and I noticed Julie was still downstairs so I decided to follow you up."

"Oh, hello," I responded awkwardly. The woman looked remarkably like Julie, even wearing a similar black dress, but all the women were wearing similar black dresses to my eye.

"How have you been?" she asked in a low, slow seductive voice.

"Just fine," I responded quickly. "I was just exploring a bit. They've done some renovations and I'm interested in design so…"

"You don't remember me, do you?" she asked knowingly.

"I'm really quite sorry, Ma'am. I meet so many people in my business. It's hard to remember all of them."

"I'm not one of your patients, silly," she said, laughing. "You remember… the beach… It was raining the whole weekend. We were forced to stay inside the entire time… You wore a faded blue cotton collared shirt with loose light linen pants and those brown sandals. Your hair was longer then. You had a beard."

For a passing moment, I was appalled that this woman was attempting to aid my memory by describing my appearance during the time in question. How narcissistic and self-absorbed did she think I was? Suggesting my memories to be based on the way I looked.

"I'm sure I don't know what you're talking about," I responded.

"Come on, Nicholas. I know I impacted you."

Disregarding the fact that she misused the word "impact" by turning a noun into a verb, I said, "I really am quite sorry. I do *not* know what you are talking about."

"I suppose I can understand why you wouldn't want to speak of it here. It makes sense, Nicholas."

"Okay," I said slowly.

Then she said, "I'll head back downstairs. You follow in a couple minutes… so no one suspects anything." And, with that, she descended into the party.

Fully confused, I decided that she mistook me for someone else. It amazed me how certain some people were that their memories were perfect, without fault.

"And I'll be avoiding that lunatic…" I said aloud to myself before searching for the light-switch. I gave up quickly then made my way down the steps.

Closest to the bottom of the steps was a group of six, four men and two women, all listening to the words of a tall well-built man with a chiseled square jaw. He appeared perfectly manicured with well styled, medium length dark hair, and a soft clean face. I did not recognize him so I assumed he was nobody. As I approached, I heard more and more of what he was saying to his audience.

"It was by luck I pulled out when I did! Well, more intuition really… I just wasn't feeling like the kind of consistent upward growth it was exhibiting, that kind of excessive growth, would last. Minutes later, those stocks were down by a half. At the end of the day, down by three quarters. One of my buddies, Justin, he and I compare notes at the end of the day. I had made almost a 40 percent return for my clients while Justin, poor guy, was down by about the same. If his clients found out, he would be done. I told him to create some very specific options contracts; get short what he still had in a couple choice stocks and go long in others. I'll spare you all the technical jargon and details, but next day he made it all back and then some. In and out quick like a fox! Let me tell you, I was a lucky duck. Justin was a lucky duck. Quack quack!"

The entire group to which he was recalling his self-endorsing self-indulgent self-important story, to my dismay, broke into laughter.

What are they laughing at? I asked myself perplexed.

Then, my answer. "I like the quack quack!" a man called out.

The tall conceited man responded, "I felt like I had been slowly slipping into an entirely too serious tone and I'm not the serious kind. I wanted to convey my lack of seriousness in some way.

The personification of my metaphor using an onomatopoeia was, I felt, appropriate."

I wanted to throw up after hearing this fool spew out his idiocy. The only thing that stopped me was my admiration for The Martins' beautiful floors. His pompous stupidity, however, did encourage me to leave that floor completely and slip into the elevator.

Desperate for escape, I pressed the top button on the keypad, the button marked "RT." Had it not been situated above all the actual numbers, I would not have pressed it.

The elevator was slowly pulled up past each floor of the magnificent residence. I considered getting off at another floor, the third, maybe fourth, to explore, but I decided that may be too intrusive.

"Roof Top!" I shouted, right before the doors opened. It had taken me the entire trip up to break the code of "RT."

I do not know what I was expecting, but there was not a chance that my expectations could possibly have come close to what I experienced when I stepped out of the elevator and into The Martins' lush oasis atop their mansion on the Upper West Side of Manhattan.

———

Roof Top

There were small trees of all kinds, some bearing fruit, some offering flowers, the rest were of all shades of brown, red, orange, yellow. Green was the overarching theme with the square manicured shrubs lining most of the circumference of the space, but every color in the visual spectrum was present.

Lights in the ground glowed, illuminating perfectly the plants, furniture, gazebo, bar, grill, and covered kitchen area. Twenty or so people milled around, admiring the beautiful flowers placed carefully in perfectly sized planters, all with small black and golden plaques describing their origins.

I stood for an extended duration in front of the open elevator before it began to close abruptly behind me, pulling me out of my state of awe and reminding me of the fact that I was there and not seeing this on a computer screen. Looking around as I walked, I saw more plants and flowers than I did in Central Park. And this was much more beautiful than Central Park; it was private. No chance of a homeless man ruining one's day here.

I had decided that this was where I was going to spend the remainder of my time at the party. It was quiet, somewhat secluded, and dangerously beautiful and serene. The choice was an easy one to make.

Near to the back west corner lived some cast-iron outdoor furniture with thick tan cushions which called out to me. They were even more comfortable than I had anticipated. I sunk far far into them and drifted far far away.

It did not, however, take long for people to start to meander around that area. They came not to talk to me, but because they noticed that I was there. They wanted nothing more than to experience at least as much as the next guest.

I ignored them and they ignored me. It felt as though we had an unspoken understanding that we had all come to the top of the Townhouse to rid ourselves of others. "Why then should we bother one another?" was the overarching consensus.

Looking up revealed a sky much brighter than it appeared from the street level. It felt hours earlier. I longed to spend my days with a vast private garden but steps away, awaiting my midday fatigue, ready to alleviate the pain of life—although what pain of life would I have possessed had I this vast private garden but steps away?

There I sat, so very relaxed, on the tan cushion in front of a large outdoor table, but the table, I soon learned was not a full table. The top was presumed to be glass by, not just me, but by all who passed. Glass was the presumed material for the tabletop because, when glass is present and when glass is absent, the table often appears the same.

For an unknown reason, the glass which should have sat atop this cast-iron table frame had been surreptitiously removed. In the glorious time that I spent admiring the beauty of the rooftop from my comfortable vantage point, six separate people placed their wineglasses on the nonexistent glass.

I knew very well that I was fully capable of stopping each one of them, but I found it much more entertaining to sit back and observe. The sixth person who made the embarrassing mistake of assuming a table to have a top exited then returned with yellow caution tape and ruined the fun by wrapping it around the top of the frame.

"Where did he get that from?" I asked myself.

But still, I sat in front of what many likely assumed to be some kind of crime scene. I was comfortable; I cared in no way how undesirable my space appeared.

Many times the elevator doors opened and closed across the garden, taking guests up and down through the floors. On its eighteenth open, Julie emerged with three other women, none of whom I recognized. She excused herself from them and walked over to me with her head inquisitively cocked to the left.

"What did you do?" she asked, assuming the yellow caution tape had something to do with my actions as opposed to my inaction.

"Oh, this," I said, pointing to the broken wineglasses and wine all over the ground beneath the yellow caution-tape-wrapped table frame. "Couldn't tell ya."

She squinted a glare at me for a while, knowing that I was up to something, but gave up and walked back to her companions who were admiring some flowers in a planter.

I stood up and slowly followed her, more for the purpose of stretching my stiff legs than for the purpose of attempted interaction.

"Look," Julie said loudly for all to hear. "It's a Calliope Hummingbird!"

A small bird darted back and forth, zigzagging toward a grouping of flowers.

"How did it get here?" someone asked.

Then Edward's voice rang out. "It just came when we planted up the roof."

All atop the roof watched the hummingbird hover around, sticking its head into several flowers, one after the other. Its wings moved invisibly quickly, it was merely a small colorful oval suspended in the air. After indulging in the flowers of its choice, the bird zipped off toward the stone wall lining the sides of the roof beneath the shrubs. It then landed and hopped into one of the rectangular drainage holes at the bottom of the wall.

"Does it live in there?" someone asked.

"Yes, I suppose," Edward answered. "That's where it goes to and comes from."

"Does it have a nest?" someone else asked.

Then I responded jokingly, "I think that's where the hummingbird hive is; where the honey is made."

Everyone nodded in agreement. "Oh yes, of course," someone said. "Ahhh, right," another added.

In an attempt to diffuse my joke and not allow anyone else to be fooled, Julie added, "They live in nests, Nicholas. They're birds, not bees..."

There was a moment of silent embarrassment before everyone who had quietly agreed with my ridiculous statement bashfully and shamefully pushed out a laugh.

"Come, Nicholas," Julie said, summoning my pride with her tone.

I approached tentatively, like a child who knew he had done something wrong and was about to be reprimanded. "Yes, dear?" I said quietly.

"Here," she said, pointing to one of the planters. "Can you smell the roses?"

I bent, nose near, and attempted, but had to admit, "No, I cannot smell the roses."

"I didn't think so," she said before turning again to her female companions. "Looks like rain, ladies." At that, they all followed her to the elevator giving to me not even a glance.

"New York's reliably unpredictable weather," I offered in an apologetic way, but still I was ignored.

Relieved to have avoided public humiliation, but slightly saddened over being left out to be rained upon, I made my way back to my thick cushioned chair and sat down comfortably, forgetting about what had just passed. It was not long before my calm was disrupted by a thud, followed by some shouting from a direction which I felt obligated to travel.

A thin woman, far older than I and wearing far too much makeup, was squirming on the ground and holding her left foot, left black high-heeled shoe three or four feet away.

"Oh, thank God," Edward shouted frantically with the fear of a lawsuit in his eyes. "Nicholas, you're here. Please, help her."

I stood there motionless for a moment before pointing to myself, verifying that Edward was indeed referring to me.

"Nicholas, please!" he said.

"Umm, okay," I said as I crouched down. "Are you okay?"

"No, I tripped and hurt my ankle," the woman responded with a fussy tone. "This uneven ground makes for a deathtrap!"

"Is it broken?" I asked.

"I hope not," she responded, again fussy.

"Me too," I agreed.

"Well, what should I do?" she asked, her tone a bit condescending and frustrated.

The foot was very pale so I suggested, "Try to get some blood to it, maybe?"

"How?" she asked.

"Elevate it," I suggested.

The woman seemed, for some reason, dissatisfied with me. "What do you mean 'elevate it'? That would make it harder for the blood to get there. I thought you were a doctor."

"I have a PhD, not an MD," I snapped. "They're completely different."

"Yes, I know that. I thought you were a *real* doctor. Someone told me you were a *real* doctor." Her tone was, at that point, unmistakably condescending.

"Ma'am, I am a *real* doctor," I said insulted. "I'm just not a *medical* doctor."

"Can someone please find me a *real* doctor," the woman shouted.

I decided to politely excuse myself and take the elevator down to the first floor. The roof no longer held its previous allure, especially since it allegedly "looked like rain."

———

The Mistress

I traveled alone vertically and it felt that way, down and down, but as the elevator doors opened, the brief ray of sunshine that was my focal point caught me from my fall. There she stood, in the middle of the magnificent room, a perfect sculpture placed for all to admire.

The elevator door blocked my view as it closed slowly in front of me. I pressed the first floor button, hoping no one had noticed me apparently forgetting how to exit an elevator. The doors again opened and, this time, I stepped out, but still stood motionless.

I watched the brown-eyed radiant beauty, her appearance enchanting me immediately, seducing me, whispering gently to my eyes. For a dozen minutes I stood speechless, admiring in awe as she captivated a group of three men, two of which were standing with their disinterested wives. The men smiled and laughed, swooning in amazement at her charm.

I fell in love with every part of her. Her long, thick, soft, straight dirty-blond hair. Her big beautiful smile, white but not glowing like many of the artificially whitened teeth which illuminated many mouths in the room. Her perfectly long legs partially hidden by the slant cut of her perfectly fitted red silky dress, seamless, strapless. Her small purse, red as her dress, dangled off her right forearm, wrist turned to the sky.

Just looking at her, I knew she was the kind of girl who had never lifted a finger in her entire life. Everything was given to her, came to her without her even having to ask, solicited by her beauty, her undeniable attractiveness. Because of this, she was so obviously demanding that no normal self-respecting man could possibly maintain any kind of self-worth or pride in his pursuit of her perfection. Her expectations: so outlandishly high that his frustrating pursuit would be certain to end in failure and possibly bankruptcy.

But, despite the obvious, I had an overwhelming feeling that she and I absolutely needed to meet one another. The words "fate" and "destiny" bounced around in my head, but I knew using them would paint me as just another man ready to impress with offers of endless wealth, jewelry, vacations, boats, planes…

As I approached, she came into clearer focus. Perfection is even more striking up close; I began to have my doubts. Then anxiety emerged. *This one must be trouble.* Shakespeare's words from *Hamlet* replaced "fate" and "destiny" in my mind. *The devil hath power to assume a pleasing shape.* Still, I moved toward her.

Noticing me approach, she excused herself from the five with whom she stood; the men, disappointed, while the women were visibly elated; they would look much better when she was not their aesthetic competition. I was startled that she was suddenly alone. *Did they bore her or was she clearing the stage for me?* I thought. Either way, the pressure was rapidly building.

Finally, I reached her. She looked at me, just looked, and I said nothing. The seconds combined, adding up until I lost count.

"Can I help you?" she finally asked.

"I'm sorry," I said with a confidence that surprised me. "But I have to say that you are the most beautiful woman I ever have seen."

"Oh, well thank you," she said modestly, blushing slightly.

"I just had to get that out. I couldn't think of anything else to say," I confessed with a worldly chuckle.

She smiled and said, "Can you think of anything now?"

"No, not really," I responded.

She had never stopped smiling, but, at this point, she did it with her entire body.

"I'm Dr. Nicholas Thesiger," I said, extending my right hand, palm up awaiting hers.

"What's in a name…" she said with such amazing perfection, I had trouble concentrating on an appropriate response.

"Well," I said, "this looks like the beginning of a beautiful friendship…"

My hand never met hers. She merely glanced down once then ignored it.

"My husband is here," she began.

My heart sank down toward my wife when she said that.

Then she added, "But we see other people."

Shocked that she started our conversation with a confession of infidelity, I could only joke with honesty. "I'm seeing someone right now," I told her. "But I don't see her *right now...*"

She smiled at my own confession, almost equal to hers.

"You know," I added, "if we had met in different stages of our lives, we might enjoy cheating slightly less."

She laughed a soft genuine laugh.

"So tell me," I began, "what is it that you do with your time?" I anticipated an answer that included art or travel, maybe part owner of a restaurant or small exclusive winery.

"I'm a plastic surgeon," she said.

"Really? That's interesting. I know a plastic surgeon—"

Then she interrupted. "Actually, I'm an actress. My latest part is a plastic surgeon."

"Oh, I see," I said. "You're an actress... which restaurant?"

She smiled slightly, less so than she had earlier and with a bit of contention. "Want to go to the roof deck? Someone told me it was quiet..." She startled me by asking.

I frowned. "I was just there and I have a feeling that I'm not welcome back."

"What did you do?" she asked.

"Hopefully killed someone," I responded before raising my eyebrows.

Her laugh was soft and mesmerizing. "How am I supposed to know you're a gentleman?" she said smoothly.

"I don't claim to be a gentleman, but I do favor Bonds."

Her smile was back to a full one, beautiful, perfect. She understood both the joke and the reference.

"And what kind of doctor are you, Dr. Thesiger?"

"I'm a psychologist," I said proudly.

"Oh, you're probably analyzing me right now then," she responded, feeding the cliché.

"Tell me this," I began. "Does a plastic surgeon take a taste of her own medicine?"

She looked away and around the room, as if to acknowledge her own building boredom with our conversation before responding. "What do you think?"

"Oh, the impossible question for a man to answer correctly…" I responded.

Then she leaned in and said, "I suppose I could say the same thing to you, Sir. How am I supposed to answer it correctly? Pretty stupid question, don't you think?"

"Come on. I'm just trying to be interesting… memorable…" I said, almost pleaded.

"Oh, listen to you. Dr. Thesiger, this isn't a game," she said seductively.

"I'm just trying to buy some real estate in your mind," I responded charmingly.

"Clever…" she said with a hint of patronization. She was clearly my match or better in pointed sarcasm and in the façade of confidence, but she had fair justification for her demeanor which made her appear so highly unobtainable that I felt little enjoyment in our conversation.

"In your professional opinion, what's my problem?" she asked in a tone which even more clearly than her body language indicated her increasing boredom.

"I couldn't say," I responded. "I would have to have you in a couple sessions before I could determine much of anything. You know; lay you down on my couch."

"And therein lies the problem with psychology," she said, ignoring my clever advance. "It takes just entirely too long for you to do what you do, but you don't have the luxury of time; I'll just go get a fast-acting pill. That'll fix me. Game over, Dr. Thesiger." And with that, she was gone, gliding away on her immense ego fueled by her arrogance and sourced in her endless beauty.

Part of me had known things would inevitably go in that direction, but the other part enjoyed the pursuit and was angered by her cutting it short. And that was it really, the pursuit. It was all I wanted from the interaction. It was what I fed off, from what I took strength, the thing I enjoyed most. I never intended on taking it further, but it was I who was the only one who knew it.

"What the hell was that?" I heard from behind me. I turned to see Julie, fists on hips, doing the polar opposite of smiling happily.

"What are you talking about?" I asked.

"You were flirting with her."

"No, I was not. But, what's her name? She never told me."

"Nick, you amaze me…" Julie said, looking in no way hurt, just angry. "Her name is Marie. Marie Walter."

It struck me that her name was the same as that of Picasso's mistress and muse, but that thought left my head as quickly as it had entered.

I continued to address Julie's concern. "I didn't even get a chance to write her a prescription to 'take one Nick every four hours and apply to sensitive area'!"

Julie was visibly and physically unamused, but I expected nothing different.

"I'm just joking around," I said as I walked closer and put my right arm around her shoulders. "I can't help it if women find me *terribly* cute and *dangerously* charming."

Trying as hard as her lips allowed, Julie failed in not letting a smile creep through. But she was still clearly very angry.

"I need you to meet somebody," she said, changing the conversation.

"Sure, why not?"

She pulled me through groups of people and different rooms, around pillars, tables, couches, past windows, paintings, curtains, and fireplaces only to reach the overbearing man with whom I had already decided I was not going to interact.

"Julie!" the pompous moron who had earlier quacked now screeched. "I thought I had lost you. What were you doing running off like that?"

"Richard, this is Nicholas," Julie said, presenting me like a pet dog to this idiot of a man.

He looked at me for several seconds, judging and smacking his lips. He held a short glass, half empty, in his left hand, secured only with his thumb and ring finger. The remaining fingers dangled freely in the air far from the glass. He wore a well fitted black suit with shoes that I suspected cost as much as the designer suit.

"I don't know you," he declared with no remorse.

I extended my left hand to him, knowing his glass resided in his left, but he quickly switched the orientation of the beverage while flipping his hand around. The glass came to rest gracefully on a coaster previously placed on the table behind him, then his hand slammed powerfully into mine, his eyes fixed directly on mine throughout the movement.

I was caught off guard, expecting him to fumble with the glass before shaking my hand, but he missed not a beat in the maneuver. As a result of my ill-preparedness, his handshake was tighter than mine. I increased my grasp to better match his, but he increased his at the same pace, exerting a grip always slightly tighter than my own. Soon we were squeezing each other's hands as hard as we could. Looking at each other in the eye, we simultaneously let go, pulling away our mangled hands. He had, no doubt, won this idiotic measure of dominance.

"I'm Julie's husband," I said as I rubbed my left hand with my right.

"Oh yes! Julie has mentioned you once or twice."

"Is that right?" I asked, feeling somewhat threatened. "And how is it that you know my wife?"

"Oh, Julie and me? We've known each other for our whole lives. Family friends. But my business moved over to London shortly after our college years so we hardly see each other anymore." Then he turned to Julie. "Those were the days, weren't they, Jewels?"

" 'Jewels'?" I questioned angrily.

"Oh, Jewels and I dated in college. Just a little nickname, Jewels. I'm sure you've got one for her."

"Yes, but it's inappropriate to use profanity in polite company," I said with an angry but rather joshing smile in Julie's direction. "It's strange, Julie has never mentioned you," I said to Richard.

"Oh no?" he replied. "We see one another at least four times each year; toward the end of each quarter, I come to my NY office to check up on things." He said the letters "N" and "Y" instead of saying "New York."

"Oh, is that right?" I said toward Julie, smile on her face. "I suppose I should start listening to her rambling to try to pick out the very few important pieces. Maybe I'll learn something."

Richard paused awkwardly at my rude words. "Yes, well... we actually went to the opera this past Monday. It was a powerful performance, wonderful really."

"Oh *the opera*?" I questioned obnoxiously. "Is that so?"

"Yes, Nick. I told you about it several times," Julie interjected in an attempt to keep the peace.

"So, what do you do, Nick?" he asked as he reached behind himself without looking to snare his short glass back into his left hand. He stood confidently with his entire body, open torso and legs, facing me. His feet were spread two dozen inches apart on the floor, but he was still slightly taller than I.

"Really?" I said. "Julie hasn't ever mentioned what her husband does?"

"No, I don't think so…" he said, seemingly oblivious to how insulting that information was to me.

"Well, I'm a private mental health consultant," I informed him.

"You're a shrink?" he asked condescendingly. "You guys are a waste of time and money. I read that psychologists use whatever therapy method they want instead of those that are scientifically proven to be effective. Plus people who get better in therapy would have gotten better anyway, and the others should just take medication. Your profession is either obsolete or it's a charade or some combination of the two. If you pee in your pants, you'll only stay warm for so long."

There were a number of different things for me to contemplate during my time of shock following the end of his rant. "Who does he think he is?" "How could he possibly say to my face the first time he meets me that I am a waste of time?" "What does urinating in one's pants have to do with anything?"

Julie broke the short silence during which I was lost in thought as opposed to planning my response.

"Ha!" Julie laughed.

Why is she laughing? I thought.

"Haha!" Richard pompously laughed.

It was a joke? I thought, very confused.

I forced a halfhearted laugh while my eyes searched the visual field for some kind of explanation.

"I'm funny," Richard proclaimed without an ounce of modesty or accuracy.

"Yes?" I said, elongating the word to make it into a question.

"You don't think so?" he asked, challenging my sense of humor.

"No, no," I responded, still a bit confused. "That was funny. You just caught me off guard."

"Haha, sorry, old boy," he said, not meaning it at all. "I'm like Superman. My powers don't work as well when I'm not in direct sunlight."

At that, Julie laughed again, no doubt remembering her days of being lovingly referred to as "Jewels."

"You always were the funniest guy around," Julie said, gazing up at Richard and infuriating me; hitting me where it hurt the most.

Richard then turned to me and asked, "Democrat or Republican?"

"Excuse me?" I said, confused by his quick change of topic.

"Your political affiliation. You're a Democrat, am I right?"

I was sure his question was leading somewhere so I adjusted to spar with this moving target.

"Do you intend to judge me based on the political group with which I identify? Someone who takes a small part of you and makes a decision, assumption, or a judgment about your character; that's the definition of a snob, is it not?"

"Well done!" Richard laughed condescendingly. "You're catching on quickly to this thing we call *humor!*"

Julie laughed along with Richard as I stood there, straight faced.

"I'm going to find the bathroom," I said unimpressed with the direction of the conversation.

Julie and Richard appeared to care not in the slightest about my impending absence. *They deserve each other*, I thought as I walked away.

"Oh, Nicholas," Julie called after me.

I turned to see her standing far closer to Richard than appropriate.

"Richard said he would go to the Spa with me. Remember the free day at the Spa passes I received all those months ago as a birthday gift from the Hoffmans? You said you wouldn't go with me, so I asked Richard."

"Alrighty," I responded with as much sarcasm as the smile on my face would allow. "Enjoy my wife! I'm glad my free day at the Spa can bring you two together. I've been planning on replacing myself for years now anyway." I continued to walk away.

Julie excused herself and darted after me. "Nick! What are you doing?"

"Why didn't you invite me to the opera?" I asked, unable to think of a better question.

"Because the last time you came to the opera, you had a terrible time. You couldn't stop telling me how much you hated it. Then, when you grew bored of the whole thing, you started making fun of my father's friend, Theodore."

"The man was wearing a wristwatch with a tuxedo! You're not supposed to do that. That kind of behavior is only appropriate when your date is Cinderella." I could not help but chuckle at my hilarity. "Now *that* was funny," I added.

"Is that really what's bothering you? The opera?" Julie questioned.

I thought for a moment before responding. "I'm going to go and find the bathroom." This time Julie did not follow.

Since I had no intention of searching for the bathroom, I found myself aimlessly wandering around in and out of rooms, all brightly lit and filled with well-heeled guests conversing about their wealth and critiquing and complaining about the most trivial of topics imaginable.

I caught a snippet of one odd conversation in which a woman was discussing her hobby. "I opened a boutique floral shop," she was telling a group of older women, all impeccably attired; well-fitting dresses and discreet but expensive jewelry. "And, one thing you would never guess about being a florist; you see a large number of dead bodies." The conversation put me in an uneasy mood, a cloudy and confused state of mind.

I scanned the room to notice Edward had finished his short glass that was previously filled with scotch, no ice, and had begun touching up the guest with whom he was speaking and to whom he was standing very close. I feared for his ancient liver.

Finally, I found a comfortable, empty, and secluded space on the wall to lean against and gaze through a window. I intended to forget where I was and what I was doing, but I found it difficult. In the window's reflection, I saw several people pass whom I recognized, but thankfully none approached.

A small group stood in the left corner of the window's reflection. Most recognizable was Clement Alfred Bishop, a fund manager who invested heavily in Argentina and worked tirelessly on his polo game in his free time. He was standing with Charlotte, his most recent wife, the former sister-in-law to a high level White House official. Just joining their conversation was William Theodore Hoffman, a prominent Broadway producer and sculptor whose work was on display at countless galleries all over the world.

Above them and to the right in the window was Emily Beatrice Allen, whose family's wealth came from Russian oil. Walking by her was Edmund Nelson Frederick, whose law firm handled all the large international private equity mergers; his most recent, a merger of an American private equity firm and a fund that invested heavily in Chinese metals.

Years before, Edmund's was also the premiere law firm that handled high end zoning in the city, but not land zoning. The firm specialized in air rights; light and air easements. They would buy and sell the space above shorter buildings so that taller buildings could ensure that their expansive views would last forever, thus yielding higher apartment values. I never trusted Edmund in the least. He always struck me as the highest level con artist imaginable. He literally sold air to people for millions and millions of dollars.

When I switched positions to the other side of the window, I saw the McAllister brothers, Joseph, Kane, and Charles IV, toward the far right top corner of the reflection. They dealt exclusively in high-end art. There was word that they forged several pieces, but the analyses were inconclusive and the suits against them were either dropped or settled quietly out of the courts. Despite that scandal, they were able to continue buying and selling pieces that most buyers were never even advised could be purchased.

Then Richard. He stood dead center of the reflection in the window, appearing there as if by magic, startling me out of my somewhat relaxed state. I turned quickly to see him standing six feet from me, staring directly at me, but not moving. His arms were crossed, flat vertical palms in his armpits with his thumbs straight up. He stood there with a menacing look on his face.

———

Richard

"Richard..." I said, feeling obligated to say something.

A server then walked up to him with a round serving tray on his right hand. Atop were four bottles of beer which Richard grabbed by the neck between his forefinger, middle finger, and ring finger on each hand, face suddenly in a smile.

He extended his right hand to me, holding two bottles of beer by the neck, and I compulsively relieved him of the load.

"Julie said you preferred beer to wine, so I figured I'd bring you some," he explained in a friendly manner. "I couldn't agree with you more on that."

"Oh... thanks," I managed to get out in a broken, surprised manner.

Then he pulled the cap off the bottle. "Twist off," he said. "I guess it's more convenient than the other kind, but now what am I supposed to do with all these bottle openers I have at home?"

I laughed at his terrible attempt at an opening joke. It appeared that he had realized that we had gotten off on the wrong foot so he was attempting to fix it with this peace offering.

"I decided to move back into the city," he confessed without prelude.

"Oh yeah?" I questioned feigning interest. "Why is that?"

288

"Well, I'm in the city four times each year and, every time I'm here, it's always work work work. You know how that is?"

I did not but nodded anyway.

"But, when I'm back here, every time I have a little taste of heaven; lunch or dinner with Julie..."

I looked at him, truly afraid of what he was about to confess to me.

"In that short amount of time, I remember how great the city can be, what I left behind. The museums, the galleries, the life I used to love..."

"Um... okay," I said, unsure I wanted him in the same city as my wife. "But, London, that's a pretty great place too. It'll be hard to leave that behind, right?"

"Not really. It's beautiful and the culture and history and all, but I've pretty much experienced everything I needed to over there. It's time for a change. I'm sure you see this type of thing all the time in your profession; people becoming jaded with life, in need of something new?"

"Yes, I suppose I do..." I said reluctantly.

"And what do you tell them to do?"

"Well, I generally help lead them to the best decision for them which is often the one they didn't think of..." I knew my attempt to indirectly sway his decision was a futile one, but I still tried.

"Interesting," he began. "This is the decision I hadn't thought of and I'm doing it! This is where my life was once great, happy, and I haven't reached that level of joy since I left."

"What about your business?" I asked, knowing he already had a solution.

"I can monitor things with four trips to the UK during the year. It's actually no problem at all." He said the letters "U" and "K" instead of saying "United Kingdom."

"Well, it sounds like you made up your mind then…" I said, trying to hide my dissatisfaction.

"I already bought a place, actually."

"Is that right?" I asked.

"A loft, on the park. It's great! Wide open space, no interior walls, high ceilings, two walls of windows, great views. The realtor said there was nothing out there like this place anymore; something open like this. You should come see it sometime. Julie already has. She loves it!"

"Is that right?" I asked again.

Richard's face had a consistent smile on it as he spoke. He appeared truly satisfied with his decision to relocate to the city. But his face dropped slightly when he noticed the not-so-well hidden sadness behind my eyes. He changed the subject quickly.

"So, you're a psychologist," he said rather than asked. "That must be pretty interesting. Meeting a lot of unique people, hearing their problems and about their lives…"

"Yes, I guess so," I said without any enthusiasm at all.

"What made you decide to be a psychologist? Smart guy like you could have done anything, I'm sure."

Richard was clearly trying to flatter me, be friendly with me, but I was yet to learn what his motives were. I thought about keeping my enemies closer; assuming he was setting up to steal my only connection to anyone in that Townhouse. But I let my paranoid thoughts fall away just as I allowed my guard to do the same, it was nice to have someone to talk to.

"Well, at college, I was pre-med and pre-law. I took the Admission Test for medical school and the one for law school and scored in the same percentile on both. I was hoping to do better on one of them, then just take that path, but that didn't happen so I decided to get a PhD in psychology instead. I came to a fork in the road and went straight."

"Wow," he gasped, genuinely impressed by my fictitious story. "That's amazing!"

"Thank you. And you, how did you decide to do whatever it is that you do?"

"Oh, I manage money, invest in stocks, start-ups, real estate, that kind of thing. And my reasons for doing it? Well, to tell you the truth, I wanted to get rich. My parents were pretty well off, but I wanted to do better than they did, much better. Managing a fund was the best route."

"Oh," I said to his unremarkable, shallow, but honest response.

Looks like I won this one, I congratulated myself.

"Hey, look at this guy," Richard said quietly indicating a man behind me. I complied by rotating slowly.

"Which one?" I asked out of the corner of my mouth.

"That guy over there who's wearing sunglasses and holding that tiny little dog."

I started to chuckle, facing directly at the man, then I turned around and continued my chuckle toward Richard. "Not only is it night and he's wearing sunglasses," I said, "but that man brought a dog to a cocktail party!"

Richard laughed. "That combination is only okay if you're blind and that little thing does not look like a seeing-eye dog!"

Richard and I laughed for a minute before calming ourselves. The atmosphere became comfortable and jocular; something I never would have expected after hearing him quack.

"See that guy over there?" I said, pointing to a tall skinny man who was jumping up and down as he spoke, swinging his arms around gesticulating his words, then rubbing his head and chest at the same time.

"Fred?" he asked.

"The energetic guy?" I attempted to confirm.

"Yes, Fred. What about him?"

"Your friend Fred, is most definitely a cocaine user," I said.

"What? What are you talking about? How do you know that?" he asked, not believing a word.

"I know because of my love of the game…" I said proudly.

"What game?" he asked.

"Football," I exclaimed. "American football, that is."

"Please explain," Richard requested in disbelief.

"Well, at college, Bio Lab was scheduled right before the intramural football games so I would always rush through the lab, then run to the field. In my haste, I would frequently neglect to thoroughly wash my hands. And so it was a recurring problem, having the chemical residue on my hands, because I needed to put in my contacts to play. My eyes would always be burning and tearing and red because of it.

"Most of the guys on the team thought that I was doing drugs before games, but they didn't bother me about it because I always made the plays, led the team to a win. But, there was one guy, Will, who was big into drugs and he assumed I too was a user. He was a little disappointed when he found out I was clean, but we remained friends anyway.

"Junior year we actually ended up living together off campus with a bunch of his friends, but, because they were his friends, they were all users. So, this is why I know a lot about drugs and how to spot the symptoms. Your buddy Fred; he does cocaine."

"Wow," Richard exclaimed again. "Amazing…"

"Richard!" I heard from behind me.

I turned to spot Popeye, the skinny man with the large mustache, loose clothes, taut suspenders, tall black top hat, and cartoonish bow tie.

"Popeye!" Richard responded. "How are you? Do you know Nicholas?"

"Popeye!" I exclaimed, half laughing. "It's nice to meet you."

"Good to meet you too, Nicholas," he said in a scratchy rough voice before tipping his tall black top hat then awkwardly and oddly shaking my right hand with his limp little shriveled left.

I looked his tall black top hat and, stifling a laugh, asked, "So… what do you do, Popeye?" I enjoyed saying his name so much that I feared he might assume I went to the same business school as Ivan.

"I'm an architect," he said proudly.

I immediately pictured Popeye drawing up blueprints for a house that resembled an Escher painting. I laughed inappropriately.

"Is that so?" I asked noticing Popeye's uncomfortable expression, brought on by my bout of out-of-place laughter. "Everyone else here is a banker or into finance in some way. It's nice to see something different, some originality."

"Well, I am what I am," he informed me.

This time, my laughter was uncontrollably boisterous. Had he really just used an expression made popular by the eponymous 1930s comic strip character and cartoon?

"Well," he said awkwardly. "It's good to see you, Richard."

"Good to see you too, Popeye," Richard responded.

"Nice to meet you, Popeye," I said, still chuckling a bit.

Popeye tipped his tall black top hat with a nod then walked down the hall and into the elevator.

"I wish I could pull off that look. That man just has so much style," Richard said, I assumed sarcastically.

"I wish nobody had that kind of style," I responded.

After we had a good laugh at Popeye's expense, Richard looked at his large platinum old-fashioned wristwatch and said, "It's getting late. I should really be going. I need to start the trading day on the other side of the world."

"Oh, that sounds pretty stressful," I said without genuine sympathy.

"It is, but it brings in the money so… you know how it is." Richard moved his head around as he spoke to locate our hosts. I spotted Edward first so directed Richard's attention toward Edward's graceful figure slipping and stumbling about in the main room.

"Some of us are playing squash tomorrow morning. Are you in?" Richard asked.

"What time?" I said without much thought of if I actually would play regardless of the time.

"Daybreak!" he shouted. "After the trading day, or trading night as it were. I'll meet you at the club, yes?"

"Daybreak?" I questioned. "That sounds a bit early for me. Maybe next time. I need to prepare for something like that, waking up so early."

"Yes, of course," he said as he picked up his empty bottles of beer from the windowsill. "Let me get yours too," he said, pointing to my two empties.

I don't even remember drinking them, I thought as I handed them off. I was likely so accustomed to drinking without thinking with Bill that the act had become commonplace enough to perform without attention and thus without memory.

"Nice meeting you, Richard. Best of luck with the move."

"Same, Nick," he said, waving his elbow in the air.

———

The Piano Falls from the Stage

After Richard departed, I felt that I too had been at The Martins' Townhouse for far too long. Prying myself away from the wall, my feet brought me into and out of four magnificent rooms before finding Julie.

In a small room off the main room, she was entertaining six other women roughly our age, younger than most there. They, on two wide antique couches, and she, on a wide love seat. I stood behind her without her knowledge and listened as she, I assumed, described me.

"The first thing I noticed about him, the first thing that drew me to him was his intelligence. He's a genius. You could ask him anything and he had an answer or something intelligent to say about it. Whenever he was talking, I could hardly listen to what he was saying. I just kept thinking to myself, 'Gosh, he's so much smarter than me.' "

"So much smarter than *I*, dear," I said, startling Julie.

"Oh yes," she said awkwardly. "Thank you, Nicholas."

An odd silence came over the small group of women, the kind of quiet that people adopt when the object of conversation enters the room. Or, more accurately, when he who enters the room was not meant to hear the previous conversation about another.

"And when did you two know the other was the one for you?" someone asked, breaking the silence.

"Oh," I said delightedly. "Would you like to take this one or should I, Julie?"

"Go right ahead, Nicholas…" she said, somewhat reluctantly.

"Well, probably at first sight," I said to the group.

My words were met with boos and hisses. "Come on, you have to give us more than that," someone shouted.

"Well, I suppose the story is more entertaining than the answer," I responded.

The crowd cheered in anticipation, adjusting their positions on the wide antique couches upon which they all sat.

I slipped into the love seat next to Julie, sitting with my legs spread and elbows on my thighs, ready to articulate the story with my busy hands. Julie scrunched to the side with her legs crossed, elbows and hands pulled in, articulating to me quite clearly.

"Julie and I met through a mutual friend. We hit it off after a short conversation then ended up meeting for lunch two days later. We talked at that restaurant until they served us dinner." I turned to Julie and asked, "What did I say to you, hun?" And, without giving her a chance to respond, I answered, " 'This night already feels like a memory…' "

A collective smile wafted over the crowd.

I continued. "Some people remember what they ordered when they first dined with their significant other; I have no recollection whatsoever. I was paying too much attention to the woman I knew I would eventually marry. After dinner, then dessert, we continued sitting, talking, laughing, loving, all until the restaurant owner interrupted to escort us out. We looked around to see chairs were on tables. We had been sitting there through closing and hadn't even realized.

"We mutually decided a cab would only rob us of precious moments together, so I walked her to her apartment. The connection just became more and more intense as we moved slowly down the sidewalk. At her building's door, we bid a fond farewell; I couldn't help but steal a kiss on her left cheek."

I turned slightly to Julie while still addressing the group. "Julie has attempted to describe her emotions following our date on separate occasions for years, but she fails every time. There just aren't words to describe what she felt... and what I felt. She told me that it was twisting and energetic, the feeling wouldn't go away. That night, she was just smiling constantly and uncontrollably, laughing and skipping through her bedtime routine.

"Her mood wouldn't allow her to surrender to the night. Tossing and turning in bed in a mass of joy and loose blankets, she suddenly sat up and said aloud, 'I love him...' She knew that I felt the same way and she knew that I wouldn't be able to sleep either so she picked up her phone and dialed the number.

"I, lying in my own bed in my apartment, turned over and looked at my vibrating phone. 'Julie D,' it read. Then I looked at my clock. 3:47 a.m. I picked up... 'Julie, are you okay? What's going on?' I asked frantically. 'Oh, Nick, I knew you couldn't sleep either,' she said. Little did she know I had actually been fast asleep since I got back. Still quite drowsy and unsure if this was a dream I asked again, 'What's going on?' Throwing all caution to the wind, Julie said to me, 'I think I love you.'

"That's when I knew I was dreaming.... And, thankfully, the dream hasn't ended."

To seal the deal on my amazing story, I then wrapped my right arm around Julie and kissed her on her left cheek.

The crowd exhaled together in a soft "Aaawwwww."

"When I'm with her," I said to them, "I feel like I can do anything. Nothing can bring me down. I'm Superman, because she's Lois Lane."

Each woman listening was teary-eyed and smiling. Julie too was smiling, but likely because she was laughing inside and not because she was moved by the fabricated story of our moment of emotional realization.

"I must steal her away, ladies," I said as I stood up. I pulled Julie up to stand, right and left hands interlocked with their opposite counterparts.

"Have a wonderful evening, you two," someone in the crowd said.

I waved as Julie said, "Thank you. Good seeing you, ladies."

After we had left the room, Julie turned to me and said, "Lois Lane? Where did you get that one from?"

"I don't know," I responded. "I think from a song or something…"

Julie laughed. "I take it you're ready to go?"

"You know me better than I do, dear," I said somewhat sarcastically. "Just let me find a bathroom. You'll locate The Martins?"

"You know the drill…" she said condescendingly.

The Martins' Townhouse was, by a good margin, the most beautiful of those I had been inside, but it was by no means the first. Over twenty years of marriage, Julie had dragged me to dozens of gatherings in wealthy New Yorkers' private Brownstones and Townhouses. Some were more up to date than others, but almost all place their powder rooms in the same location.

I walked quickly down the hall and toward the stairs. Beneath the upward slope of the steps was a small wooden door made of six vertical pieces held tightly together for over one hundred years by two horizontal wooden vises. I inspected the old door before pulling it open then turning on the light inside and finding my reflection in the mirror.

The room was cramped with a steeply slanting ceiling, a result of the steps above. The sink was small; a bowl shape atop a low dark wooden cabinet. Filled, it would hold little water, but it was heavy and marble, maybe six inches at its thickest point. The tiles were a mix of very small beige mosaic tiles and large muted green ceramic pieces.

The walls were covered with beautiful paintings, but I was surprised to recognize almost all of them. A Monet, a Picasso, a Klimt, a Van Gogh, a Renoir, a Cezanne. I was shocked that the most valuable of their paintings filled the walls of the powder room under their staircase.

This little room must be worth millions, I thought. *The Martins aren't the type to have replicas or fake paintings, but why would they be in the bathroom? Is this their attempt at modesty?* I began to question if this was a secret storage room instead of a bathroom.

On closer inspection, I discovered that these beautiful, valuable works of art were, in reality, framed puzzles. I looked in the mirror and smiled at my reflection despite the widening differences between how I attempted to see myself and the reality that was becoming more and more difficult to ignore.

A security guard for my graduate school dorm, with whom I used to spend time at a bar far uptown, once told me that I would learn the most about myself by looking at myself in other people's mirrors, sleeping in their beds, using their shampoo and their towels. He told me that I would learn far more about myself if I never returned to my own room. That night, under The Martins' staircase, I saw nothing in the mirror except the wall behind me riddled with puzzles.

On the slow walk back into the main room, where I assumed Edward resided, I looked at the walls trying to find more puzzles, but only the bathroom held them. Instead I noticed, lining the entire hall, drawings of cows on what appeared to be some kind of farm or in a field, some were even walking down a dirt road. Everything seemed normal about the drawings except for the fact that these cows were all severely underweight. I had never seen such oddly skinny cows before and it spawned a disquieting turmoil in my mind.

Slim cows? I questioned to myself.

I found Julie in the main room with Edward looking very uncomfortable. He was gesturing spastically with his drink, spilling splashes of scotch, no ice, on his magnificent floors. I quickened my pace and put my hand on his shoulder to let him know I was there.

"Edward," I said. "Thank you very much for your hospitality."

"W-wha?" he asked in a slur before correcting himself and over pronouncing the "t." "Wha*t*?"

"Julie and I were just thanking you for your hospitality. It's getting late and we have an early morning tomorrow."

"Wha*t*?" he asked, again emphasizing the "t."

"Edward, are you alright?" I asked, a bit concerned.

"Ohhh, I you tought sumfing," he slurred forcefully. "Heyyy, I'm gung to say heyyy. I'm gunna do sumfing to now and I'm gunna do now."

"Would you like to sit down?" Julie asked as she politely placed her hands on his left arm and attempted to lead him toward a nearby chair.

"My damn wiff, wife," he pushed out struggling. "She fuellif. She thinkskss I woll. Wait! Is everything watching? Is everyone watching? Wow. Ahhh. Yyyuuhhh!"

Edward shook from Julie's hold on his left arm and my grasp on his right shoulder and stumbled his way to the back corner of the room by the piano. His unintentionally zigzagging path and his propensity to bump into whomever and whatever happened to be unlucky enough to be positioned on that erratic path suggested the man had surrendered all dignity some time before.

Edward then did something that I do not think anyone could have predicted. He sat down behind the piano and began to play and sing Jim Henson and Sam Pottle's "The Muppet Show Theme."

—

It's time to play the music.
It's time to light the lights.
It's time to meet the Muppets on the Muppet Show tonight.
It's time to put on makeup.
It's time to dress up right...
It's time to raise the curtain on the most sensational inspirational celebrational
Muppetational...
This is what we call the Muppet Show!

—

I was laughing hysterically throughout. Edward played all the way to the last note before Elisabeth was able to get two servers together to help her pull him away. The rest of the room was shocked silent as they stared. Edward fought his wife and the servers, swinging his elbows around, then stumbled off the piano seat. Unfazed, he jumped up from the floor only to find himself without balance before stumbling into the wall behind him.

"Can we get closer?" I asked Julie, as the crowd became dense in front of us, blocking our view.

"Nicholas!" she scolded. "After the piano falls off the stage, you don't sit in the front row."

I laughed in surprise at her unexpectedly inappropriate metaphor.

"Fair enough," I said still chuckling.

Edward then somehow managed to pull himself upright and stumble to a closed antique chest in the corner, which he then opened and pulled out a skull.

Gasps overtook the room before Elisabeth informed everyone, "It's just a fake skull. Merely a prop from years past. Be not alarmed."

But, if anyone listened to the hostess's attempt to introduce calm, no one heeded it and the surreal atmosphere of anticipation persisted. Our host did not disappoint.

Edward, holding the skull far above his head and staring deeply into its eye sockets, shouted, "Alas, poor Yorick!"

Seeing the hilarity in it, I laughed aloud, but I was the only one. A hushed silence had bounced from one side of the room to the other and back.

Two of the servers began handing out coats to guests and two other servers took Edward by each arm and began leading him toward the door with Elisabeth attempting to calm him with whispers that I had trouble making out from our not front row seats.

But Edward continued to struggle. "I will *not* go quietly into the night!" he shouted, fighting for independence.

The display had become rather pathetic at that point, which sadly sucked all of the humor out, leaving me only a slight smile as I cringed.

"Honey," Elisabeth said to him. "We're just going to get you a cab so you can go downtown and sleep there, okay?"

Quietly and awkwardly, each one of the guests slowly made their way outside and dispersed in different directions to their waiting drivers or to hail a cab on the next street.

Without words, Julie and I did the same, walking toward the park.

Seeing Edward like that was hard for her to take in; Julie had known him her entire life, speaking fondly of him always, he was like an uncle to her. She was likely thinking about what she would say to her parents, if she should tell them at all. How this would affect things with her family. The Martins and Julie's family were very close. For those reasons and more, Julie and I said nothing to one another as we walked away from The Martins' Townhouse, waited on Central Park West, traveled in the cab across the park, and we walked silently up the stairs into our apartment.

We both slowly and sadly readied ourselves for bed, then just laid there. No words exchanged, not a sound in the other's direction. There we laid, on our backs, eyes wide open but looking at nothing, both knowing that neither she nor I had anything to say that had not already been thought by the other.

I kept looking over my left cheek to see if she had fallen asleep, but each time all I saw was her staring, staring at nothing, staring at everything. Part of me wanted to ask, but the other part wanted nothing more than to leave her in her own head.

I watched the longer arm on my phone's analog clock spin and spin and spin and spin, wasting its time away. At almost 4 a.m., I heard quiet sniffles. I turned to see tears trickling down Julie's face in the twinkle of the lights of the city night and onto the white T-shirt she wore to bed most nights, absorbing them immediately. For an hour afterward, the tears fell from her eyes without the accompanying sobs to which I had grown so well accustomed.

I wanted to say, do, something but I could do only nothing. I was tired but it was not the fatigue which ultimately stopped me from acting. It was the realization that the resulting conversation would lead toward what I knew to be inevitable; the complete loss of the bond that used to keep us together, but now held us only tenuously.

It's over, I thought, the words I feared she would use if I inquired about the weeping. But I could not allow that. Before it could end, I needed to be sure that I could not mend what I knew to be broken. First I needed to give it my all, a zealous all-out effort to regain what we once had, before I would give up the little we had left. I just needed the motivation. I hoped it would come tomorrow.

So I said nothing, did nothing, but rather attempted to drift off, concentrated on nothing, and allowed my mind to put sounds with similar sounds, letters with similar letters, words with similar words until I, in my fatigued state, could perceive it as an illusion of my fatigued state or rather ceased to perceive it as I slipped into a slumber.

During the hours of endless tears, my interest drifts elsewhere, senses sensing less and less, mind minding less and less, awareness of awakeness in crying wife fading, concentration on conception of ideas wading: brain, wife, work, less patients, rain , scotch, birds, less patience, beer, Muppets, Yorick, less pay, senselessness; simultaneous mental experience leading to the absence of consciousness.

Not Quite Top of the List

[Two weeks later]

Dear Nick,

Given that you became so angry the last few times that I visited you with nothing in hand/nothing to report, I have decided to take your advice. "You could have just sent me a note, Bill!" is what I recall you telling me yesterday.

I regret to inform you that this is unfortunately not an update note because there is nothing new about which to update you. Yesterday ended up being a very busy day and, unfortunately, I was unable to read what you have already written. So, not quite top of the list. Sorry about that, but this may be helpful to us. I realized that, if the people I am working with and I read through your account of the first part of the week then have to wait to read about the remaining days of the week, it will only make things more difficult regarding statements, events, facts, and consistencies/potential inconsistencies.

Having your entire account of the week together to read before we decide on appropriate steps forward is preferable, so you are receiving this note as opposed to meeting with me when I have nothing "productive" to say. Once you have completed your account and sent the last sections to me, I will read through thoroughly then make an appointment to meet with you. So expect me a day or so after you send the final sections.

And make sure to put additional thought into what has happened beyond a "straight recounting of the week" so we can discuss your perspective and perception when we meet. I believe we will be able to get to the bottom of it all and really make some significant progress toward our goal if we have more than just fact-checking to accomplish.

I look forward to reading your perspective of any noticeable connection between Courtland's passing and the unfortunate events of the end of the week having to do with Julie, her family, the ducks, the crash, the fire, and everything else that led you to the current situation.

-Bill

P.S. Also, please be sure to slip this note into your writing. You know, just to keep a comprehensive record.

CPSIA information can be obtained at www.ICGtesting.com
Printed in the USA
BVOW11s1956010914

365076BV00011B/181/P